I0653336

A Pride & Prejudice Reimagining

Pride & Peace

Pride, Prejudice, & New Adventures
Volume IV

NEY MITCH

Reader,

Welcome to Book IV of the *Pride, Prejudice & New Adventures* Series. This volume is a *second edition* of the original publication.

I hope that you enjoy this installment of the series, and remember that as you pick up this book, enjoy something that is dedicated to you—for it was through you that I have been able to continue on. Thanks especially to Jane Austen, whose classic novel 'Pride and Prejudice' continues to be a great inspiration to me.

Special thanks: to my publisher, my editor, and the cover artist for their continual belief in my writing.

Ney Mitch

❦ I ❦

CONFLICTS ON THE RISE

I t's a theory, not universally accepted, that family bonds are the most fragile of all. Whether the ties be temporarily strained or permanently severed, they are not unbreakable, even though we all would so wish to believe it otherwise.

This knowledge, this awareness at how familial wounds could hurt the most, made me apprehensive, and I was not alone in my fears.

For there we all were, Mr. Darcy, Jane, Georgiana, Mr. Bingley, Miriam, Lord and Lady Fitzwilliam, Acton, Kitty, Henry, Colonel Fitzwilliam, and I in the sitting room. Richard had just finished announcing his proposal to Kitty to our company, and Henry's response was even more chilling than we had anticipated.

There Henry was, a man in between the purgatory that was heartbreak and the hell that was from feeling betrayed, and therefore what were his feelings but one of revenge, I assumed. Of bitterness from feeling ill-used. Despite the obvious fact that Kitty had never done anything to entice him, Richard had never initially known about his brother's infatuation, nor did Henry ever make his intentions toward Kitty known to anyone. Our awareness was through implication, no more.

Yet turning from Darcy and staring at Henry as he looked on his brother, anger flashing across his eyes, I secretly concurred with Darcy: it now was just beginning.

Lady Fitzwilliam, moving silently and approaching her eldest son as if he were a cornered beast that would pounce at any moment, said quietly, "Henry, son, please, you must calm yourself."

"Calm myself?" Henry growled, turning to her. "Mother do not let your favoritism for Richard—"

"Enough!" Lord Fitzwilliam shouted, standing up. Henry Fitzwilliam silenced himself, but his quietness was still bubbling with rage. "Henry, your brother is getting married. Congratulate him."

"I will not—"

"Henry!"

Henry looked down as if he were a petulant child while Lord Fitzwilliam turned to his second son. "Richard, is this the path you truly wish to take?"

"Yes, it is," Richard replied firmly.

"And yet, are you certain? This is not the best match for you."

"I beg your pardon?" Kitty stood up, offended. "And what of me is not suitable?"

"What indeed?" Richard asked. "That is my future wife, Father, therefore respect is something you will offer her and moderation of your cheek, I beg you."

"On the contrary, Richard," Kitty exclaimed, spirited. "I am curious." She turned toward her future father-in-law. "Lord Fitzwilliam, since honesty is your preference, tell me, what makes me an unsuitable match for your heroic son?"

"Kitty," Darcy began, yet he was interrupted by Lord Fitzwilliam.

"Your family lacks the economy that my son needs to—"

"Money, or lack thereof, should not be the sole purpose behind matrimony," Kitty argued. "And if you read the book that is attached to the religion that you presume to believe in, then you would know that it is very much the opposite. And the pursuit of wealth itself was considered to be a hindrance often."

"Do not question our society."

"Lord Fitzwilliam," his wife interrupted. "Desist in this."

"I question and oppose anything that will stand in the way of me wedding your son," Kitty stated, "even if that is you, sir."

"You—you cannot say anything in your defense. You draw in both my sons and then turned from the first you enticed with your arts and allurements, then choose another, which leads to the basest and most vile of all actions and I am sorry for it."

"Indeed, you have used me ill!" Henry bellowed.

"Kitty is not to blame." I stood up and faced the pair. "And if you had any common sense, then you would be aware of this. Yet you lack it, when you need confess to yourself, is it your heart that is wounded or your pride? Kitty never flirted with you or gave you any encouragement. Whatever you felt, that was within you, and you alone."

"Precisely," Darcy said, venomous. "Henry, you and Kitty only spoke little. Does it not occur to you just how foolish it was for you to believe she should wait for you to make some form of gesture towards her? I was present, Henry, as so many of us were. What did Kitty do but speak to you, for she was now your family, in an attempt to reach you from a congenial standpoint?"

"Do not pretend yourself an idiot, Darcy," Henry answered. "Though you can be pig-headed often, and more importantly, do not think to take me for a fool as well. Implication was everything." Henry turned his attention back to Kitty. "I paid attention to you. I clearly favored you."

"Speaking to me twice," Kitty countered, "and then not doing so for weeks upon end is your way of affection and courtship? You expected me to wait and pine away here at Pemberly, fixating on you. And Richard, when we fell in love, was not even aware of your feelings for me, for that is how little you made anyone aware of the depth of the feelings. Even if I were to think on your potential affection, how was I not to regard it as a fleeting emotion? Something made of air, yet no substance?"

"Richard may not have been aware before, yet he is now," Henry spat. "However, your awareness and lack of delicacy and sensitivity has shown that the woman I admired for so long has been a creature of my imagination. You are a stranger to me and are a villain of the worst kind."

"How dare you say anything against her—" Richard began.

"That is enough!" Darcy bellowed with so much force that all became quiet. "Henry, you will repent every word that you have said in offense against my sister-in-law, Kitty."

"You defend a bond forged through marriage, and blood that is inferior to ours as well, over your cousin who is related to you?" Henry asked.

Lady Fitzwilliam, in a burst of emotion, slapped Henry.

Surprised at her action, and not due to her hit causing him any actual pain, Henry faltered.

"Son," she whispered, just as much taken aback by her own action as he was, "you cannot say these things, for you break my heart in doing so."

"And you break mine," Henry retorted, "in choosing Richard, as you always did."

Henry rushed out of the house and strode to the stables, where he found his spare horse being tended to.

A couple of minutes later, we all saw him riding down the road, away from Pemberly, whipping his horse into running faster. Distance was clearly all he sought, and freedom from us.

After the sounds of his horse's hooves were no longer heard, we all turned to each other.

Lady Fitzwilliam stared at the hand that she had used to slap Henry, looked up at us, and then out of embarrassment, she rushed out of the room.

"Mrs. Reynolds!" We heard her cry. "Please bring me my pelisse."

Knowing that all one could do was retreat, Lord Fitzwilliam straightened his jacket and began to leave.

"Uncle!" Darcy called, his voice cold. His uncle stopped but did not turn around, his back facing us.

"Remember that I will always care for you," Darcy continued, "yet until you learn to regret all that you have said to incriminate Kitty for following her own innocent and infallible guide in matters of the heart, I am not proud of you."

Lord Fitzwilliam's shoulders stiffened, and then he left the room, following his wife as they proceeded to exit the house and wait for their carriage to be drawn.

"What do we do?" Jane asked, at a loss. "Should we see their carriage off?"

"Believe me," Richard said, "it will be the last thing that they would want." Richard kissed Kitty's hand. "Wait for me, for even if I have caused discord, they will not turn me away, nor can I turn from them fully."

"I understand. They are, after all, your parents."

Richard left and Kitty moved toward the window. She watched as Richard approached his parents and Lord Fitzwilliam helped his wife into the carriage. Words were spoken, yet they were soft and not a heated debate.

Richard watched as their carriage left, stood there, and waited till it disappeared into the distance before he re-entered and joined us.

The rest of the day was spent in tense company. None of us knew if it were wiser to confront the situation, or to avoid discussion of it altogether. Thinking it wiser and more of ease to Kitty if we did not speak on the matter, we turned our topic of discussion toward conversations of their upcoming wedding, and they all wished to see the nursery that we had prepared for our child.

Mrs. Reynolds accompanied us there, knowing full well that there was something amiss with the Fitzwilliams' abrupt departure.

When we entered the nursery, we spoke of every bit of detail that Darcy and I put into the room, and everyone's desire to talk of lighter things was so desperate, that we remained in there for an hour, answering their questions.

We then sat down to a meal where everyone spoke of their own childhoods, from their memories of joyous events to their mishaps.

By the end of the evening, everyone knew each other's vices and sins committed under the excuse of toddler years or being a young adult.

Miriam confessed to bullying her brother mercilessly till she turned twelve years in age and finally grew a conscience. Mr. Bingley confessed to being afraid of the dark and sometimes had to sleep with his parents. Kitty confessed to one time eating a worm. Georgiana admitted to pouring ink in the tea of a girl she despised. Darcy's list was too interminable to pick out one thing in particular, Richard had acknowledged to eating a few leaves, Jane felt remorse of having no good stories to share, and I announced my love for climbing trees.

"Ah," Darcy responded. "Due to your safety, I am so happy that you ceased that habit."

"I know you are, dear." I laughed, not telling the whole truth. "I know that you are."

I had actually climbed a tree with low branches a couple days ago. For some reason, being six months pregnant did not deter me or my determination. Yet, I figured that if there was one thing that I kept from my husband, then a small matter of my climbing trees was appropriate, for it was of little significance.

The hour soon grew late, and we all retired to bed.

While Darcy helped me undress, we finally found ourselves at liberty to speak on the earlier matters, for intimacy allowed us the freedom.

"Well, that could not have gone any worse."

Darcy unfastened the buttons of my gown. "I wish to agree with you, yet it actually could have. With the look of rage on my cousin's face, I would not have been surprised if Henry tried to attack Richard."

"Thank you for defending Kitty."

"I am heartily ashamed of my family, Elizabeth. To act in such an indecorous and vulgar manner. Your mother, no matter her behavior, had never done anything to match that level of crass and baseness."

"You were not there when your Aunt Lady Catherine De Bourgh attacked me and declared me unfit to wed you. My mother scared her out of her home. It was delightful."

He chuckled softly. "I'm sure it was."

Fitzwilliam helped me get my nightgown on as well and I untied his cravat.

"Yet it still remains," he continued, "that this is a crisis that has yet to be resolved. Mark my words, Elizabeth. We have not heard the end of this."

I sat at the dressing table and brushed my hair. "Do you think so? I would have hoped that time and distance would ease Henry's emotional scars. Or at the very least, he would do what most men of his consequence do who find themselves in such a situation."

"Which is?"

"Out of a desire to spite his brother and show his worthiness, he will quickly go out among the ton. He will charm a woman into believing herself ready to accept him, then persuading himself that he is in love with her, even when it is apparent that he is not."

I replaced my brush and plaited my hair into one long braid. "He then will make a very foolish match, based on the grounds of unrequited love in another corner. Next, Henry would convince himself that he has made the superior match, and that his fiancée bested Kitty as a gentlewoman." I turned from the mirror.

"However, this action, though causing a temporary relief, will ultimately prove emotionally fatal, for there will only be desperation in the case rather than true affection. After no more than a year, both parties will sink into indifference and Henry would be left envying Richard even more."

"I can see that you haven't given this too much thought," Fitzwilliam said in jest.

I gave him a gentle punch to the shoulder. "I have seen it happen before, and Henry is in an *interesting state*. And that is always the state that begets the fate that I mentioned."

"It is possible, for Henry's anger is ill-founded, yet he will not see it, for he has told himself that he had been ill-used, because of his wounded pride."

"Pride...is that the downfall of everything?" I asked.

"I'm afraid that it is, especially in this situation. Henry Fitzwilliam is the first born of the Fitzwilliam family, heir to the estate of Matlock, inheriting the rank of being an Earl, and has never experienced the sensation of loss before. It is not in his nature. And that, mingled with his wounded and misplaced pride will be something felt most acutely."

"Will he overcome it? Do you think?"

"I hardly know. I love Henry, but we were never close, not in the least. Richard was always the one who knew how to reach out to me and make me comfortable, no matter how bashful or cold I was in nature. Henry shall not only cast his wrathful thoughts on Richard, yet he shall feel it for Kitty as well."

"And maybe even us," I added. "For we are the ones who harbor them and let them remain with us. He will look at that as siding with them."

"And therein lays another injury that he will feel, even if the injury be imagined and self-inflicted."

I gave him a solemn look. "Am I cold for confessing that I feel no pity for him?"

"Not at all. His actions today were unpardonable. And as you had so evenly argued, their acquaintance was brief, and Kitty had never attempted to draw him in. Therefore, his fixation came from his choice to dwell alone over an affection that he did not even do much to further. Good god, love makes fools of all of us."

I nodded. "Yes, it can. And it inevitably will."

"However that does not conclude our crisis. We have a house full of people who we have to entertain, and I am unaware of what to do with them after this situation."

"That is where Richard and Kitty have saved us. They wish to marry, and they will see that it is better to do it sooner rather than late. I propose that tomorrow, we help them to finalize what day their wedding shall be, and then I along with the rest of the women shall plan it." I pulled the extra pillows from the bed.

"That will preoccupy us females while you and the gentlemen organize a hunting party with some other gentlemen in the neighborhood. The sheep shearing festival is also occurring soon, which makes us able to hold that in expectation. And—though this shall make you angry—can we also send out invitations to hold a ball at Pemberly after Richard and Kitty's wedding?"

"Oh, a ball!"

"Fitz." His sarcasm made me smile in spite of myself.

"Oh, all right. As long as you promise me one thing."

I watched him undress. "And what is that?"

"Do not call me Fitz again."

"Really? Must I swear to that?"

"Yes, you must."

"Oh, very well. It is a sacrifice that I shall make in payment of being able to put on this ball."

Darcy looked at me fondly.

"You secretly really wish to host a ball, don't you?"

"Yes," I confessed. "Yet so does Georgiana. So, I do not feel selfish in any way."

"Well, this day continues to bear gifts," Darcy scoffed. "I have a cousin who announced his engagement, his brother who ruined it, the paroxysm caused a rift in our family peace, and now we might host a ball. I pray no more conflicts on the rise appear, for I do not think I could bear it."

❧ 2 ❧

A GREAT UNREST

"Mary!" Mrs. Bennet cried, moving through the hallways of Longbourn with eagerness. "Mary! Oh, where is Mary?"

Within her bedroom, Mary placed a bookmark where she was reading, closed the book and stood up. Mary knew very well that there was no urgency to her mother's errand, whatever the errand should be, and yet her mother would insist that it was anyhow. Closing the door behind her, Mary left her room and walked down the steps.

"Coming, Mama." Mary entered the sitting room and she saw her mother sitting in her chair with Hill moving around her and fanning her.

"Is everything well, Mother?" Mary asked, eying Hill with confusion. "For it is not that warm."

"Oh, dear, do you understand nothing? When you get to be my age, sometimes you shall grow to be overheated suddenly. Hill, I am quite cool now, therefore you can leave, and I shall call you again when you are needed."

"Very good, ma'am," Hill said, leaving the room and nodding to Mary as she did so. When alone, Mary turned to her mother.

"What is it, Mama?"

"Betsy has brought the mail in as well," Mrs. Bennet cried. "And a bit of it is mailed to you. Now sit down while I read it."

"It is my mail, Mama."

"Well, until you decide to find some useful employment to do, such as improve your apparel and make yourself presentable to the gentlemen in Hampshire, then I, as the woman who gave birth to you, have the right to know all your concerns."

Mary sat down and waited patiently, not caring about how her mother read her mail, for letters had almost never been a private matter in Longbourn, unless a person managed to check the mail before their mother did.

"It is from Jane, at Pemberly,"

"How is she?" Mary asked.

"Oh, she is well, though still has not managed to catch herself a husband, which vexes me greatly."

"Jane has a chance, Mama."

"She is not getting any younger and is already of the age when she is regarded as an old maid. All hope is lost."

"Elizabeth was of supposed spinster age when Mr. Darcy married her," Mary pointed out delicately, "and I find it very hard that a woman has a narrow window of age before her chances at making a match expire. Why should it be that to be close to thirty means one is passed all hope? I think it should be otherwise, that only at almost thirty should we begin to hope and have our options open to matrimony."

"Oh, dear, do not speak nonsense. That mode of thinking shall never catch on, now here we go." Mrs. Bennet opened the letter and began reading.

Dear Mary, and if you are reading this as well, hello Mama.

Mrs. Bennet then lowered the letter, exclaimed happily that Jane knew she would be reading the letter, and then picked it up again.

We have the best news. Kitty offered to write to you as well, yet I believed that one sister could speak for all in this case, and I believe that she will very soon be occupied with other concerns and will not have time for missives. Five days ago, Colonel Fitzwilliam had returned from the continent after serving heroically in the Peninsular War, and upon arrival, he did a most gallant and romantic thing. With our whole family present except for you who were at Longbourn, he announced his undying love for Kitty, proposed to her, she has accepted and now they are engaged to be married. In the absence of our father, Mr. Darcy gave his consent; however, we would like our father to do as well. Kindly write back to us all, to Kitty especially, who I know will be happy to hear that you are all proud of her, as we all are.

I miss you all, though at Pemberly, I dare say that we are all quite in heaven.

Your loving daughter,

Jane

Mrs. Bennet lowered the letter and sat there at first, in shock apparently, and not saying a word.

"Mama?" Mary asked, not at all fazed by the news, or caring one way or the other on the state of matrimony and the importance of it.

"Your sister," Mrs. Bennet said, astounded, "your sister...Kitty, she is getting married."

"Yes, she is."

Hearing Mary confirm it seemed to have released her from her shocked state and the next second she was all in an uproar.

"Kitty is getting married! Oh, my goodness, I am all in a twitter. Kitty? To Colonel Fitzwilliam. Mr. Darcy's cousin. I could not believe it, for after Mr. Collins, I thought her headstrong ways would make her unfit to be married to anyone. Can you believe it, Mary, the one who I thought would die an old maid, and to be wed to such a distinguished gentleman. My nerves shall never recover."

"Yes, they will, Mama, they do every time," Mary replied, used to her mother's references to her nerves. "I am happy for Kitty, truly, and I shall write back to Pemberly post-haste expressing my joy. Is there something that you wish for me to say in reply?"

"Oh, of course, I want you to write for me that I demand that they come to Longbourn."

"Come here?" Mary started, thinking it an extreme request just for a proposal.

"Oh yes, of course. I want my Kitty to come here to Longbourn, and this way, her father can give his consent in person. Yes, Kitty must come."

"But mother," Mary argued, following her mother as she walked to Mr. Bennet's study. "Why should Kitty feel compelled to come to Hampshire just so that we can celebrate her engagement?"

"Because my second youngest child shall get married only once, you know. Therefore, I am going to celebrate it."

"Unless he unfortunately passes away some day and she is left to remarry."

"Mary, I hope you were speaking in jest—yet even if that were not so, that was still a terrible thing to say."

Mrs. Bennet entered Mr. Bennet's study and looked down on her husband. He lowered his book when she entered but kept his finger in the spot where he left off, intending to go back to reading immediately.

"Mr. Bennet, we have received the most wonderful news! It is about our daughter, Kitty."

"Oh, is it?" Mr. Bennet replied, amused.

"Yes, and you would not believe."

"That my second youngest daughter is engaged to Colonel Fitzwilliam, Mr. Darcy's cousin?"

"Oh, well...yes." A frown appeared between her eyes. "How did you know this?"

Mr. Bennet took off his reading glasses and looked up at his wife, grinning.

"I am so sorry, my dear, and it appears my memory has more cracks in it than Lydia's cooking skills. Did I forget to tell you that Elizabeth has also written to you and me that Kitty was to be wed?"

"What?"

"Oh yes, I received the letter yesterday, and read it while drinking my tea."

"No, you did not tell me that!"

"Old age," Mr. Bennet said to Mary, who had followed her mother into the room. "I find that I cannot recommend it to anyone." Then he turned back to his wife and continued onward. "Yes, my dear, apparently your desire to have our daughters thrown in the paths of other rich men has come to fruition. What a triumph."

"And yet you neglected to tell me such news?" Mrs. Bennet cried. "Oh, you do take delight in vexing me too much. I suppose you thought it a good joke."

"I appreciate a good joke, my dear, for it has been my constant solace in the face of absurdity for these twenty years at least. Forgive me for having so many vices in which I need defense against, but so it is."

"Well," Mrs. Bennet replied, not fully understanding her husband's words, "be that as it may, do make some attempt in the future to save yourself from your poor memory. And now that I know that you know, is it not wonderful? Three daughters married! Fortune has been very good to us."

"So it would seem. It almost makes one feel giddy enough to believe in destiny and its ability to turn us a good round."

Her thoughts were way ahead of him. "We must have them at Longbourn, and I've come to tell you that I am inviting them immediately."

"I believe that they wrote to you in hopes of no other view."

"Of course, they would want it. Yes, I knew how it would be. Now, I shall be away with Mary to tell my sister Phillips, and while so, I want you to write to Pemberly, extending our invitation to all the occupants of the house and not just our family. For we do not wish to offend anyone."

"No, we do not, for that would be most objectionable."

Mrs. Bennet kissed her husband, and then rushed out of the room, calling to Hill to prepare her coat and bonnet. Before following her, Mary turned to her father.

"What do you need of me?" Mr. Bennet asked.

"You did not neglect to tell her the news of Kitty's engagement because of a simple joke. You did it in hopes of keeping our mother ignorant of it so that she would not invite our extended family here, you would not have to take part in many affairs, for our mother to make a show, and then you would let her know just long enough for us to be able to travel to Pemberly for the wedding."

"You see much in this regard, Mary," Mr. Bennet said. "My attempts have been thwarted, as you see. And yet, you look as unaffected as ever. Your sister is getting married. Do you feel any happiness for her fortune?"

"It is marriage, and marriage is a duty," Mary replied. "Therefore, Kitty is doing as she must."

"You do not expect there to be much affection in the case?"

"We are trained to marry, and it is moral, but as with Elizabeth and Mr. Darcy, it is a match made to keep us from becoming destitute."

"Is that truly all that you see to your sisters' choices, Mary?" Mr. Bennet asked softly. "Just simple 'duty'?"

"Yes, of course," Mary replied, not seeing any flaw in her

judgment, or taking any doubt in her views. "There is no other reason."

"Very well," Mr. Bennet replied, his expression unreadable. "You may go back to your reading and find your own conclusions within it. Now do me the honor of leaving me to the purpose of what my study was meant for, which was in peace."

Mary rolled her eyes, wishing to return back to her studies, then turned and followed her mother. They got their pelisses and bonnets on, and then began walking to Mrs. Phillips home.

☙❦❧

"It is a shame," Mrs. Bennet spoke of when she walked with Mary, "that neither Kitty nor Lydia shall never likely live in Hampshire and with them being such a favorite amongst the young people here. Yet imagine if they chose to live in Steventon. Hay Park might do if the Gouldings would quit it or Chatwind if the drawing-room was larger."

"Or Purvis Lodge," Mary added, trying to contribute to the conversation, even though she cared little for it.

"On no dear, not Purvis Lodge, the attics there are dreadful."

Upon arrival at the Phillips residence and regaling them with their news, Mrs. Phillips cried, "Oh, my dear sister! That is wonderful to hear."

"Yes, it is," Mrs. Bennet replied proudly. "And was I not right all the while, sister? When Mr. Collins proposed to Kitty, I was so content to have believed she was right to reject his proposal, for it was only fitting that she would make a more eligible match in another quarter. Colonel Fitzwilliam may not be wealthy, but he comes from a good family and is of noble birth."

"Yes, sister, you were right. And therefore, always commit to your purpose and be firm."

Mary stifled a groan. Her mother, as was always her way,

turned her recollections toward unreality—and the reality was that Mrs. Bennet bullied Kitty for not marrying Mr. Collins, thinking it would be the best option for Kitty. And now, she was remembering it as otherwise, all for the sake of allowing herself to feel the self-satisfaction of being right. Yet Mary had known otherwise.

As for Mr. Collins, Mary was secretly grateful to Kitty for rejecting him. For when Mr. Collins had first come to Longbourn, his piety and position in the church had made Mary believe, that of all her sisters, he would have chosen her for a courtship. Mary, who not only was attentive to his reading of Fordyce's Sermons, but also sought out Mr. Collins's company and asked his advice on many philosophies that were of the moral and metaphysical. Also, after Jane had been engaged to Mr. Brocklehurst, Elizabeth selected for Mr. Bingley at the time, it logically left Mary next in line for Mr. Collins to do his duty by. Yet he did not, and instead, looked right past Mary and had directed his attentions to her younger sister, Kitty. It therefore left Mary not only offended, but also insecure. For what did Kitty possess that Mary did not?

It was not fair, Mary often thought. *It never was so.*

Therefore, when Kitty's marriage announcement had come, Mary did not feel any joy over it especially. On the contrary, it only made her old jealousies arise. Jane may have been the beauty, yet beauty was not something Mary cared to possess. Elizabeth had her share of loveliness, yet she also had wit, which was a trait that was often looked down upon by most, therefore Mary never wished to emulate her. Lydia was just a reckless and vulgar creature—and then there was Kitty; the only sister to ever come close to achieving what Mary had so desired.

When looking back upon it, Mary could not determine that she ever was in love with Mr. Collins, yet her vanity had been most affected when the man who should have found her worthy found Kitty so instead. And while one wishes to remain rational, Mary could not help but secretly harbor resentment toward Kitty for it and feel robbed of something.

Therefore, as her mother and aunt continued to speak about Kitty's happy event, Mary sat there, dutifully, yet in internal turmoil in hearing a happiness found and that it wasn't her own.

However, back at Longbourn, Mr. Bennet was in for an unexpected arrival.

Sitting at his writing desk, he had begun writing his letter:

Dear Elizabeth, Kitty, Jane and to all else who shall be reading this letter over my daughter's shoulder,

I have received your latest missive, and I congratulate you, Kitty, on making such a fortunate alliance. While I am not acquainted with the Colonel very well, I can declare with some authority on the measure that Kitty: you and he shall be very content with each other, for your tempers, though not exactly alike, are close enough for there to be harmony, yet also comprehension of how to withstand each other in moments of discord, which is a talent all in itself in regards to matrimony.

Therefore, I heartily give my consent, even though I was not asked first, and I shall take no offense on that score as well.

Onto more news, I also must be the errand boy to a request from your mother. Out of a giddy state from hearing another daughter to wed, she expressly demanded that she would like you all to come to Hampshire before the wedding so that she can celebrate your engagement, have you all partake in parties that will be in your honor here in town, and since she is well within her rights to demand this of you—even I must admit—I shall not object on the matter.

I hope to hear from you soon and expect to do so.

Your loving father,
Mr. Bennet

When Mr. Bennet finished the letter, there was a commotion outside, where horses drawing a carriage could be overheard and then he heard a loud and boisterous voice that he was certain could only belong to one person.

Filled with dread, he stood up and walked to his door, opened it and walked down the hallway, just in time to see Hill and another servant exit the house to meet the new arrival. They did so, and then soon the visitor entered, to which Mr. Bennet met with both inner joy and also inner anger and disgust.

Feeling quite self-satisfied with herself, Mrs. Bennet had spent a whole hour with Mrs. Phillips, and when she and Mary left, she was confident that her sister would make sure to tell most of her servants, then the news would be spread over Hampshire in the matter of a couple of days. Such news could not help but swell Mrs. Bennet's sense of pride and accomplishment and she spoke of it all the way home. Eventually Mary ceased to listen even, knowing that as long as she said 'aye' or 'nay' every now and again, her mother would not take it amiss.

"They will have to remain at the inn," Mrs. Bennet said. "Yet that will be of no consequence to them. I wonder if I should invite the Gardiners to stay however, for I believe they might not want to miss this."

"Uncle Gardiner's vocation might not give him time to visit Hampshire, Mama," Mary offered.

"Oh, I suppose it must be if you put it like that."

"There is no other way to put it."

"There is, I am just not seeing it."

Eventually they came upon Longbourn again and Mary noticed that someone was in the sitting room, for she saw them through the window. Then the door burst open, and the visitor emerged.

"Mama!" Lydia Wickham cried out, excited. "And Mary, you look bored as ever."

"Oh, my lord!" Mrs. Bennet cried, rushing up to Lydia, where they had an energetic embrace. Mary faltered, holding back, and beholding her fallen sister being welcomed back on Longbourn again as if she was the heroine of a romantic story.

Having no choice, Mary approached Lydia, and even with all civilities exchanged, there was not much affection in the case, and a feeling of a great unrest in between them.

𝕊 3 𝕊

SPARKS FLY

In Mr. Darcy's study, I sat at his desk and began to write while he paced back and forth. While I liked his study in Grosvenor Square, I found the comfort in his study at Pemberly to be unparalleled.

After Darcy ceased pacing, he went over to the fireplace and warmed himself up at it, letting the flames hypnotize him. Every now and again, as I wrote, I glimpsed him out of the corner of my eye, my quill in hand suspended mid-air and wondered at him.

Even in such a neutral state, I found him to be the most elegant and stunning creature to have ever walked the earth. Memory strikes one at random moments, and my mind quickly passed over every memory we had together from the first time we met to present day. From me pouring him punch at Almacks, his almost kissing me in the park, his constant turning of his mind towards me, then his final acceptance of our love. He was such a complex figure of a man, and I felt as if I would never tire of him. And I know I never will.

Eventually I was done writing and after doing so, I looked back up at him.

"Are you ready?" I asked.

"Do not worry," he said, still looking at the fire, "I am listening."

"Very well." I began to read the letter that I had written.

Dear Cousin Thomas and Emilia,

Greetings, how are you all? We have arrived safely in England, and in coming home, we have found ourselves in the beginnings of a whirlwind of excitement. Cousin Thomas, we know you are well acquainted with knowledge of Lord Fitzwilliam, the Earl of Matlock and his three sons Henry, Richard, and Acton. Richard, titled Colonel Fitzwilliam, has served valiantly in the Peninsular War, has returned a hero and you ought to be very proud of him. Yet, we also think you ought to be even more proud of Kitty, for upon our coming back to Britain, she has found her destiny intertwined with his. They have fallen in love and are now engaged. Therefore, the family of Bennets is even more tied to the Darcys, making us forever linked once more —which is a bond that we greatly appreciate and always wish to acknowledge.

The conflict that has arisen within us was always most unwelcome and we regret how it all ended, yet never do we wish to have a breach between us. Never do we wish to be forsaken and let us take the time to now realize that our bond as a family is stronger than any rift that has occurred.

While our connection will inevitably be temporarily broken due to war, it is not so yet, and before that inevitable tragedy occurs, we wish to let you all know that we treasure you all, and that Kitty and the Colonel wish for you to be happy for them.

We never forgot the happiness we experienced at Canterbury, and we never wish to.

Sincerely,

The English Darcys

I lowered the paper and looked at Darcy.

"Well, what do you think?" I asked.

"Why do you call us the English Darcys?"

"Because, from their perspective, we are the English Darcys."

"Ah..." He nodded, returning his gaze to the fire.

"My dearest, what is it?"

"I just feel so annoyed with it all. You do not feel as if history is repeating itself?"

"Darcy?" I chided.

"No, I am not going to avoid this. Before, we wished for acceptance of our marriage, so we turned to the American Darcys. Now our sister and cousin need acceptance of their marriage, so we turn to the American Darcys. And look how it ended the first time."

"It ended that way due to the pride of a certain Henry Darcy."

"I'm certain Henry is still there."

"Yes, he is, but Cousin Thomas and Emilia are not the sort of people who wished to take sides, nor hold a grudge forever. I promise you that they regret how it ended, for it is in their nature."

"I do see your point, but does it not feel as if we are using them? We relied on them once, and now we expect to rely on them again."

I leaned toward him. "Of course we can rely on them. Is that not what makes them family? Family is meant to save each other at times like this, and since Henry Fitzwilliam has taken to Kitty's engagement to Richard in the same way that Henry Darcy took Jane's refusal of his proposal, if Cousin Thomas and Emilia show a particular desire to yield the breach, then their example will set a standard for how Lord and Lady Fitzwilliam should reply. Cousin Thomas and Emilia will not forsake us, for it is not in their nature. And their doing so will show all how no one should do so under such circumstances."

"Very well. Elizabeth?"

"Yes?"

"Do you feel as if we are always constantly saving everyone?"

"Yes, but in so doing, we perpetually save ourselves, do we not?"

He smiled at me. "Yes, I suppose that we do."

After I folded the letter, there was a knock on the door, and Darcy turned to it.

"Come in."

The door opened and Kitty entered.

"Hello, am I bothering you?"

"No, you are not. What do you need?"

"It is a request, and I know that I have been doing that often, so forgive me." Darcy's chest tightened and he was growing apprehensive about what her request could possibly be.

"Continue," Darcy said.

Kitty sat down and folded her hands in her lap.

"I know this is unorthodox, but I was wondering if maybe we did not have our wedding at Acton."

"Oh, that is all? Well then, what church do you prefer?"

"No church at all," Kitty replied evenly. "I was wondering if we might hold the wedding out of doors."

"Out of doors?"

"Yes. I know it seems strange, but I have always secretly enjoyed the idea of my wedding being outside. Instead of having it in a church, can we have a small altar built, have chairs placed, and have the wedding on the grounds of Pemberly? I do not disregard the authority of the church, but one cannot deny that nature will always have more beauty to it, do you not think?"

"Oh," I said, turning to Darcy. "So, it is simply that you wish to have it on our fields."

"Yes," Kitty continued. "And if you think on it, it might be more fitting and better on the whole. Think on it, if we have it on the grounds of Pemberly, we can invite all the tenants of Pemberly, their families can easily attend, including all of Jane's pupils, it will not feel so formal and stiff, and it will be easy to decorate."

"Well," I said to Darcy, "what do you think of this new scheme, sir?"

He raised an eyebrow at me, and I stifled a chuckle.

"Kitty," Mr. Darcy said, "give me time to think on this, for I would like to make sure that I consult Mrs. Darcy on the matter. Yet this is something that will make you happy?"

"Quite sir," Kitty replied. "Though I have not asked Richard about this, for I thought to seek your approval of it first."

"Then you shall have our answer within an hour's time," he said.

"Thank you, Mr. Darcy," she said, jumping up, kissing him on the cheek—and here he faltered—then Kitty left.

I laughed and pressed my fingers to my cheeks. "Dear lord, you are so easy to move. Kitty kisses you and you clearly are more open to saying yes to her, are you not?"

"Perhaps," he said, "my familial ties have too much of a hold on me. Yet as for you, Mrs. Darcy, you very much just put me on the spot."

"Oh did I?"

"Oh, you know you did."

"Well," I said with an impish smile, "I believe I had no choice in the matter, for though I am the mistress, Pemberly is after all still yours. How could I not turn to you and show that I regarded your opinion before anything else?"

He blushed. "Oh, that is what you were doing?"

"Yes, you imbecile." I laughed. "And you very much deserved being called that name."

"I suppose so. Well, what do you think of Kitty's idea?"

"I am jealous."

"Jealous?"

"Yes, very jealous that we did not do that ourselves."

"Oh, so you now regret that our wedding was too traditional?"

"It would have sufficed if we were two traditional people, yet we are not. And I quite like the scheme of a wedding out of doors and under the beauty of Pemberly. Besides, to have the wedding, and maybe even have the after-wedding feast outside where we serve cold meats and allow dancing, well, it might be quite beautiful... we could even have Jane have her pupils design some of the decorations. They could weave flowers, make hangings, and strings of apples. With children designing it, their parents will be proud and feel that they all have contributed in some way. It would be glorious, for it becomes a mixture of a project done through passion, community and it also shall be a labor of love."

Darcy sat down in the chair across from me. "And I won't even have to do anything."

"No." I laughed, amused at his anti-social manner. "You won't even have to speak much at the wedding, for we Bennets can do all the talking for you."

My husband sighed. "That is surprisingly delightful. And with Kitty and the Colonel, they might not have some family attending, yet the loss shall be immediately made up for by the attendance of so many of the people here in Kent."

"I do believe that I have quite convinced you."

"You did not...very well, perhaps only a mere little."

After the letter to the American Darcys had been sealed and handed to Jefferson to mail, Jane came upon Mr. Darcy, Georgiana, and I as we were all in the music room, listening to Georgiana play the pianoforte.

When we told Jane of Kitty's concept to her wedding, and asked Jane about having the children design the decorations while she oversaw them, she felt elated at the idea.

"Their families would love that!" Jane cried, elated. "And it shall give them a reprieve from their reading lessons and be more aimed at arts and craft work."

"Precisely."

"Then I shall ride out with Kitty and ask the families

individually. Yet I forget my purpose. I have just received a letter from our father."

"Then you should seek Kitty out first. Has he given his consent to the marriage?"

"Oh, he has," Jane replied, looking around.

"Jane, what is it?" I asked, sensing more coming.

"Elizabeth, you know our mother. Well, she is demanding that we all travel to Hampshire where she can host a party in honor of Kitty's engagement and maybe even hold an assembly dance in their honor."

"Oh, dear god, she would," Darcy bellowed.

"You seem surprised?" I asked lightly.

"I know I shouldn't be, but I am."

"Forgive me," I said, "but in this circumstance, I do understand our mother's reasoning. Think on it, Fitzwilliam. If we had children, and one of them got engaged in a different location, would we not demand them to return home before the happy event so that we could get acquainted with their fiancé, and to celebrate?"

Darcy looked ahead, considering my words.

"On this matter, I believe we should ask those who it concerns, which is Kitty and Richard."

"I agree, and—"

I was interrupted, for I noticed a carriage pulling along the road to Pemberly.

"Fitzwilliam, were you expecting anyone today?"

"No, I am not," he said, approaching the window. "And I know not who..."

The carriage drew closer and then Mr. Darcy groaned.

"My love," I said. "What is it?"

"It cannot be..."

"Fitz!"

"You promised you would not call me Fitz."

"I will hold to that promise if you cease to stop explaining your expression of shock to me."

"I think... I know that I recognize that carriage and who it belongs to."

"Who, then?"

The carriage pulled up, parked before the steps of the house, the footmen stepped down and opened the door.

"Oh, my goodness," I said on a sigh.

"Dear lord," Jane added.

"How could this be?" I asked.

"And yet, it is," Darcy said, firmly. "I should learn never to ask for conflicts to cease to arise in our lives, for every time that I do so, two conflicts rise up once we had solved the previous one."

"Yes, I believe that it could not get any worse than this."

"No, my dear. No, it could not."

There was nothing for it but for us to leave the security of the music room, walk down the steps, and emerge from the front doors of Pemberly.

"Ah, you were all remiss in meeting me as soon as I had arrived."

Her temper, self-consequence and pride were as I had always remembered it, and anger toward her over the months had not abated. One look between us showed that even from the start of our discourse, a fire of resentment ignited and here the sparks fly out.

Lady Catherine de Bourgh had come to Pemberly.

❄ 4 ❄

THE RASH AND THE RATIONAL

Lydia entered Longbourn as if she was a conquering hero—or at least it seemed so to Mary.

"Well, how have you been, Mary?" Lydia asked when she came upon Mary who was sitting and writing down an extract from Plato's parable of *The Cave*. "Still writing down other people's words?"

"Better than using your own words and not being very good at them," Mary retorted. "Yes, Lydia, I consider that the worse crime."

"Ha ha ha!" Lydia crowed, sitting down with her usual flare. "Mother asked me to ask you if you have heard from Maria Lucas yet? She knows that you write to each other, and right now she is staying where again?"

"Maria has visited Charlotte at Hunsford Parsonage."

"Ah," Lydia answered, "she's visiting her unfortunate sister."

"And how would she be unfortunate?" Mary asked, lowering her book. "For you cannot be so stupid as to still think marrying an officer is more respectable than marrying a clergyman."

"You have no idea what a constant excitement my life is in," Lydia argued.

"If it is a constant excitement, then why did you come back home?"

"I told you all already," Lydia argued, "it has been months and I wished to return home."

"And I know that you are hiding something."

A blush rose on Lydia's neck. "What are you on about?"

"I'm 'on' about the fact that I can tell when you are lying."

"I never lie. And if one wishes to expose a sister who conceals all, then I could do so with you and not the other way around. And in some cases, neither of us has anything to tell. I because I withhold nothing and you because you communicate nothing."

"I have heard that line before," Mary replied, startled. "From a book."

Lydia flinched and then looked down.

"You've read Jane's book, *Sense and Sensibility.* "

"Well, so what if I have?" Lydia asked defensively.

"You never read anything," Mary whispered.

"Well, it was out of necessity. When someone you know writes a book, it is one's duty to at least attempt to read it."

"That sounds loyal of you."

"Do not sound so surprised, Mary! Or must you always be against me?"

"I am only against you when you are in error, which is often the case."

"In your eyes, I often am, yet Mary you are not even correct half of the time."

"Yet I am correct that you fully read Jane Austen's novel."

Lydia flexed her hand, as a nervous tick, and then continued on.

"So, what if I did? Jane and I may not get along especially, yet not reading her book would be too cold of me."

"Then why don't you inform her that you read her novel? She would feel flattered."

"I never said that I wouldn't. I just simply haven't gotten around to it yet."

Mary leaned back in her chair, wondering what to make of Lydia at the present time. To read a full novel and to offer such support for an author she knew was not her usual way. Mary decided to change tactics and return back to the topic that was most pressing.

"Lydia, I believe that I have an idea of why you are here."

"Oh, do you then? Well, go on then and spit it out."

"Your husband's regiment was called away to serve on the Peninsula, he is now marching into war, however after sharing that news, you ceased to speak of him."

Lydia looked down and bit her lip.

"Normally, you would be boasting of your good luck in catching such a handsome husband, and of his blue coat and uniform, along with the fine figure that he has. Yet that is not so. You told us that he went off to fight, and then you never brought him up again. You have also been walking up and down Steventon as if you had been before you wed, almost as if you were attempting to turn back time. Acting as if your present state could be undone."

"What novels have you been reading?" Lydia spat out. "For it seems as if you are confusing my situation with those you have read in prose."

"No," Mary objected. "I have not. Lydia, we've been sisters our entire lives, and I think I can tell when you are hiding something behind your forced smiles and laughter. Admit it, you are now beginning to see the error of your ways and now know that Wickham does not love you and was only forced into marrying you by better men."

"What? In the way that Mr. Collins did not love you?"

Mary flinched at Lydia saying her inner feelings out loud, for while Mary's embarrassment had been known to her sisters, they always had the good grace to not ever speak of it.

Mary, however, did not see how such declarations went hand in hand. Lydia's confronting Mr. Collins's dismissal of her was no more or less vicious than Mary's acknowledging Wickham's apathy towards Lydia. Yet both sisters, intending to emotionally wound each other, looked on one another in hopes of causing the most havoc.

"Be quiet, Lydia," Mary hissed.

"I shall not. We all know how you stupidly fawned all over Mr. Collins and he chose Kitty over you—and you have been jealous all the while. I see the way that you look at Kitty. It's sad, Mary."

"Sadder than only being wed because someone had to pay a man to marry you," Mary retaliated. "And what is my jealousy in comparison to yours? Admit it; you are very jealous of Elizabeth, for you know, deep in your heart, that Mr. Darcy married her because he loved her. I don't know if she loves him back however, while Wickham married you because Mr. Darcy pressured him into it. And now it is quite plain to you, and you cannot deny it to yourself: you are beginning to learn all this little by little and it's breaking your self-confidence. Lydia Wickham wants simply to be Lydia Bennet again, but Lydia Bennet was never enough to begin with."

"Are you always bent on being so frigid and vicious?" Lydia cried. "And that is why you shall always be unlovable!"

Mary looked away from Lydia, feeling as if she had just been slapped on the face.

"That is why Mr. Collins, who is the most unlikable person imaginable, still did not choose you."

"I hate you, Lydia."

"And I feel the same, Mary. And all you ever do is make me into the villain."

"Because you are a villain, Lydia. No matter what, your story seems to always end poorly because you make the wrong choices and think yourself correct. You are headstrong without the proper philosophical platform to stand on. You ran off with a man who cared not one way or the other about you, have been labeled as the silliest flirt in all of Hampshire, are ridiculous to a fold, are thoughtless and care nothing for how you hurt others! And I will always be ashamed of you."

Lydia did her best to hold back her tears, yet they streamed down her cheeks anyway.

"Whatever my faults," Lydia said with a sob, "it will never be anything compared to you, who is a coward."

"How am I a coward?"

"Because you are afraid to live! You do not think I know what you do, yet I see it. You live hidden in your room, writing down other people's words and using them as your own, because you have no idea of how to make your own choices, no confidence in your own voice. You are dead, Mary. And you always will be. I live my life to its fullest, and it frightens you. Well, I shall take my life as it is, with all its failures and not be frightened by the mistakes that I make. Anything to not spend my life never moving, as you do."

Lydia then began to walk out of the room, yet Mary, in a fit of anger, stood up and grabbed her sister's arm.

"Ouch!" Lydia cried.

"Oh, I'm not even grabbing you that hard and—" Mary paused when she looked at the part of Lydia's arm and saw bruises on it. "What did you..."

Then Mary noticed the bruises went all up her sister's arm.

"Lydia?"

Lydia winced and forced her arm out of Mary's grasp.

"Lydia," Mary whispered, "where did you get all those bruises?"

"I sometimes bruise myself in my sleep."

"Since when? For you have never done so in this way before."

"I also fell down."

"Truly?"

"Yes."

"So first it was just that you bruised yourself in your sleep and now it's also that you fell down. Why does your story keep changing? I'm not a fool, Lydia."

"I do not really care what you are, Mary."

"Lydia, tell me the truth. How did you get those bruises?"

Lydia looked at Mary with a hollowed expression.

"Oh, so now you are trying to protect me? Now you are trying to be the older sister that you always should have been?"

"You were mother's favorite," Mary reminded her. "I was no one's favorite. So do not tell me about what you lost out on from me."

"I fell down, and bruised myself in my sleep as well," Lydia stated flatly, "no more."

She removed herself from Mary's grasp and left the room.

❦

In separate rooms, both sisters would have been surprised to find that they were feeling similar sensations. Both were left feeling exposed to the world for an inward truth and a secret pain that they both had been concealing.

With one, it was the tendency to fall away from mankind and never experience one's life in full.

With the other, it was sadness at being found out, at knowing that all of her mistakes were obvious to many when she did her best to hide them.

With the first, it pushed her into doubting whether her philosophical pursuits had led to her never forming her own thoughts, ideas, and concepts. So much of her life was bent toward study and learning, but was life passing her by before her very eyes? She desperately wished to have a superior intellect, and was it so wrong for that to be her aim? She began to doubt what was correct and what was false in her life.

With the second sister, the transformation would prove all the more shocking. For in her position, the knowledge that she might have been erroneous in her previous outlook on life had been slowly occurring to her gradually. She suspected that her husband cared nothing for her—and regarded her as less than nothing—yet for all to know it.

Now even the luxuries and distinction that came with being a married woman meant nothing at all, for all were aware of it. The facade had never fooled anyone, but herself. She was a woman who had attached herself to a sad fate and it could not be undone. Yet to hear it all mentioned out loud! It was too much to be borne, and in such moments, Lydia had to not only admit to her inner self that her husband did not love her ever, yet now she could not deny that she hated him and lived in terror of his temper.

Wickham was a charmer in public and a vicious beast in private —he was Willoughby. Only worse. And when reading that rake of a character, Lydia clung to the story that Jane Austen had written, not knowing how she could have embodied a villain that would be the foreshadowed fate to Lydia's own story. For that was why she had continued reading; for when seeing a fictitious character embody someone in your reality, it has the effect of wakening a person from their own dreams.

"And what is worse," Lydia said to herself, "is that the world will always fall in love with Wickham, for they love men like him. The world always loves people like him. I made that mistake myself."

And so, Lydia sat in a chair by the window, frightened to move or leave her room, for within there, she felt safe and secure.

'Did she ever have to leave it?' she asked herself. Why could she not remain at Longbourn, forever in a state where she was her parents' daughter and no more? Married life had proven to have failed her—or rather she failed herself. Why could she not undo it all? Even if Wickham were to return from the war, would he truly care for her to return home? Of course, he would not. Therefore, what did she have to lose if she went to her mother and told the truth? The truth about how she never wished to return to Newcastle, how she wanted to stay forever at Longbourn, using whatever lie to remain there and stay far away from Wickham. She could grow old there and be at peace. Now that was all that she wanted: peace.

However, that was the very detail that haunted her; she would have to tell the truth. She would have to tear down the wall of happiness that she built around herself that had kept her appearing so secure always. She would have to admit that she had made a mistake, and that she had been in the wrong. To confess such a thing was too much for her sensibilities at the moment, and she still felt like she could not commit herself.

Therefore, all she could do was sit there, wondering how long she could remain there, outrunning the reality that she was beginning to understand that she could not fully escape.

With Mary however, the revelation was not as keenly or deeply felt. It was the first time that anyone had come forward and made her aware of her faults, and while it is always the wish that one person's critique of another's flaws will lead to an immediate transformation of their character, it does not. It often takes many corrections and reminders before a person learns how to take advice and improve themselves.

Therefore, everything that Lydia said, while it had an impact on Mary's self-assurance, it still would take more days to come to realize that Lydia Wickham did, in all fairness, have a point.

In two separate rooms in Longbourn, both sisters sat, one picked up her book while the other remained in a silence that was most unlike her, a mixture of the rash and the rational connecting them both.

5

ONE MOMENT OF DOMINANCE

The arrival of Lady Catherine de Bourgh could not have been more frightening to all of us. What was more amazing was that behind her appeared Anne de Bourgh.

"Well," she said, moving from her carriage, "as I am of the highest rank, it is my duty to walk into the house foremost, and though you all seem to have let propriety and order go to the wayside, you will at least oblige me in keeping that sacred. Come along, Anne!"

With an air of self-possession, Lady Catherine sauntered past us all and into the house with Anne behind her. Anne, however, had the good grace to nod to us all as she followed behind.

When we all entered the sitting room, Lady Catherine chose the most illustrious sofa in the room and sat down on it. Before seating herself in the chair next to the sofa, Anne turned to us all as we entered and gaped at us.

"Mrs. Darcy," Anne said. "I have heard much about you."

"And I about you," I replied. "It is a pleasure to meet you."

"And I as well. I also take it that is your sisters, there?"

"Yes," I said. "This is my sister Jane Bennet, Kitty Bennet, who has now had the good fortune to become engaged to the Colonel here" —and here I noticed Lady Catherine roll her eyes— "And this is Mrs. Miriam Bingley."

Miriam bowed as well.

"Well," Lady Catherine said, "as you all know, I have often been praised for my frankness and desire for honesty, therefore upon receiving a report of *another* most alarming nature."

"Aunt Catherine," Darcy said, "while I am happy to have you in my house, if you have heard something, why did you not simply write about your concerns to me in a letter?"

"I feared the response would be delayed."

"When have I given you reason to believe me to be hesitant, unless I don't wish to speak to the person? Which is always a possibility if that person has forever lost my good opinion."

"Are you getting cheeky with me, Fitzwilliam?" Lady Catherine asked.

"Never...if not needed so."

"Well," she said, "I do not wish to stay where I have come unannounced, though my coming was highly necessary. I have heard, coming from a most reliable source that Colonel Fitzwilliam, my nephew, is now engaged to Miss Kitty Bennet."

"And by a reliable source," Colonel Fitzwilliam began. "You mean that my brother has sent word to you."

"Not just him alone," Lady Catherine said, her eyes turning to slits. "Lady Fitzwilliam has sent me a letter as well, asking me to offer my congratulations."

"It is true that I am to wed Miss Kitty here," Colonel Fitzwilliam confirmed, coming forward. "Have you come to give me your congratulations then, aunt?"

"Of course not. I have arrived to urge you to come to your senses."

"I never knew they left me."

"They have clearly," she said, standing up. Anne, sitting beside her, remained seated, staring at her hands. "I do not know nor understand what these Bennet women have to recommend them, yet their arts and allurements have drawn in one of my nephews, who was so headstrong as to not heed my advice, and I shall not fail with the other."

"Your words were not advice, aunt," Darcy said. "They were verbal poison."

"Fitzwilliam!"

"No, aunt. I am not candid, just as you are not. And do not insult Elizabeth or any of her family in my presence. As well as do not speak about me as if I am not in the room."

"What has occurred that has made you believe you ought to speak to me so, Fitzwilliam? There was a time where you were of sound mind and obeyed me, for you knew my logic was undeniable."

"Logic?" Colonel Fitzwilliam said. "Perhaps in one light. Yet your logic leads to domestic misery, an emotional state fit for hell, and I echo Darcy in his sentiments. Aunt, before you speak any longer, I shall tell you that your words shall fall on deaf ears. I am marrying Miss Kitty, and we shall be content."

"Have you no consideration for your future?" Lady Catherine asked. "She has nothing to offer you, for she has no consequence in family or fortune."

"I have consequence." Kitty spoke up. "Yet it is simply not the way in which you judge things of any value. I have no monetary gain, yet I care for your nephew. As my sister cares for Mr. Darcy, and if you had their own interests at heart, their true interests, then you would not be putting so much of your energy in keeping them from their domestic joy."

"What does joy have to do with success and advantage in marriage?" Lady Catherine said. "Headstrong and foolish child."

"That is enough!" I shouted in such a volume that everyone turned to me.

"Lady Catherine," I said, quieting my voice, "you are my husband's aunt, and he loves you. I wish for there to be peace between us, therefore if you can gather the sense of humbleness and humility to tear down this desire to rule everyone's lives with an iron fist even when you ought not to rule them at all, then I will accept you, and welcome you in our house." I had to stop and take a breath.

"Yet if you continue to ruin my sister's happiness, and then attempt to offend us in every possible method that you can concoct, I will have not only every satisfaction in throwing you out, yet I will also never wish to let you return if you were to later have a change of heart."

"I ought to take my leave of you all!"

"Nothing is stopping you, Lady Catherine," Jane said. We all turned to her, surprised, for we never thought that Jane would have been the person to have spoken up in the end.

"And who are you to speak to me?" Lady Catherine hissed.

"I am Jane Bennet, the oldest of my set of sisters, and since you have forgotten me, you have just done the worst thing in the presence of an older sister, which was offending her siblings with accusations that were not deserving of them."

Jane stood, bringing herself to her full height. "My sisters have not drawn anyone in, but have won the hearts of the men fairly, which is better than you plan which is for a woman to lure them in through the size of their pocketbook. Men should not be bought. Just as we woman should not. We are not cattle. Therefore, to marry based on the merit of the person is cheap in your eyes, yet it is priceless in those who know what love is. And my love for family is clearly more well-placed than yours. I will not stand for any more meanness of opinion from you, any harsh words spoken against them, not while I am Jane Bennet. And I will always be Jane Bennet, ma'am."

"Jane," Miriam cried. "That was bloody brilliant!"

Jane took a deep breath, surprising herself. "Yes, that did feel quite exhilarating."

"I..." I gasped. "Well, my word, I never knew you had that in you as well."

"This has been a year of revelations, indeed."

We all turned to Lady Catherine, who felt all eyes on her at the moment. Lady Catherine had a will of iron, that much was certain, yet there was faith in numbers, and with all of us looking down on her, in complete objection to her views, there was hope that she would stir, that she could be moved to change.

"Well," she said, looking away from us, "I can see that this is how I am repaid for placing all of your concerns close to my heart. This is how I am to be betrayed."

"You are not being betrayed." Anne's voice squeaked to her left. We all turned to her as she looked up and at first bit her lip, but then continued on. "Mama, you were never so."

"Anne," Lady Catherine cried. "Be quiet and do not defend them."

"Let her speak," I said. Anne looked towards me, nodded and continued on.

"My cousins are grateful to you, Mama," Anne began. "Yet their lives are their own. How would you feel if every move you made, you were hounded by a person, oppressed by them, and made to adapt to their views? You would hate it, Mother. For your independent spirit would compel you to loathe it. Well, this is what you are doing to them now. And it's what you do to me."

Lady Catherine closed her eyes, and then looked away.

"Freedom, Mother," Anne said. "It is all that anyone ever desires. And, if you oppress someone enough, even if that oppression is out of affection, they will break free. They will want their liberty and do anything to obtain it. Therefore, Mother, what else have you done but push them into wishing to rebel against you, and then be surprised at their revolution?"

I turned to Colonel Fitzwilliam who blinked, recalling saying something similar about the American Revolutionary War. It was an extreme example, yet a good example in many ways to show a parent what would happen if one clung too hard on their child. All things in moderation then...

Lady Catherine then stood up and walked toward the pianoforte, and we saw her shoulders rise and fall as she contemplated what the best move for her to make was. Then she turned back to us.

"I am not used to not being rightly understood or being objected to. Yet if this is everyone's will, then I shall believe that the right course of action is to—accept all of your decisions after all."

"Truly?" Mr. Darcy asked, amazed.

"For the moment. I know when I have lost, and I admit that I am quite defeated in this case. I do not wish for it to happen again, yet if you are all determined to have your way, then for now, you may have it," she added, raising her chin proudly and as if she was making a great sacrifice on her part. "Now, since you are determined to have your Miss Kitty, Richard, then so be it, and since you have already chosen your Miss Elizabeth, Fitzwilliam, then I have no choice but to allow it."

"Well, thank you, aunt."

"Now, I did not come all this way to not have my way about something. Let me speak to Mrs. Reynolds, who I wish to inform her of what I think we ought to have for dinner."

While I did not like her taking charge even in that way, I decided to check my pride at the door and allow her that one moment of dominance.

"Very well," I replied. "Mrs. Reynolds!"

I didn't need to call again, for Mrs. Reynolds was right where I knew she was...on the other side of the door.

❧ 6 ❧

THE SHADES OF PEMBERLY

Throughout the dinner, Lady Catherine dominated the conversation. Even though she asked questions, she often did not wait for a reply before she began to speak again, and we all, just happy with her losing ground, allowed this.

After dinner, we all sat down to hear Georgiana play on the pianoforte, which she was so proficient in that even Lady Catherine could not find one objection to.

As we conversed, I managed to grow close to Anne de Bourgh, and when she caught my eye, she nodded to me. Taking that as encouragement, I walked over to her and sat down beside her.

"We have never had the chance to get better acquainted," I began.

"No, we have not," Anne replied. "And we find ourselves in a strange predicament where we were both once engaged to the same man."

"I hope that you bear no ill will toward me."

"None at all, Mrs. Darcy. I did not lose Fitzwilliam because I was obliged to, but rather because I knew that it was not correct nor sound. You need have no fear of me. We are family, and I wish you both nothing but joy."

"Thank you, Miss de Bourgh. And also special thanks to turning your mother's mind, for you did it to a large success."

"I was surprised that I could be so determined. Yet now that I know my own strength, hopefully I shall cling to it."

"Yes, we hope too. If you do, I believe that you shall find happiness."

"Thank you, I believe that I shall."

❦

Lady Catherine de Bourgh left for Rosing's Park the very next day, and only would have stayed if she were allowed to organize the whole wedding between Kitty and the Colonel. Therefore, out of desperation, Darcy searched his mind to find an excuse to not allow her to do so without rejecting her outright, and then a miracle found him.

"Thank you so much for your offerings, aunt," Colonel Fitzwilliam said, "yet we have received word that Kitty's family wishes us to return to Hampshire where they can celebrate our engagement."

"Oh," Lady Catherine said. "Then you shall write to them and tell them that it must be delayed, or that they should come here."

"Forgive me, aunt," Darcy added eagerly, catching onto his cousin's scheme. "Yet I have already sent our confirmation that we shall be going, and they have begun preparing our journey."

"Indeed," Mr. Bingley added. "I have already sent word to my servants to re-open Aginfield Park so that we shall have a place to stay."

"Precisely," Kitty said.

"Very much so," Jane added.

"With regrets, yes, it is so," Georgiana also added.

"And I have also sent forward order to our servants," Miriam furthered.

"Therefore, we must go, to be obliging," I said with finality.

"Oh, so now you all gather a desire to follow propriety." Lady Catherine said. "Well then, since you prefer your family to me, I shall most definitely make my exit."

"You need not worry, Aunt Catherine," Georgiana offered. "For if or when I get married, I shall let you design it to your heart's content."

"I shall do so," Lady Catherine said. "For no one has better taste in regards to marital traditions as me. Yet you had best make a match soon, for I do not wish for you to turn into an old maid."

Lady Catherine and Anne stepped into their carriage, and then they were off back to Rosings. We all watched the carriage drive along, and each of us felt a great weight roll off our shoulders. For the moment, we had escaped the wrath of Lady Catherine de Bourgh and we were on her more favorable side, though we knew perfectly well that we could always lose it the next day—or the day after that.

৩୬ঃ

The good luck that fell on the occupants of Pemberly was clearly not meant to last, however. That day had ended without any mishap and we were all preparing our items once more, packing them in our travel cases, for we would proceed to Aginfield and Longbourn in two days' time. Yet those two days could not have come sooner, we would learn in the very near future.

The next day, Colonel Fitzwilliam and Kitty were riding their horses along the grounds beside Pemberly. I was walking along, enjoying my solitude before having no choice but to be overwhelmed by company, when I saw a rider approaching Pemberly from the road. I turned and watched as the rider became recognizable and for the second time in only three days, another unpleasant surprise was approaching the house.

"Richard!" I cried. Colonel Fitzwilliam turned to me and rode his horse closer.

"What is it, Elizabeth? Are you well?"

"Your brother. Down the road there. It's your brother, Henry."

Colonel Fitzwilliam turned and then watched as his brother approached. When Henry Fitzwilliam drew close enough, he dismounted his horse, and I noticed a rapier sword was in its sheath at his side.

"Henry?" Colonel Fitzwilliam began, eying his brother with distrust. "What is it that you—"

Henry took out the sword and tossed it at the Colonel.

"Pick up the sword, Richard."

"Oh, Henry, do not do this."

"I challenge you to a duel! Now pick up your sword," he shouted, taking another sword from his horse's back and brandishing it.

"Henry," Kitty cried. "Stop this!"

"I am not speaking to you."

"But you will speak to me," I yelled, turning to him. "Henry Fitzwilliam, you are the oldest son of an Earl, you will inherit a fortune, and you can have any woman that you desire—and you must desist immediately. No one will call out anyone on my fields."

Henry ignored me and raised his sword to Richard.

"Pick up your sword, damn you!"

"I do not wish to harm you, Henry."

"Harm me? Who taught you fencing, little brother?"

Colonel Fitzwilliam picked up the sword, sneering.

"And who has been fighting in a war, Henry!"

"Richard!" Kitty cried.

Yet our pleas were to no avail.

Henry delivered the first strike and Colonel Fitzwilliam parried, then counter attacked. They continued to fight on the lawn, their swords clashing against each other while Kitty and I kept crying out for them to cease.

Back and forth they went, one gaining the higher ground then the other gaining so.

"Why resort to this, Henry?" Colonel Fitzwilliam cried out. "What do you have to gain from this?"

"My honor."

"Your honor was never taken from you! This loss is all in your mind."

"This is always as it must be, shouldn't it? For you've always been jealous of me."

"Jealous! Precisely. You were given everything. Destiny favored you Henry—but not me. And now for the first time ever, I am given something, and you attempt to seize it from me? Am I to have nothing?"

"There were many women in the world. Go to them and leave Kitty to me."

"She is not a possession! Or at least not yours, for all you are is a spoiled brat who is angry because a toy was taken from you."

They continued fighting while they argued and Kitty and I remained there, feeling quite helpless. Suddenly I felt a figure rush beside me with two swords in his hand, and I saw that it was Darcy. Moving as quickly as a cat, he ran to the two men and stabbed Henry in his sword hand. Henry dropped his sword and grabbed his wounded palm while glaring at Darcy. Darcy then raised his sword to Colonel Fitzwilliam's's shoulder, threatening him to lower his sword.

"That is enough!" my husband roared to his two cousins. Both Henry and the Colonel froze and remained still while Darcy glared down at them.

"Are you mad?" Darcy cried out. "Is this what you two have reduced yourselves to?"

"I will not—" Henry began.

"Shut up!" Darcy interrupted viciously. "Do you have no consideration for not only decorum, but also your own names? Have you any idea how many of my servants see this from the windows and now they will know everything—and they will speak, meaning your names will be linked for weeks with two brothers who fenced over the same woman. You embarrass her; you embarrass yourselves, your family, and me as well. To start with you," he said turning to Colonel Fitzwilliam. "Do not let yourself be so easily batted in, won't you? And as for you," he said turning to Henry. "How dare you come on my lands and challenge your own brother all because of your misguided pride and ruined humility.

"Face the truth, Henry, you are spoiled and have always been given everything, therefore you have grown to be unsatisfied unless everything is yours. Kitty was not yours, therefore it had to be something that you had to have. Richard gained her fairly, and now you want her even more. Wake up! It's not love that you feel for her. It's obsession. It's a desire to rule over everything that you even kind-of desire, which is why you cling to her now, even when you barely knew her. And I will not suffer foolishness to pass. Therefore, by all means, continue to indulge such foolish notions and see how I shall respond. Yet before it comes to that, I offer you congratulations for because of your decisions, now it can fully be said that the shades of Pemberly are thus polluted. I hope you are content."

"I merely wish to re-establish my honor," Henry Fitzwilliam declared.

"And I merely wish to keep both my cousins alive," Darcy hissed. "Which intention do you think is more noble? Yet if I have to choose one, then I shall do so. Henry, if you do not leave my grounds now, but continue to threaten violence upon Richard's person, then I shall run you through, and no one would blame me for it."

Henry glared at my husband, and a part of me did wish that Darcy would at least stab him again for daring to look at him venomously.

"I repeat, cousin, what will your choice be?"

❀ 7 ❀

SANCTUARY

Henry and Richard looked at one another while we all stared at them in contemplation. Richard's look masked resentment mixed in with bloodlust, and Henry's was wrath mingled with embarrassment.

Henry then went over to the swords, picked them up and turned away from us.

"I yield not out of cowardice or desire for the conflict to end unresolved," he whispered evenly, "yet only because of the damage this will do to our names. Not out of love for any of you."

"Don't walk away talking, Henry," Richard replied. "Just walk away."

"And heed my reply to your parting words," Darcy added. "Henry, until you have overcome your wounded pride and ceased to threaten your own family members, then you are not welcome here, and are banished from Pemberly."

"I will not forget this, Darcy."

"Nor will I."

Henry turned away, walked across the grass to his horse,

mounted it and then was off, riding down the road and what felt like into oblivion.

We all turned to each other, not knowing what to say in regards to Henry and Richard's altercation.

"I," Kitty began. "Richard, I am so sorry."

Richard did not even speak but grabbed her hand and led her along back to Pemberly. He did not even look at us nor care to explain or define his feelings. Yet maybe his attitude and actions were normal for men under such a circumstance, because I felt Darcy grab my hand and pull me back to Pemberly as well. We entered and I allowed him to lead me to his study, where he closed the doors behind us.

"My husband," I began. "I am so sorry. I tried to stop them, I did."

"Why did you not immediately come to get me?"

"I have never seen a duel before. I was at a loss of what to do is all."

"You're right, I am sorry."

I rushed to him and hugged him tenderly, and he wrapped his arms around me, where I felt secure in his embrace.

"How did you handle that with such strength? That was heroic."

"I... I don't know really. In truth, it all came from a place of rage and I did not even recall half of what I said."

"It was brilliant!"

"Was it?" He smiled, holding me even tighter. "Was it really?"

"Of course, it was. You've given me many reasons to be proud of you, but that moment just eclipsed them all. Upon my word, I am so amazed by you."

"Then I am glad to have made you so."

Richard and Henry's duel proved to have been observed by many eyes and word had spread all over the house, meaning Georgiana, Jane, Mr. and Mrs. Bingley and Mrs. Reynolds also received word of it.

While it was improper for us to allow Richard and Kitty time alone, we in all honestly did nothing on the matter because we understood that they needed each other's company. This however presented a wonderful time to bring forth the idea of going to Longbourn and accept our mother's invitation with alacrity.

Due to a desire to put the incident of the duel behind all of us, we welcomed the idea of traveling to Hampshire.

"That would be splendid," Mr. Bingley said when we informed him. "I will send word to my men to open Aginfield sooner than expected so that it will all be prepared for us."

"While Miriam shall be allowed to remain at Aginfield," Jane said, "our mother will require Kitty, Georgiana and I to remain at Longbourn."

"Me as well?" Georgiana asked. "Why so?"

"You are unmarried, and she will enjoy the compliment of you remaining with us so that she can look after you. Believe me; I know our mother and she will like the idea of that. She wanted to have you stay with us before when last you came, but Aginfield was not filled with so many residents. Now that there are, she will want you to stay."

"Oh," Georgiana said, self-satisfied with the idea of being considered so. "Fine enough with me."

Mrs. Reynolds had the servants prepare our luggage and we all, who once regarded my mother's invitation to come to Longbourn as a necessary obligation, now regarded it as a godsend.

"And do not worry about all the wedding preparations," Mrs. Reynolds said. "I shall oversee it all in your absence and have it complete in time."

"Thank you, Mrs. Reynolds," I said as we were all getting our coats on and the carriages were being drawn up for us.

And so, with Mrs. Bingley, Mr. Bingley, Georgiana, and Jane in one carriage, then Darcy, Kitty, Colonel Fitzwilliam, and myself in the second, and Jefferson, Lucy, and a couple other servants as well in the third with all of our luggage, Mrs. Reynolds offered us farewell as our coachmen urged the horses onward.

While we rode along, I turned to my husband.

"Dearest, I forgot something."

"We have to turn around?"

"Oh, nothing in that regard, I mean I did not remember to tell Georgiana something."

"Such as what?"

"I forgot to tell her that Lydia is now at Longbourn."

"What?"

"Yes, she is."

"Oh dear," Kitty said.

"Well, this week continues to bear gifts," Darcy said. "We shall just have to inform her when we break our journey at the inn at our first stopping point."

"Thank you. And when we reach Longbourn, I shall speak to Lydia again."

"Thank you, that is all that we can do."

"And something tells me that it will not be so hard," Kitty added.

"What do you mean?"

"Lydia had sent me another letter since the last one," Kitty said.

"Why did you not tell us?"

"I did not think it was worth mentioning. Her words were forced, and I felt that there was a hidden despair behind them. I think she is beginning to regret her marriage to Wickham terribly. Before it was subtle, now it seems apparent. In the letter, Lydia did not even mention Wickham and only wished to reminisce about our lives when we were back at Longbourn, single and free. When Georgiana arrives, she will not wish to speak of Wickham, believe me, especially since she wants to impress you all."

"She wants to impress us?" Darcy asked.

"Well, yes. She wants to come to Pemberly, does she not? I believe now that she has learned that her actions have led to an unfortunate turn, she might have learned to care a bit. In other words, she will do whatever that she can to impress you, I believe."

"I hope so."

"Unless I am completely in error, and I am seeing things that are better than the reality that is."

"I hope not."

Silence fell between us all and we began to fall into the private lives that are our daydreams.

We stopped at two inns along our journey, but in four days' time, we found ourselves looking back on the familiar face of Steventon, Hampshire. When we had come upon Aginfield, it felt as if we came closest to a safe haven, for my memories of Aginfield Park were all positive ones. When we arrived, the servants had prepared everything, and Jefferson took a horse to ride off and inform our family in Longbourn that we all had arrived at Aginfield.

After we all exited the carriages, I immediately felt weary, and Darcy, worried about our child as well as me, requested to Bingley that we all be allowed to retire to our guest rooms till dinner time. Mr. Bingley, who also saw that Miriam was exhausted, allowed this of all of us, except for Jane, Kitty and Georgiana, who were immediately taken to Longbourn.

When we got to our bedroom, I asked Darcy to tell Mr. Bingley to order some food for me because the baby was demanding more nourishment. While it was being prepared, I got into my nightgown, lie down, and fell asleep. When I awoke, the sun had not set, and Darcy's arms were around me.

"Don't worry," he said, his eyes closed. He startled me because I thought he was asleep. "The food was just brought in and you have only been asleep for half an hour."

"Thank you." I sighed, rolled over and kissed him. Behind him I saw the food on the table. "Food is a beautiful thing, but now this makes me too happy." I rolled over him and moved towards the food.

"Please be careful," he said. "Mind the baby."

"I promise you that I don't hinder it by rolling over your figure, though you do have a chiseled form."

"You flatter me."

"Yes."

"Good."

I began to eat, then I climbed on the bed and put some of the food into his mouth, showing that I was willing to share—despite the fact that I could have eaten it all myself and still have felt hungry.

"Eating for two is quite wonderful," I said. "I like having every excuse in the world to sit on my bottom often, eat all that I like and still be called beautiful for it."

"You do look beautiful."

"All because of her," I said, patting my belly.

"Or him."

"Yes, or him. You must understand that being raised in a family of five girls, one naturally expects to have a girl for one's first time. Would it not be amusing if we ended up having all girls?"

"It would feel redundant, but I could see destiny doing that to us." Darcy laughed heartily.

"If it is a girl, what should we name her?"

"I like Elizabeth, if you don't mind."

"No, I do not mind, though if we have two girls, I also very much like the name Helena."

"Helena?"

"Yes, from *A Midsummer's Night Dream*. I like the character Hermia most, but I hate that name!"

"Helena Darcy...yes I do like that."

"Well, what about if it's a boy? Can I name him Fitzwilliam?"

"Dear god no, my love. I hate my name...with a passion that consumes my soul!"

"Then what shall we name him?"

"I...well, how about Victor?"

"Victor? Well, that is a lovely one. I also like the names Dorian, or Hector."

"Hector?"

"I admired Hector's love for his wife in the Trojan War, Andromache."

"Well, when the time comes, if it's a boy, we have our three choices and we can choose them."

"That we are agreed upon."

Darcy then rubbed my belly.

"Elizabeth, I worry about you."

"You are worried about when I go into labor with the child, aren't you?"

"Yes, I cannot help but fear for you."

"I understand your apprehension. No matter what, it is a dangerous necessity in life. Yet we must be content nonetheless, and happy for our situation, no matter what the future holds."

"I know, but... I would not be able to do this without you."

I thought on what would happen if I were to pass away in childbirth, and while the idea frightened me terribly, I was worried most about leaving him alone with a child that he would have to take care of all alone.

I took his hands in my own.

"I will fight, Darcy, and always do my best to never leave you alone. Yet, if tragedy was to befall me, and I do not survive, then you must remarry."

"Elizabeth, I could not."

"You must. Live, Darcy, and you will and must begin to love again. For the sake of our child."

"Let us not think of this now. And I should not have begun to discuss it."

"Yet you did, and you were wise to. However, you must hope— for think on it, my mother survived seven successful pregnancies."

"Seven?"

"Yes, two were stillborns. She survived seven of them somehow and never experienced any health side-effects nor did it prove to even be possibly fatal to her. I come from a woman of that much strength, so hopefully I have it in my own right. Yet, if you so much desire to not get me in the same situation so soon after, then I propose that no wet nurse be brought in to look after our child, and that I should be permitted to nurse them."

"Yet that is improper."

"What is natural should not be. Our mother breastfed me and Jane for our first two years, and it was to her benefit, for when you nurse your own child, a woman cannot get pregnant during that time."

"Is this true?" Darcy turned to me.

"Quite true. Therefore, *when* I successfully give birth to our baby and if you are wishing me to not undergo pregnancy again for quite some time, to protect me, then allow me to nurse them myself. Also, it does create a strong bond between a mother and their child. Therefore, how is something so natural at all improper?"

"Well then, if that be the case, then I approve of that scheme."

"And once again, we are in agreement."

I finished eating the food and when done, I jumped back onto the bed and embraced Darcy once again, enjoying his warm touch.

"I must say Elizabeth; I never met a more energetic pregnant woman in my life. From what I recall, when my mother was pregnant with Georgiana, she could not move quickly at all, and did not wish to."

"I feel more sluggish because I am growing so huge. Yet it only makes me livelier. However, how are my feet looking to you, for I honestly miss seeing them?"

"Oh, dear, I had not thought of that."

"Yes, I cannot see my feet at this point. At first, when I noticed that my belly was growing, but the rest of me was not, I was worried. For with me, I actually do recall how my mother looked when she was pregnant with Lydia. And she was massive all around. Her arms, legs and thighs were four times the size she is now. Then she had Lydia, and I do not understand how she lost all the weight again, yet she did for quite some time."

"Some women gather mass only in their bellies and others grow it everywhere. When my mother was pregnant with me, she said that she was larger than my father was. She never understood why she remained thin for Georgiana. However, she did say that her labor with me went smoother than with my sister, therefore maybe all the mass she gained was for the better."

"Yes, and I hoped that I would follow suit, yet I still feel strong and resilient, so I am not angry with myself."

"Elizabeth, if she be a girl, may she look like you."

"I'm not certain, for I do quite like your nose more than mine." I laughed.

Darcy tickled my belly as I nibbled his chin.

"This always feels best," I said, "just falling into your arms."

"Yes, this is where home always is it seems. Lying here, with the world outside, as if our affection can keep it at bay...it is the best sanctuary of all."

8

MY FATE

The next day our mother was excited to see us, and most of all she was ecstatic to see the Colonel.

"Oh, there you all are!" she called out as we rode to the front of Longbourn. Our carriages halted and our entire party dismounted. Our father appeared as did Jane, Georgiana, Mary, Kitty and Lydia. It was so strange seeing Georgiana amongst them, for she was standing where I usually did in the line of them. It was quite an interesting concept to consider, for what would have happened if our destinies had been switched, with me the daughter of Pemberly and her as a daughter of Longbourn. For she did look quite comfortable in the lineup of the Bennets and our mother also seemed to be very considerate of her.

"I know why you did not come here immediately upon arrival," she said, "yet it still does feel very hard upon me that I had to wait a whole day before I saw my third son-in-law."

"Second son-in-law," our father said, exiting the house.

"Third son-in-law," our mother argued.

"Oh, correct, I forget about Wickham sometimes. He always has that forgettable appeal to him."

I saw Georgiana chuckle at this.

"Now," our mother said, turning to Mr. Bingley. "Is that the new Mrs. Bingley?"

"It is, indeed, Mrs. Bennet," Mr. Bingley said. "Allow me to introduce my wife, Mrs. Miriam Bingley."

"Mr. and Mrs. Bennet," Miriam said, curtsying. "I have heard nothing but the highest praises of you."

"That will raise people's expectations of us too high," our father replied. "Yet still it is nice to meet you as well. I have seen Mr. Bingley look happy, yet he seems to be glowing now, therefore I believe you are as lovely as you appear."

"Oh, thank you, sir."

"Now, let us all gather inside," our mother said, for our cooks have made the most wonderful mid-day meal. You shall love it."

We all entered, and our mother began immediately addressing me.

"And Elizabeth, you look wonderful."

I patted my huge belly. "Oh, thank you, Mama!"

"Yes, by the size of you, it will not be long now." Then she turned to our father. "Do you remember how many times I was that size?"

"Seven, my dear, and as a loving father, I remember each day of them."

"Oh, you always say that, and I never believe you."

"It's good that you don't, my dear. For no one should ever lose their wits to that degree."

We all stifled our laughter at that.

"So," I said, "how have you been, Mother and Father? You both look well."

"Yes, I daresay that we both do," Mrs. Bennet said. "But all my girls back under one roof with their beaus and two extra lovely women, I shall be quite distracted. Only one thing is needed to complete this scene and I do not even know what that is. Have you any idea, Mr. Bennet?"

"Of course, I know, my dear. We need a little bit of Irish Whiskey."

"And what does that have to do with anything, Mr. Bennet?"

"I was wrong, oh, I'm sorry. I hadn't the slightest idea of what I should have said instead."

She swatted his chest with her handkerchief. "The answer should have been 'grandchildren', my dear. Only the fond sounds of grandchildren could have improved the scene."

"I still prefer the idea of Irish Whiskey."

"Oh Mr. Bennet, the way you carry on, you would think our daughters were to look forward to a grand inheritance as well as a lot of children in the making. And we only have one at present, and Elizabeth, may it all come out well."

"Thank you, Mama."

"Yet I hope for your sake, it is a boy. It always gives the husband comfort in knowing that his line is secure. When it does not happen, a bit of his soul is lost."

"When have I ever parted with half of my soul, Mrs. Bennet?"

"Every day, dear, every day you do."

"I shall be happy whether our infant is a boy or girl," Darcy said, not annoyed with my mother's comments or my father's sardonic humor—I daresay that he had gotten used to it by that point. "And I need not fear, for our family always saw to it that if there were never any male heirs, it would be handed down to the next heiress. Therefore if we were to best you, Mr. and Mrs. Bennet, and have ten daughters, the oldest would be able to protect her younger siblings by being the mistress of Pemberly."

We all chuckled and then we sat down to dinner.

Supper went well, for all were used to my parents and were able to see the humor in them—all except Miriam, who was new to Longbourn. However, Miriam, coming from a large family where her father could be emotionally remote and the mother affectionately talkative and very forward, grew accustomed to my family very quickly and even felt comfortable with them.

By the end of the dinner, while my family did have this ability to be vulgar, base and a little crass, they did give one the feeling of warm family life—as well as being at home. Those who pride themselves on sophistication, cold prudence and serenity would not find it in Longbourn, and would despise us Bennets, yet I believed that there was a place for our family in the eyes of goodness, no matter how rambunctious we sometimes were.

What frightened me through the afternoon was Lydia and how she would behave. Yet to my surprise, she was animated without pushing through the boundaries of propriety and falling into being disgraceful. I worried she would attempt to flirt with Colonel Fitzwilliam, yet she did not. I thought she would do her best to dominate the conversation with talks of Newcastle and all the friends she had, yet she only mentioned Newcastle if she were asked about it. I also feared that she would mention Mr. Wickham, yet she didn't even wish to hear reference of him, which was both heartbreaking and pleasing.

One time I even saw her look down on her wedding ring with disgust. Not only did it become inherently obvious that she knew Wickham was not a good man, yet she also had experienced the only things that would have taught her humility... she had learned loss and regret. Despite being two things that people loathed to experience, they were the two things that people mostly learned from. With Lydia, it clearly had been so.

That evening we all returned to Aginfield, where we offered to have the residents of Longbourn over for the next day.

In two days' time, there was the assembly in the banquet hall of the Red Lion, and that our entire party arrived to the sight of many familiar faces. Naturally, Charlotte Collins was not there, yet Maria Lucas was with Samuel Lucas, Sir William, and Lady Lucas as well with the rest of their family. Also there were the Phillips, the Pratts, Longs, Jenkinsons, Asters, Campbells, Westons, and the Austens.

Upon entering, people enjoyed seeing Mr. Bingley, Darcy and Georgiana again, yet they were immediately taken with the Colonel who was always well-qualified at recommending himself to strangers. Also, being an officer in his majesty's army made him a hero, therefore every woman was quick to not only like him, despite that he was not as handsome as Darcy or Mr. Bingley, but they were also quick to be jealous over Kitty for catching him.

As for myself, I had just gotten done telling the Austen sisters about the little bit of our time in America that I had not mentioned before, under the strict confidence that they would not tell anyone else about Jane's rejection of Henry Darcy.

"It is quite a curiosity though," Cassandra commented, "that Henry Darcy should have pressed the matter, and not accepted her refusal, and then claimed that she had denied him with so little effort at civility. Especially since he wondered why with so evident a design to offend and insult her, he chose to tell her that he liked her for such paltry and false reasons."

"Aye, it should have been against his judgment, his reason and his better character," Jane Austen added. "Jane had every reason to think ill of him. And as she said, what consideration should tempt her to accept a man who had been the means of insulting her most beloved sister? Did he deny it?"

"He had no wish to deny it," I replied. "He claimed that he did anything and everything to get me to see his bigoted idea of reason, and that if I listened, he would rejoice in his success. Towards himself he had been kinder than toward me."

"But it is not only that on which I am decided against this other Mr. Darcy," Jane Austen said. "My opinion on him was decided when you told me of his jilting you when you first met. How did he defend himself on that subject?"

"You take an eager interest in this *other Mr. Darcy*, Jane?" I teased.

"Who that has heard of him can't help feeling an interest in him? I know little, but I can tell you that he is probably in America now thinking of his misfortune in being rejected."

"The guilty always think themselves ill-used and innocent," I answered. "His misfortunes. His misfortunes have been great indeed. And knowing him, he possibly regards this set down in his life as a great affliction. He has reduced our family to our state of a family divided and strained, and he might regard us with contempt and ridicule."

"And is this your opinion of him?" Cassandra asked. "By your calculation, his faults must be great indeed. And they are, for I have no pity for him. But perhaps these faults might have been overlooked had not his pride been affected so early into your acquaintance. He is a man knocked down; hopefully, he will see clearly when he has to get back up again."

"You do not blame Jane for refusing him, do you?"

"Blame her? Oh no, how could she have attached herself to his vicious character? If he is so very bad. Yet you have seen it with your eyes, so it must be true. Unless there is some mistake."

Jane Austen laughed. "Oh, Cassandra! That will not do. You cannot defend and justify both characters. There is only room enough for one good sort of man, and for my part, I am inclined to think it all Mr. Darcy. Your Mr. Darcy, I mean, Lizzy, and not the other one."

"Thank you."

"And from what you told us," she continued, "the turn of his countenance I will never forget when he said, 'Had you behaved in a more gentleman-like manner'. Very fitting for a proper set down. Though I daresay, as far as ending a speech can go, 'You are the last man in the world who my sisters should ever be prevailed upon to marry', will always be my favorite."

I looked Jane in the eye.

"You are going to use that line in some way or the other, aren't you?"

"Some words should not go to waste by being spoken once and then never being uttered again. No, Elizabeth, some sentences must and should last forever."

⚬⚬⚬

All throughout the assembly, Colonel Fitzwilliam, Mr. Bingley and Darcy had many dance partners. While people could say that Darcy was growing to be loved by the people of Hampshire, most always loved Mr. Bingley and most were quick to adore the Colonel. Kitty felt all the distinction of being engaged to such a pleasing gentleman, I was happy to see that Darcy was showing all around him how wonderful he was, and we all felt the comforts of the world outside remaining *the world outside*. At the assembly, all was perfect, all were happy. And the woes and memories that haunted us could be outrun, it felt, and could be in our past.

⚬⚬⚬

That evening, our company split, some went to Longbourn and the rest went to Aginfield.

"I am happy to stay at Longbourn as it turns out," Georgiana whispered to me. "I am sleeping in your old room. And your sisters tell me secrets about pranks you pulled when you were younger."

67

"They would do that. But Georgiana, please, you must tell me, how has Lydia been? I never got the moment to talk to her and I neglected to tell her how she ought to behave."

"It is quite shocking, but she and I get along well."

Rather surprised, I asked, "Do you?"

"Yes. She has not mentioned Wickham at all so far. It's almost as if she does not wish to speak of him. He has done something, I fear. Something awful, for she pretends to be free, in every sense of the word. Yet Elizabeth, there is something that she does not know that I am aware of."

"What?"

"She was changing into her chemise and I saw scars on her back. And while they could have come from anything, I am not certain that they were not wounds from passion. She also has some bruises on her arms."

Despite the size of my stomach, it felt empty all of a sudden.

"Have you spoken to anyone about what you suspect?"

"No, but Mary seems to know something is wrong. I cannot tell because she and I do not speak often—we are too different—but there is a certain look in her eye, a sense of knowing. She is aware that Lydia is hiding something."

"You can see all this?"

"A trick of living with a man such as my brother. You have to learn how to read people through the emotions they hide rather than reveal, and the words they don't say instead of say. And he's given me much practice."

"Yes, I dare say he would."

"Yes. Mind you, I could be wrong about all this."

"It is fine, Georgiana, and thank you for being so observant. I believe, had life turned out different for you, you would have been a great spy."

"Thank you, but I know."

I grinned.

"And if you are wrong or right, I shall find out what is happening underneath it all."

"I hope I am wrong, but I fear the most frightening thing of all."

"And what is that?"

"That I am right."

Georgiana then left and joined the Longbourn party.

⚜

It was strange how Georgiana and I had switched places. With her being on the inside of Longbourn and I was on the outside, looking inward. And judging from what I had witnessed, she may have greatly enjoyed the swap.

The next day, I decided to walk from Aginfield to Longbourn.

"You cannot be serious?" Darcy asked me as I was getting dressed that morning.

"Serious? *Moi?*"

"Yes, you"

"Why so? Wasn't it my journey from Longbourn to Aginfield that was the beginning of you falling in love with me?"

"Your fine eyes were brightened by the exercise, yes, but still we were not married then."

"Admit it, you are worried about me."

He ran his fingers through his hair, rumpling it. "Yes, I am. And in your pregnant state."

"Oh, very well, you are correct on that score. I am carrying a greater load now and it might weigh me down."

"That is one fear that a person could have, or you might grow ill."

"Very well then, after breakfast, can you draw the carriage for me so that I may go?"

"And why do you wish for me to not join you?" he asked.

"Because I need to speak to Lydia," I replied in honesty. "I want to know the truth about what has changed in her, for something is amiss. Also, I want to know the truth about her life with Wickham. I know he is not treating her well."

"It is not in his way to treat any woman well once she gets to see the truth of him," Darcy growled.

"Precisely, and if you come with me, then there is no chance that I can get her to speak to me if you are present. She is too intimidated by you and will only wish to talk of frivolous things that make her appear light and breezy."

"Fair enough. And though I hate to sound overbearing and demanding right now, but if you learn the truth, will you tell me it?"

"Yes," I replied. "I shall communicate all, that I can assure you —as long as you promise to always ask me such things by request and not by ways of command."

"I can agree to that."

We kissed and then separated.

"You had better!"

⚜

After dinner, the carriage was drawn, I journeyed the distance to Longbourn and then Nicholson pulled up before it.

"Thank you, Nicholson," I said as he helped me down. "Would you like to come in and take some tea or refreshment?"

"Thank you, Mrs. Darcy," Nicholson said. "Yet I should like to just rest at the stables. To be honest, I'm a little bashful and I will not know how to make conversation."

"Very well," I said as our servant Hill was the first to exit the house to meet me while Nicholson nodded to her and moved the carriage down the lane. "Hello, Hill."

"Oh, Mrs. Darcy, it is nice to see you, as you very well know. But you come without Mr. Darcy? Still independent I see. I wonder if you still even climb trees."

"Not in my wider state." I drew closer to her. "Hill, I need you to do me a favor."

"You're going to ask me to hide something, aren't you?"

"Yes. Has anyone noticed my carriage?"

"We servants have seen it, but the rest of the family is in the dining-parlor, having a late breakfast."

"Oh, I miss those. Well, do me the favor of telling Mary, as soon as she is done, to come around to the back of our yard by the yew tree, for I wish to speak to her. Yet make it very clear that I do not wish for her to inform anyone else about my being here just yet."

"Ah, you are planning something."

"Always, Hill. Always."

I went around our lawn and waited by the tree yet was not left to wait long. After ten minutes, I saw Mary emerge from the back door from the kitchens and then see me. She walked across the lawn and we met under the branches.

"You wish to know something?" she said.

"Good day to you too, Mary."

She looked at me with a slight pause.

"Good day," she said.

"Thank you, Mary."

"Forgive me, Elizabeth. I just did not believe that you needed me to come in such a clandestine fashion if you did not immediately wish to get to the heart of the matter. Also, we do not have much time before I'm sure that we shall be come upon, so I think you might wish for me to be pertinent."

"Very well," I said rolling my eyes. "Still, you can look more comfortable. We are sisters, Mary, and not attorneys at law."

"I thought I did look comfortable."

"Right, sorry. Mary, how long has Lydia been here at Longbourn?"

"A little over a fortnight."

"And in that time, has she spoken to you at all—about her time in Newcastle?"

"She seems to not wish to talk about it," Mary said, avoiding my gaze.

"Mary, is that the whole truth? There is something about your nature that is not good at dissembling and being untruthful. Or maybe it has to do with your desire to be forever moral. Mary, please, remember your principles now and help me. Is there something that you know?"

"I..." Mary began, her voice losing its monotone self-absorbed tone, "I have no proof of this."

Alarmed I asked, "No proof of what?"

"When Lydia came here, she had many bruises on her body, and she gave excuses that I did not believe matched the lacerations. Elizabeth, I could be wrong, and I am afraid to speak of such a terrible act, yet I had to consider."

"You think Wickham may have abused her?"

"Aye. I think Lydia's husband is violent toward her."

⁂

"I want to believe that I am wrong," Mary rushed out.

"Yet you are also afraid that you are correct," I finished for her.

"Precisely. I am very afraid."

"So am I."

"Elizabeth?"

"Yes?"

"I know that Wickham is a worthless libertine," Mary whispered, "but do you believe that he could be so very bad?"

"Yes, he has it in him to be anything. And the question then becomes, how is such a man to be worked on?"

"And she had to marry him, even though he was such a man."

"Yes, there was nothing for it."

"She brought this on herself."

"Mary, I do not approve of Lydia's actions any more than you do, but sometimes we all bring some form of trial on ourselves. It shall happen to you one day, and all we can hope for is to weather it."

"Should I reject Lydia forever?" Mary asked. "Before, I thought that I ought to, yet now I am confused."

"Mary, please. If she is in such a state all because she foolishly loved the wrong man, then do not deny her forever. She has suffered for her ignorance, and now her own punishment is making her pay enough clearly. Thank you for telling me all that you know."

"What will you do?"

"I have no choice, apparently. I will have to speak with our sister."

❦

"And why did you need this to be a secret?" Lydia complained as I closed the door to her bedroom. "From what I recall, I have done nothing of late to make you angry with me."

"Precisely. You have done nothing to offend or embarrass anyone. You have also ceased to flirt as much as you did before."

"Well, propriety commands me to."

"Because you are a married woman."

Lydia's smile faltered.

"Yes, I am really."

"Yes, you are. And I can tell that it causes you grief."

"It does not. I was the first to marry and I have a handsome husband."

"Who mistreats you."

"I..."

"If you are afraid to allow me into your confidence Lydia, then I know there is nothing I can do to persuade you but know now that you lose nothing by trusting me. I know that Wickham only appears as a charming and perfect match, but he is heartless, ruthless, and selfish to a fault. I know that he is cruel sometimes, and that he married you because of the money he was offered to do so. And what is most painful for you is that you are beginning to learn all this."

Lydia looked down.

"I know that you are going to try and cling to the facade that you have built so well around yourself, but that facade has now put you in danger. Lydia, I know that he has committed violence upon you."

Lydia looked up, shocked.

"How did you... Mary! How could she?"

"Mary did not tell me anything," I lied. "No one has told me anything. And I did not know that he was abusive at all actually...yet your reaction has just told me everything."

"It is not—"

"Why do you protect him, Lydia?" I cried, at my wit's end. "What brings you to feel as if you have to conceal this?"

"Because there is nothing that anyone can do."

Lydia sat quietly for a moment, then stood up. She walked to the window of the room and looked out.

"Because this is my fate, apparently, and I have to endure it."

9

BECAUSE THEY ARE FAMILY

"This is my lot," Lydia sighed. "And that is the end of it."

"By god," I whispered. "While I am happy that your mind has improved, Lydia, it still frightens me. What has he done to you that he has turned you into this? You are a shade of your past self. And in this moment I can hardly recognize you."

"Well then do what you will, Elizabeth. Enjoy your happy ending and knowledge that your destiny brought you peace. You had better you stayed home. Condolence is insufferable in my case. Let you triumph at a distance and be satisfied."

"Lydia that is unkind."

"That is from the sister who can never hope to have your good fortune, therefore at least let me have an insult. At least let me have my jealousy."

"Lydia, there is no need to be jealous of me."

"Elizabeth, there is every reason. We fell in love with men who were villains in some way, yet mine remained a villain, and yours decided to open his eyes and turn into a hero that saved you and everyone around you, including me. Yes, Lizzy, you are right. I am broken, and I want nothing more than to become the girl I once was again: single, savage and hearty. I was wild, yes, but I was still innocent. I meant well, I did, I was just foolish. And should I really have been damned for all time for it?"

"You are not damned because of his wickedness alone, but out of your own choices, and your failure to see that they were the wrong ones. That you ridiculed others, laughed at many, and did not care, calling anyone who did their best to improve yourself as being high-minded or prudish."

"Whatever my faults, I am suffering for all eternity for it. Therefore, so it is..."

"I did not say that you deserve a man who is violent to you. I am simply saying that you cannot think to improve your situation, if you do not improve yourself."

"Why do you think I have fled here?" Lydia shouted. "I am doing my best to remain away from the problem for as long as I can. When Wickham and his regiment marched out, traveling to the Peninsula to join the Portuguese, I gladly rushed down here. I am free for the moment and I cannot deny that I am in heaven. I come here and I can act as if my mistake never happened."

"That is not the answer. It did happen, and only by confronting it will you change for the best in full."

"I am changing. You see this. At first, I worried that I would have to return once Wickham's regiment returned, yet he will not need me, nor desire me. Truly, Lizzy, my own husband doesn't care if I am dead or alive. Therefore, if he returns and I were to inform him that I wish to remain at Longbourn, he would not send for me, and even rejoice in his freedom from me. I can stay here, Lizzy, and grow to be a married maiden who is exiled, but content to be so."

"And what will the people in Hampshire say about your prolonged visit?"

"Well, I figured that I could form some excuse. I could say that my mother's health has led to me wishing to remain and wish to look after her, and my husband accepts it. There may be talk, yet nothing scandalous will come of it."

I sighed. "Well, I will not deny that I want you to never return to him, and this seems to be the best way to do it. Therefore, in hopes that you find what you need to be, and out of a desire for your safety and a hatred for Mr. Wickham, I am happy that you have found this course of action."

"Thank you, Lizzy."

Lydia turned from the window and began to leave.

"And if you ever were to invite me to Pemberly," she added, "I should admit to liking to visit there."

"I shall ask Darcy."

"Thank you."

All throughout the carriage ride home, I confess to wishing all sorts of violent actions on Wickham—some of which I wished to do to him myself, out of a desire to make sure he felt immense pain. Yet he was separated by a large body of water and bits of a continent. He was safe from me, and what I would ask Darcy to do to him.

When arriving back at Aginfield Park, I found Darcy sitting in the library, reading some letters. Upon my entrance, he looked up, but took one look upon my face and his demeanor changed. As I sat down beside him, I unfolded all that Lydia had told me, and he met it with rage.

"I wish to kill him," he snarled.

"And I wish that you could, I admit," I replied, "even my own thoughts toward him are quite belligerent, and I do not fear sounding indelicate for wishing to do so."

"You are being protective. No less can be said of so. Lizzy, we have to do our best to make certain that she does not return to him when he comes home."

"That will not be hard. If we concoct any scheme to keep Lydia away from Newcastle, he will not care one way or the other. Lydia, now that she is far away from him, is safe, and he will not return to England looking for her or caring about her at all."

"Then we are lucky at the moment because he is so coldhearted that Lydia will be able to slip out of his fingertips in the same way that she had fallen into it; with ease."

"Then if finding liberty from such a libertine is so simple, there is hope for her after all."

"Yes, lots of hope. Your sister, whether by her luck or not, is not forsaken. And apparently," he said, holding up a letter, "neither are we."

"What is that?"

"It's a letter from the American Darcys."

"Really? Wait, how did they know to send the letter here?"

"They didn't. Before we left, Jefferson was worried we would miss letters of importance, so he ordered certain letters from certain senders to be forwarded here from Pemberly. This letter arrived at Pemberly four days ago, and Mrs. Reynolds forwarded it here."

"Oh, thank you, Jefferson," I said, despite that he was not present.

"Yes, and now the letter has just arrived, and I have read it."

"Well, do not leave me in suspense. What did it say?"

"Since you were so courteous as to be honest with me about what Lydia has disclosed to you, I think it only fitting that I return the compliment."

He handed me the letter, I sat on his lap and began to read it aloud.

Dear Mr. and Mrs. Darcy,

We are happy to hear of your good news and we are certain that you will be a most loving set of parents. While I do not know of your desires, I hope that you are as productive as I am, for a house full of children, though loud and in constant disarray, still is a jovial and uplifting place.

In regards to Kitty's marriage to Colonel Fitzwilliam, that is also wonderful news and we offer our congratulations. In truth, I have not seen the Colonel since he was a child, and I am curious to see the man he has turned into. If he is a good man, then Kitty deserves him, and he deserves Kitty.

Yet dear cousins, you know that we desperately wish to resolve the rift that had formed at the end of your stay with us, and we are in hope that this might be the ideal situation to yield the breach. We know that you both cannot travel, for your pregnant state does not allow that, yet Kitty and the Colonel, like yourselves, could celebrate their honeymoon here by going on holiday in Philadelphia. The Colonel's appearance might offer us a new acquaintance and give us the chance to start over, and then little by little, we can form a stronger bond. We shall also make it so that our eldest son, Henry, will treat them with the respect that is their due. Please inform them of our invitation. For this next war is clearly going to occur—and we very much still want to have you as our family before the Great Divider that is war causes our families to break contact once more.

Hope to hear from you soon,
Cousin Thomas and Cousin Emilia

I lowered the letter.

"I believe that they wish to offer us the olive branch," I said, "and I wish to gain it from them."

"Yes, I agree," he said. "Yet one thing that I do not understand is their constant efforts. Why do they try so hard? Why do they wish to maintain this bond?"

"Because they are family, my love. That's what family does."

✦ 10 ✦

THAT IS THE WAY WITH FAMILY

When we told Kitty and Richard about the letter, they agreed to the scheme with great enthusiasm. Despite how our last visit had ended, Kitty did have many fond memories of Cousin Thomas and Emilia, therefore she was willing to try once more.

"Even at the expense of seeing Henry Darcy again," she said. "Oh, hateful man!"

"Then I can write back in the affirmative," Darcy said.

"Aye," Colonel Fitzwilliam said. "For I have been quite curious to always see them again. And after the latest skirmish with my own brother, I look for peace anywhere at this point. One family embarrassment can help you forgive another. Whatever this Henry Darcy did, it was not nearly as irksome as my brother challenging me to a duel. I may not be disposed to like him, yet I could handle him, I bet."

"Yes, Henry Darcy is a strong man," I said. "But he's no fighter."

"And I am." Darcy then wrote the letter to the American Darcys and had Jefferson send it express, with the date for the couples' arrival and all else that needed to be spoken of.

When he was done, we prepared to go to Longbourn for our afternoon luncheon.

Yet before we had done so, I was in my bedroom, making sure my hair looked presentable, when I noticed a book was open. I went closer to it and noticed that it was a diary, and even closer inspection showed that it belonged to my husband. A part of me knew the wisdom of not reading it, yet I was a wife, and not a saint. Curiosity ate away at me and I wished to know what was on the page that was open. Telling myself that I should and would only read that one page, I, much to my shame, gave into the temptation, picked up the diary and read it.

This morning, when I awoke, I rolled over, and her eyes were the very first things that greeted me. The sun shone all around her from the windows. Call our marriage unorthodox, call us forever falling toward the edge of impropriety, but from the day that we became man and wife, Elizabeth and I have never slept in separate beds, but in one, united, always in the presence and company of each other. For months we have been man and wife, and yet still, I can only find completion in her eyes, by her form. There's never been a day where I felt that if we were separated by mountains, oceans, and hell itself, I would not journey until I found her. She is my life. She is in my very soul, and I fear the day that I might lose her. I fear us ever having children, for the birth of a child will every now and again lead to the death of the mother. If it were to be so, I fear I would hate the child. I fear that I would never forgive it for robbing me of the one human that I cannot be without. I fear the evil in me that would erupt if I were driven from her. A demon might arise inside my soul—a demon that would not care if the whole world burned, for if I didn't have her, nothing would matter. This morning, she turned, looking at me fondly, her eyes still sleepy, her nude form only covered by our sheets. She leaned forward and ran her hand gently down my cheek.

'Good morning my love,' she said, smiling in a way that she only did for me.

I rolled over and kissed her passionately. I felt all my fears subside. She was still mine for another day. I was still blessed. The animal inside of me is still tame, and I am still a good man, for I have her by my side. The evil, the anger that is in me, is still at bay. May I never lose her. For if that were to happen, I fear that I would not care if the whole world burned.

I closed the diary and put it down gently. Stirred by his words, I felt rooted to the spot.

His confession about his apathy toward the world if I were not in it did not rattle my sensibilities nor did it frighten me. It was altogether strange of me, yet I felt moved by his words, amazed by the power of his love. I could not believe that so deep an affection and a bond could find me, yet it had. And every instinct to never be parted from him, because I loved him so was not in error, but of perfect harmony and correctness. Our tempers and natures could not help but be each other's foil as well as each other's complement. Our souls were different, yet they also were the same.

And yet, he feared losing me still to childbirth. While I believed myself to be a strong and robust woman, there was and always would be that danger that came along with the deed. If Darcy were to lose me, would he truly despise the child? It made me frightened for my baby somewhat. I wished to believe Darcy was exaggerating, yet I feared that he might not be. However, even in utter despair over losing me, he would not forsake our child, nor would he blame them. Oh no, for in the throes of heartbreak, he always finds his way out of the darkness that is his emotional abyss. My husband is the rocks beneath while also being the flicker of light in the darkness...he always remains, and he always finds his way to sunlight.

Therefore, whatever befell me, I knew there would be much good left in him. Until then, I would have to wonder at where our destinies would lead us: to hope or to bitterness.

My hair looked presentable and then I left my room to join the others.

⚘

The rest of the day went well, and the next day it was our turn to have the residents of Longbourn over for dinner. While preparing everything for dinnertime, Miriam confided in me about her ease of being mistress of Aginfield.

"I at first thought it would be daunting, yet now that I have adjusted to it, I find that I can bear the position quite cheerfully. And Mr. Bingley has expressed joy over it for one main reason."

"What is that?" I asked.

"Now that I am the mistress, he does not have to bring his sister, Caroline Bingley, everywhere with him. So now that is a great weight lifted from his shoulders."

"Yes," I agreed. "A great weight."

That night I tried on a gown that I had ordered made especially for an evening amongst friends, and while I was wide in the belly, I had hoped that it would still find a way to flatter me. After Lucy had managed to place it on me, Darcy entered, and he stopped in his tracks.

"Mrs. Darcy, you look radiant this evening."

I gave him a curtsy. "Thank you. I was hoping to impress you."

"And you have."

When done, he offered me his arm.

"Now, let me escort my perfect wife to the dining-parlor."

"She would be delighted."

Together, we walked down to dinner and met the others.

That night, the dinner proved successful until the grand unveiling of an inappropriate action occurred. After dinner, Kitty said that she had to go and fix her hair which was falling down. Yet after she left, Colonel Fitzwilliam was asked by Jefferson to go to the stables, because his horse was having a fit, and the Colonel had influence on his stead. The Colonel left, however after a few moments, Kitty did not return. I was worried over this, but it was a shout that had startled all of us. A few of us rushed into the hallway and we saw my mother screaming in a doorway.

"Take your hands off my daughter, Colonel! And Kitty, move away from him this instant."

"Mother," I cried, walking forward. "What is the matter?" I was being followed by Darcy, Mr. Bingley, Jane, and our father.

"It is of the greatest error to even think that you would get away with this!" she cried. "They were alone, and I walked in on them—" Our mother covered her mouth in shock.

I walked up to the door and saw Kitty and the Colonel standing next to each other, looking red in the face before our mother.

"Richard?" Darcy bellowed. "What is the meaning of this?"

"Darcy, forgive me," Colonel Fitzwilliam said. "And you must not be angry with your daughter, Mrs. Bennet. She simply allowed me liberties out of her feelings for me, and I took advantage of it."

"You never should be alone with a lady before you marry her!" our mother cried. "And you should never dare kiss her. This is outrageous, Colonel, and I expected better from you. And Kitty, move away from him this instant and gather your shawl, for we are leaving for Longbourn immediately."

"Mother, he is my fiancé and has apologized," Kitty argued.

"And I am still your mother. Now do as I say, and stop being such a headstrong and foolish child."

"Kitty," Mr. Bennet said, resigned. "Do as your mother bids and gather your things."

Kitty, torn between submission and remaining obstinate, walked away from the Colonel, moved around us, and left the room to collect her shawl. Colonel Fitzwilliam stubbornly bit his lip but refused to look ashamed.

"And Colonel," Mr. Bennet said, "I do not pretend to be a saint myself. Yet when giving into temptation, was it really worth it? I dare say that it was not."

Taking our mother's arm, they followed after Kitty, then collected Jane, Lydia and Georgiana.

"I suppose you wish of me to apologize," Colonel Fitzwilliam said.

"That is a start."

"And yet, I cannot. It was a kiss, and I love her."

"I know, but still, Richard!" Darcy said. "Look what it has led to."

"And yet, Fitz, while I am sorry for the trouble that I caused you, I cannot apologize for the rest of it. Forgive me for that."

Darcy bit his lip, then turned and walked away.

◈❦◈

My family left, with my mother in a huff, and Colonel Fitzwilliam retired early. Mr. Bingley, though claiming to be ashamed, was not upset that the Colonel kissed Kitty. He was only vexed that the Colonel was foolish enough to do it when her parents were in the vicinity and under the worst circumstances where it would be easy for them to get caught.

"There are some things that can always be understood," he said to me in confidence, "and that is always a man and woman kissing before their nuptials, for it is a very natural thing. In truth, I kissed Miriam often before we wed, just as I know that Fitz kissed you as well. However, who kisses when there are so many chances to be found out? That is where thought flies out of the window."

"Affection always can lead to thought going on holiday," I offered. "I'm not excusing their actions, yet you and I can comprehend it."

"Yes."

Later that evening, Darcy and I were in bed and we had exhausted the discussion of what would happen as a result of Kitty and Colonel's discovery.

"My mother is going to fly into hysterics," I said, "and her demands might become extreme as a result."

"Tis true. I want to reprimand Richard..."

"Yet you cannot," I concluded, "because if you did, then you would feel like a hypocrite."

"Precisely. And did you notice how the very room that they were found in—"

"Was the same room where we kissed in after the Aginfield Ball? Oh yes, I noticed very much. We should chastise them, yet our own actions being similar to theirs make it impossible to do so."

"I am therefore at a loss."

"And that's where the power of parents comes in. We need do nothing, for my mother and father will throw the book at them, and that will be chastisement enough."

"Well, that is a great weight lifted off my shoulders."

"Yes, let's just see how this shall unfold. For we do not rule their lives, nor do we have reign over it. When we are ready, we shall be our own children's parents, and until then, we need to stop having to be forced to be everyone else's."

"Yes, that would be a great comfort. Too much we have to tend to others."

"I agree—too much."

"And I worry over it. Elizabeth, our family seems to always be struggling to remain on the right side of dignity, and also rendering itself ridiculous. From Lady Catherine's constant meddling to Henry Fitzwilliam's duel with Richard, and now this? It does seem as if we never have much time to find serenity and enjoy the peace that comes along with it."

"And then there is this," I added, patting my belly. "Yes, you are right, there is a story to our family: a series of trials and tribulations. Yet that is the way with family, I suppose. And with my family I have grown used to it, and with bringing another individual into the world, I believe we must prepare ourselves, for the wild events shall follow us from now on.

II

THE PAINS OF LIVING

The next day, Darcy, Colonel Fitzwilliam and I traveled to Longbourn, knowing that not to do so would be highly offensive. Upon our arrival, we were told to enter the study where my father was. After we did so, he bade us to sit down and then had Kitty enter with our mother.

"Well then," Mr. Bennet said, "let us begin."

"Kitty," our mother started, "I cannot believe this. For you are not the sort of girl to do such a thing."

"That sentence sounds familiar," Kitty answered, "for it was the same thing that you had said about Lydia when she had eloped with Wickham. Yes, I remember very well, for you had claimed that she wasn't the sort of girl to do such a thing, had she been properly looked after."

"Kitty..." I began, but Kitty stumbled onward.

"No, I will not be silenced! You chastise me for this, yet I recall how Lydia went off and did a most dreadful thing and all you felt was sorrow for her, then acceptance when she was prevailed upon by the most worthless man in Britain. Does the satisfaction of her most terrible fate rest now in its proper place? Why, Mother and

Father? Why is my kissing my fiancé so very dreadful, yet you thought Lydia still lovely in your eyes, Mother? So, you ask me what is wrong with me, then I ask in return, what is wrong with you?"

Our mother looked between us, not knowing what to say. Our father folded his hands in his lap and sighed.

"Kitty, you are correct in that our lack of punishment toward Lydia was a large fault, and we have no choice but to remember that it was so. Even my unwillingness to see her after her marriage was not a severe enough punishment. Yet our misstep elsewhere should not stop us from being proper parents now, for at last I have learned to be cautious. I do not pretend that you are not a great deal less in error than Lydia was, and you also are not to be chastised as you have been, yet we have to be more proper now. And we have to follow suit. We have therefore decided that it would be best for Kitty to remain in Longbourn for the duration of your engagement while the rest of you return to Pemberly, and then we shall travel and arrive in Kent two days before the wedding."

"You are separating us!" Colonel Fitzwilliam roared, his voice echoing in the room.

"Yes, we are," my father said staunchly. "And to ensure that you learn from this incident, we have decided that Kitty shall remain here in Longbourn, while the Colonel returns with you all to Pemberly, and there they shall have the wedding in two months' time."

The Colonel was beside himself. "Two months? Why so long from now? It is nonsense!"

"Is it?" My father replied, cynically.

"Father," I began, "forgive me, but is that decision not counter-productive to what your aim should be at this point? Kitty and the Colonel were found in a compromising position. Therefore, it should be only fitting that you would wish to move up the date of the wedding, which we can do most easily. Also, at Pemberly, all of our decorations and preparations will be set up in no more than two weeks' time, which was the set date. We should not do anything to alter it, especially since the invitations have already been sent out."

"The Gardiners and Phillips shall have no worries in making this new time," our mother exclaimed. "Believe me on that score."

"Yet what of Richard's family?" Kitty objected. "Did you not think of them? And with your mission being to marry off your five daughters, no matter how foolish the match might be, why has your intention changed so suddenly to one of hesitancy? At one point, would you not have wished for me to rush to exchange vows? Why this sudden change?"

"Because," my father replied, sounding resigned, "for too long it took me to learn to be cautious, and I have. And I failed with Lydia, yet you will feel the effects of it. I know that it sounds unjust of us, especially given that Lydia did far worse, but if you recall, I refused to see her for a time after that. Do not argue with us, any of you, and let me be a father while I still can. And Colonel? When you marry my daughter, and you finally become a father yourself, you shall understand what I am experiencing now. You will not want your daughter to rush, but rather, you would instinctively order for a separation of the couple until the man who calls for your daughter learns that he must adhere to decorum."

"She is soon to be my wife," the Colonel reminded him. "If anyone is allowed to take liberties, it should be me. Or do you feel so impotent, Mr. and Mrs. Bennet, because of what you let your youngest child, Lydia, get away with?"

"Richard!" Darcy cried.

My father leaned forward in his chair, looking over his spectacles.

"Making an enemy of your future father-in-law is not a wise way of starting out the relationship."

"No, it is not. Yet I must ask you, sir, to allow the wedding to resume in two weeks' time. Not two months."

"Two months, sir. That is my final word."

"If that be the case, then I shall not leave Hampshire, and I will not leave Kitty."

"Are you afraid that you will forget her in two months' time?"

The colonel's eyes were dark with anger. "You toy with me."

"Yes, I do. And I shall make it plain for you. Either you leave Hampshire and let her remain here while you all sojourn to Kent without her and she learns restraint while you are away—or I withdraw my consent for the marriage."

"You wouldn't!" Kitty cried.

"Father, be reasonable," I urged.

"Wait, Mr. Bennet," our mother cried. "Even I admit that is extreme. We do not want Kitty to lose a husband."

"Then are we all agreed?" he said. "For I know that I am so."

We all looked between each other and we saw that we had no choice but to comply. Kitty and the Colonel grudgingly agreed, and my father felt the satisfaction of his point carrying him through.

"A valuable lesson to be learned in the end, believe me," he said, "the pains of living: having to submit to your family."

12

LOSE MY TEMPER

Before submitting completely, Kitty threatened to run off with Richard to Gretna Green to get married if our parents did not relent. Yet she was able to be coaxed out of her temper and was only allowed the permission to escort the Colonel to our carriage while we all were in their company.

However, once the moment came, Kitty grabbed the Colonel's hand as they walked, and I wondered why she dared to do it.

"Kitty, let your fiancé's hand go this instant!" our mother cried. Truly, I did not understand the change that had come over my mother who would have loved to have seen the deep bond a man had for her daughter, as well as revel in his eagerness to have a swift wedding date on the rise. But there was no reasoning with her. To add to this strange picture, Lydia was there and was watching the whole interaction, most amused. The little imp.

Kitty let go of the Colonel's hand, but I noticed that it was still balled up in a fist. I wondered if he kept it so to remember her touch, but I wondered at it for some reason—thinking that there might be something more behind it.

When our carriage departed for Aginfield, the Colonel was livid.

"Who are they to lecture me?" he groused. "When they are the fools who thought it wise to send their youngest daughter to Brighton without any of you to supervise her, and then had nothing else to do but resign her to wed the worst man in Europe. Forgive me, Mrs. Darcy, yet I have no patience for them."

"And I am sorry for this turn of events, Colonel," I said. "Indeed, I do not know what they are about in this situation."

"I do," Darcy said, to my surprise. "They failed as parents in Lydia's case and now they are trying to make up for their failure tenfold, by coming down on you and Kitty. However, they are doing their best efforts to the point where they cannot see that they are overdoing it—to the very most extreme."

I rubbed my hand across my eyes. "I mean no disrespect to either of them, yet they are being great fools."

"And I will not stand for it," the Colonel said. "I will not leave Hampshire, but I shall remain at the inn, and come every day till they let me see her. What harm can we cause by my calling on her?"

"Richard, while I understand your wounded pride," Darcy allowed, "I believe that in this case you should retreat to fight another day. Come back to Kent with no objection, and the two months will go swiftly."

"Fitz," Richard said, his eyes narrow and appearing frozen over with bitterness, "you know retreating is not in my nature. And it never will be."

⚜

We returned to Aginfield, where we were met by the Bingleys. Colonel Fitzwilliam however did not wish to sit with us, but took a mid-day ride on his horse, Hector.

"Two months?" Mr. Bingley said when we told him the news. "That is the reverse of what I expected, for instead of it being two weeks away, we thought they would wish to push it for two days instead. This is quite unprecedented."

"Yes," Darcy replied, "it is. Yet it is all out of our hands."

"Indeed it is. And how is the Colonel taking such news?"

"How do you think he is taking it?"

"Oh," Mr. Bingley groaned, coming to a revelation. "That bad, huh?"

"Yes, that bad."

Before dinner, we all went to our rooms to change our clothes and Darcy was helping me tie up my dress.

"What did Mr. Bingley mean by 'that bad'?" I asked. "Is the Colonel going to be unruly, do you think?"

"I know that he is."

"Yet Richard is such a kind and obliging man."

"Kind, yes. Obliging, yes. Yet he is a soldier, and therefore, he has a large sense of confidence, pride, and desire to have his way. He will not take this well, Elizabeth, oh no, he will not take this."

"Then you believe that his threat to remain in Hampshire to be sincere?"

"Oh, I know that it is."

"Yet that cannot be. We have to persuade him to do otherwise."

"I have one solution."

"What is it?"

"I shall inform you of what it is when I see that it has potential to be a success. Do not fear, I shall let you know by the time I come into bed."

"You promise?"

"Yes, I promise."

"Darcy?" I asked, a little suspicious. "There will be nothing *foul* about your plan, will it?"

He leaned down and kissed me.

"My love, I cannot answer that question truthfully at the present time."

After dinner that evening, Mr. Bingley and Darcy informed us ladies that, while usually when they would join us after the meal in the sitting room, they needed a night relief and would leave for the evening. They were very ambiguous about their plans, and when they left, Miriam and I spent a whole two hours berating them for their lack of manners while we sewed some pillow sleeves.

"I tell you this, Miriam," I said, "my husband had better have a reason for why they left us alone, or I shall never let him hear the end of it when they return from wherever they came from."

"Nor I with Charles," she added. "For I am a paranoid woman, and now he is playing on my sensibilities. I am so going to kick him in his kneecap when he returns. Well... I would never do that, yet I was thinking of doing it."

After the two hours, Miriam and I went to bed, yet as Lucy assisted me in getting into my nightgown, there was a knock on the door. Lucy opened it and it was another servant who communicated something. When the servant finished, Lucy turned to me.

"Mistress, Mr. Darcy has returned. And he is asking for you and Mrs. Bingley."

Miriam and I followed the servant down the steps, followed by Lucy. However, as we walked, we did not head to the entrance or the sitting room, but to a random room in the left wing of Aginfield.

"Why do they wish to meet us here?" I asked Lucy.

"I am not certain, Mistress."

When we entered the room, we saw Mr. Bingley and Darcy—and Colonel Fitzwilliam lying on the floor with a large sack next to him.

"Oh my god!" Miriam cried. "What has happened?"

"Is the Colonel all right?" I gasped.

"Oh, it is fine," Mr. Bingley said, waving his hand at us dismissively. "He is just heavily inebriated."

"He is drunk?" Miriam repeated.

"Very *very* heavily so," Darcy added.

"And why is he drunk?" I asked.

"Because we needed him to be."

"What do you mean, you *needed him to be*?"

"I mean that... this was the plan."

"The plan?" I reiterated.

"Yes, my love."

"Are we both speaking of the same 'plan'? The plan that you assured me you would tell me when you thought it would work?"

"Yes, that plan," he said, going red in the face. "Well, sorry— but look! It worked."

"Darcy," I began, my lips getting pressed thin, "all that I see is a drunken man on the floor of your friend's home. What worked precisely?"

"My sentiments exactly," Miriam cried. "Charles, what is the meaning of this? And speak your words up sharp before I get very vexed with you."

"Oh," Mr. Bingley said, looking unnerved and a little terrified. His eyes searched around and then he sounded his retreat.

"It was all Darcy's idea!" he shouted, pointing at my husband.

"Oh, thank you, Bingley," Darcy replied. "Now I know that you cannot be relied upon for anything regarding an accomplice."

"I refuse to get in trouble with my wife because I was simply aiding you."

"I was going to explain, if you had only waited a moment before you—"

"Both of you be quiet!" I thundered.

"Right," they both replied, looking a bit abashed.

"Very well," I said. "Charles please get the Colonel off the floor and sit him in a seat. And Darcy, my love, please tell me what you did."

"Very well," Charles said, happy not to talk and he began to get Richard off the floor while my husband began to give his explanation.

"Well, you see, this is an old prank that Richard pulled on me a couple of times when we were at school together," he began.

"At Oxford?"

"Yes, at Oxford. He would get me drunk sometimes and then pull a prank on me while I was inebriated."

"Oh, that is very amusing," I replied, still stone-faced. "Now please continue."

"Well, tomorrow we are leaving for Kent, for not only to prepare for the wedding, but also for your laying in. I wanted the Colonel to come willingly, but I worried that he would still be resolute. Over the years, I have proven to be a better drinker than Richard, who after the third bottle of wine, can fall into a deep sleep for almost fifteen hours sometimes. Truly, my dear, I have seen it. And when he wakes, he is much disoriented, it takes him long to remember things, and therefore if he didn't wake up till we were mid-journey, then he would be more compliant."

"This was your plan then, to get him drunk? So drunk that we would have to carry his limp form into the carriage tomorrow morning in front of the servants, so that we can get him to leave Hampshire compliantly?"

"Affirmative, dear, that was the plan."

"Well, as much as I despise this," Miriam said, "why did you call us here then instead of just telling us? We did not need to see his drunken state."

"No," Darcy said, "we actually need you for the sewing."

"Sewing? What sewing?"

Mr. Bingley then held up the canvas sack.

"Wait," I objected. "Is that what I believe it to be?"

"Yes," Darcy replied. "A canvas sack that is used for men to be sewn in so that they cannot crawl out and try and escape."

"Yet you said that he was so drunk that he was not going to wake."

"Yes, but just in case he does, this way he will not be a harm to himself or wander out of Aginfield and try and find his way to Kitty in a drunken stupor. That would just be counter-productive to our mission. So, in this way, I am just being thorough."

"Yes, you clearly thought of everything," I said, my voice dripping with sarcasm.

"Elizabeth, now do not look at me that way. Richard did this to me four times back at Oxford, where he would challenge me to drinking contests and then make me into a fool. The way that I see it, I am doing what is best for the family, while also getting my revenge."

"Getting your revenge? That is a senseless reason for this incredibly senseless plan. And I—I..." Unable to contain my inner frustration, I paced back and forth and then burst out laughing. I sat down, not able to contain myself ultimately.

"Forgive me," Darcy said. "Yet is that funny laughter or angry laughter?"

"My husband," I said, trying to contain myself, "you must be quiet now."

"Well then," Miriam said. "Charles, I will not stand for this again, yet in the meantime, I need a servant to bring me my needle and thread so that I can sew the canvas sack closed."

Lucy produced the needle and thread from her apron, which resulted in Miriam and I gaping at her.

"I was told to bring it," she said by way of explanation.

"Oh," Miriam said with a nod, "right. That would make sense."

Miriam and I threaded two needles and then got to work. Charles and Darcy placed Richard's limp form in the sack, and Miriam and I began to sew the opening of it around Richard's neck.

We stopped at the point where it would have been too snug for him to breathe comfortably, yet also not loose enough for him to get free if he so desired it.

When we finished, he was carried to his bedroom by Charles and Darcy, then we closed his bedroom door behind him. I bade Charles and Miriam goodnight and both couples parted. When we reached the privacy of our bedroom, I turned to Darcy.

"All right, here is where I lose my temper," I said.

"When?" Was his reply.

"Right now."

"Right now?"

And then I slapped him.

13

VALUABLE LESSON TO BE LEARNED

After I slapped him, he grabbed his face, caressing the spot that still stung.

"I can see why you would do that. And I could see why I deserved that."

"Yes, yes you did."

"And maybe I could have found a better plan, if I had more time, yet my dear, I had to act quickly, and therefore I was in a rush."

I ground my teeth, frustrated. I saw his point, yet it was all just so ridiculous.

"Fitzwilliam, you are the master of Pemberly! I simply... I would never have expected this of you. I truly am amazed that you even had this instinct within you."

"Still waters run deep is all that I can say by way of explanation and in my defense."

"Yes. And this reminds me now to never underestimate you."

"I suppose that it is better that you know me in full. Yet also know that I would never do this to anyone unless I was very close to them."

"So, you justify pulling such pranks and using such trickery by only doing it to those who have no choice but to forgive you?"

"Yes."

I flinched.

"Oh, my love, you replied with such finality, that I have no idea what to even say to that."

"I know. That was what I was hoping to achieve."

"I want to slap you again."

"I know dear. I know. Yet you forgive me though?"

I did slap him once more.

❧

The next morning, I awoke to Darcy looking on me as he lay in bed next to me. He grinned shyly, and I smiled, and then ran my hand down his face.

"Does it still hurt from when I slapped you?"

"Four times. You slapped me four times."

"Well, after the second time, I figured what was two more times but to help my point sink in more."

The night before, after my slapping him ceased, he grabbed me, and we began to kiss savagely. It was quite a strange thing, yet I never knew that an argument could lead to such passionate affection afterwards.

"How did we end up being intimate with one another immediately after our argument?"

"It is actually often a natural reaction to arguing with one's spouse. So do not think us abnormal for doing so. We were having a heated debate and as a result, emotion rose, and we rose with it."

I rolled on top of him as he wrapped his arms around my body and his hands rested on my thighs, stroking me over and over.

"I'm happy my slaps did not lead to any scars on your face."

"They were not that hard. They just stung a little."

He raised me up a bit, kissed one of my breasts and then caressed my lips with his fingers.

"Well," I said, "as much as I wish to not leave this room, for the outside world seems to offer us many obstacles, it is already 6:30. Now we must dress, so that we can breakfast at the appointed time of 7:30 and be on the road to leave for Pemberly by 8:30."

"Yes, time is always of the essence."

We rose, put on our robes and called for our servants. I went to my adjoining room where Lucy helped me dress and do my hair. Although, the next second there was a knock on Darcy's door. I heard him go to it, open it up, and then I heard hushed voices. Leaving Lucy, I went to my door, opened it, and saw that it was Mr. Bingley who was speaking with my husband.

"Yes," Mr. Bingley rushed out. "He won't let me in and..."

"Bingley, what is it?" Darcy demanded.

"She is in there."

"She?"

"Kitty is with him."

"Kitty is with whom?" I interrupted.

"Elizabeth, have you been listening in?" Darcy asked.

"Yes!" I stated boldly. "And I will not feel bad about it under the circumstances. Charles, where is Kitty and who were you talking about?"

Darcy walked to me.

"We should speak of this in secret." He took my hand and we walked into a nearby room that was empty. Once the door was closed, I looked at both of them, expectant.

"It turns out that Richard was not as inebriated as we had assumed," Charles Bingley said.

"And what does that imply?" I asked, folding my arms, and still a little angry with them both over the situation of the night before.

"It means that he woke up a lot sooner than expected and he managed to get out of his satchel."

"But he was sewn into it! And Miriam and I stitched it strongly, I swear."

"Yes, and as it turns out, he was not alone. He had an accomplice."

"An accomplice?" I almost stuttered. "How could he..." It took me a second and then I grew to recall what I had seen yesterday before Colonel Fitzwilliam left Kitty at Longbourn. "Oh, those little devils."

"Devils?"

"Yes, before we left Longbourn, Kitty and Richard held hands. When they parted, Richard's hand was still closed. She must've given him a note and they had planned a rendezvous."

"Then that explains how she got in last night. Richard must've made certain to keep the servant's door open, and she naturally would have known which bedroom he was in."

"Which bedroom?" I reiterated.

"The Colonel's, Elizabeth," Darcy said reluctantly. "Apparently, Kitty took a horse from Longbourn, at night, traveled here, and snuck into Aginfield through the servants' entrance, which we can assume Richard left open for her. However, he did not expect us to get him drunk, and sewed into a sack, confined to his room. Yet Kitty must've entered anyway, even though he did not meet her, traveled to his room and saw the state that he was in."

"And she cut the sack open then," I finished, filled with horror.

"That is the easy part of this situation." Charles ran his fingers through his fair hair.

"What do you mean when you say easy?"

"I mean that when I went to retrieve him, he was not only awake, aware—but he has Kitty in his bedroom with him, he has locked the door, and barricaded them both within."

"That is outrageous!" I cried. "Has everyone gone mad?"

"Come, Elizabeth," Darcy said, walking to Richard's room. "We shall make short work of this."

"Shall we?" I asked, following after him. "The Colonel seems to have lost his senses."

"He'll regain it once the alcohol wears off."

"He is still drunk then?"

"No, he just is not clear-sighted because he is still suffering the after-effects of the wine. Too much of it can make one temporarily out of one's mind. And as for Kitty, well, I am aware that she will do anything for him. But how could she—"

"Do as I had done?" I offered. "Yes, even I did not foresee this."

"Oh Elizabeth, I did not mean to admonish you."

"And you still have not. Yet I cannot judge Kitty, for I did the same thing out of love. Although, I can blame the Colonel for encouraging it, for if he had told her to wait, then she would have done so. This outrageousness comes with too much allowance on his side. Kitty was only doing what she felt to keep him by her side. In that, she is not Lydia yet—she is simply as bad as I am."

"You are not bad, Elizabeth."

"No, but I was reckless. I can therefore not judge Kitty for coming for him, but for only allowing Richard to go this far in his extreme actions. Now all the servants will know of it."

"And if I know Richard, he is counting on that."

Shocked, I said, "You cannot be sincere."

"Oh, I am. I believe that this was all precisely what Richard wanted, and our getting him drunk was a minor setback for him that he rectified by his own cleverness."

"You make him sound strategic in his views."

"He is a colonel in war, Elizabeth. Strategy is something he knows very well, I am sure."

We reached Richard's room and Darcy tried the door at first, which was locked steady.

"See," Mr. Bingley said, coming from up behind us. "Locked fast."

"And enforced by my dresser, chests and a few chairs." Richard said from within. "Therefore, any attempt to come in will be futile and impossible as well."

"Richard," Darcy said, going up to the door, "I demand that you desist in this behavior this instant."

"I understand why you tell me so, Darcy, and I know that I look foolish, yet I have done too much to turn back now."

"You are correct, you are being foolish."

"And it will change nothing."

"Richard, what do you plan? How is this all to end, and to what purpose are you aiming for?"

"My requests are simple. I shall not exit, nor shall Kitty until their father is notified that I demand our wedding be moved to no more than a month away, just in enough time for us to return to Pemberly and the wedding to be done as soon as may be, but still in a style to suit Kitty's desires."

"Richard!" Darcy shouted. "I am appalled and ashamed. Have you any idea how childish and immature you are being?"

"No more immature than getting me drunk and then sewing me into a satchel because you did not trust me, so that you could drag me away like a slave."

"And clearly I had been correct to do so." Darcy's tone then lightened, and he grew curious. "Though actually, I am confused to no end. I'm the better drinker than you, so how are you even awake now?"

"Fitz, are you serious? I was a worse drinker when we were in school together, but it's been years and I have served in a war. You think in all that time of seeing such carnage, I never learned how to be a better drinker? War makes men of high tolerance where there were once none. Therefore, I woke up very soon."

"Oh, move over," I said to Darcy and Charles, moving in front of them and knocking on the door. "And by that you mean that you woke up when Kitty found you, did you not, Richard?"

"Hello, Elizabeth."

"Hello, Colonel, and I believe that you have my sister in there with you, do you not?"

"Yes," he replied shakily. "Aye, I do."

"Well, since you are beyond reason, then I shall appeal to her. Richard, please tell Kitty to come forward and speak to me through the door."

"Elizabeth, I know you must hate me."

"You are correct, I do. Now let me speak to my sister."

"Right."

After a second, I heard shuffling and then Kitty spoke.

"Good morning, Elizabeth."

"Good morning." I sighed. "Kitty why did you agree to do this?"

"I have no excuse to give you. I was simply angry at my parents for separating us, and I will not be torn from Richard, even for a little bit."

"Being headstrong is no sin, yet when driven to such extremes as this."

"Elizabeth, what have I done that you did not do? You walked toward your destiny, and I rode to mine. I want to be with Richard, and I will not bear two months of separation for some foolish reason. And I know that this must look scandalous and reflect poorly on you all, yet if we marry soon, will it?"

"And that was the plan," I finished. "You agreed to this because this way you could force our parents' hand and not only allow you to leave with the Colonel but agree to a swift wedding date."

"Elizabeth, Richard is correct. It is the best course of action. I could not rely upon our family to be reasonable, as usual, and so the only answer there could be was to reply by being equally unreasonable."

"Kitty, I was hoping that you would have acted better than I have proven to act in my past, yet you have the mistake of following in my footsteps."

"That mistake you made clearly led to you gaining everything."

"I was rash!"

"Because you believed the risk was worth the costs. Richard is worth everything, including the loss of my esteem in people's eyes."

I looked at Darcy and he looked resentful to say the least, yet I could not help but be torn. I knew Kitty and the Colonel were wrong to do what they had done, yet if their actions would clearly lead to the fate that Darcy and I shared, did it take their wrong to find a right?

"Kitty," I said, turning back to the door. "What do you want me to do?"

"I want you to go to our parents. Inform them of our situation and the potential scandal behind it if we delay any further, to which they can only remedy it by letting me leave with you all today. My things are already packed away in my room, making the addition of me being no hindrance to you. And all the servants here will follow after Mr. Bingley and Mrs. Bingley to London, which means there will be no time for any rumors of our ill-conduct to spread here in Hampshire."

"You mean to force their hand by threatening notorious gossip upon them if not otherwise."

"Precisely."

"Well, Kitty, when you come out of there, I cannot pretend that I might not strike you, yet at the very least, you both did think on this clearly."

"We have spent many words on it—and be sure to let our father know that."

"They what?" our mother shrieked after I finished telling her the news. Our father sat there, still as stone, while Darcy stood behind me. We had arrived there ten minutes ago, and we had just finished telling them what had occurred the night before at Aginfield.

"This is all so absurd!" our mother cried. "The fools, what could they be thinking?"

"For once, I am in agreement with you, my dear," our father finally said. "What could those fools be about?"

"Just that," Darcy answered. "And no matter how irrational and unexpected this all seems, it can be remedied well enough if the wedding can be moved to a much earlier date. If you allow Kitty to leave with us, then the rumor shall not spread in Hampshire, for the servants will not linger as well, but will be transferred to London."

"All of this can be accomplished," I added, "if you keep it silent as well and do not think to speak of it here."

"Why would we let something such as this be exposed?" my mother objected, affronted.

"Because you gossip, mother," I replied. "You speak so loud and so much on all that you hear, there is a chance that the servants might hear it already from your proclamations through me telling my tale. Mother, please, remember that this is not safe to speak on, so do not inform anyone here at Longbourn. If you do, then you will be responsible for the very rumors that you wish not to suffer under."

"And why should we let you leave with Kitty?" our mother said, her voice tight. "You have done a terrible duty at being her chaperones."

"First," Darcy said, "do you not recall that it was under your supervision that Kitty got away and came all the way to Aginfield? Or does your memory lapse that much? We restrained Colonel Fitzwilliam, and I made good work of it, so explain to me just how your daughter was missing, the whole night, and you never noticed!"

My parents were silent at this.

"And also tell me, how people who claim to be intelligent, thought it would be wise to send their most reckless daughter to Brighton, where there would be officers everywhere, and thought it would all turn out for the better?"

"Lydia was not the kind of girl to do that sort of thing," my mother argued, "if she had been properly looked after."

"Except that she *did* do it," I replied, exasperated. "And she was properly looked after. Mother, stop making excuses for Lydia this instant and see that you let her go when it was foolish to do and that it was not wise at all."

"Well..."

"And furthermore," Darcy argued, "what possessed you both to agree to postpone the wedding? All because they were caught kissing once during their engagement? Does it occur to either of you that was an extreme reaction, and now because of it, they have met it with an extreme reaction of their own? This means that your actions inspired theirs. Yes, I applaud you for just learning now that idiocy is contagious, and one dimwitted action can lead to another in a separate quarter."

"So this is our fault, then?" my father roared, who rarely ever raised his voice. "Is that what you are implying?"

"Yes," Darcy said in a way that brooked no opposition. "It is plain as day to see. And honestly, how can you not have known that one of your daughters had been missing for so long?"

"We were sleeping," my mother argued.

"Did you not check their rooms before you did so? Did you not say goodnight to them and make certain that they were asleep before you did so?"

My parents looked at each other, their confidence shaken.

"Does it not occur to you that you are negligent parents?" Darcy bellowed. At his wit's end, he stood up and straightened his waistcoat. "You have only one choice, you either accept this scheme, where we take them both to Pemberly, the marriage occurs no more than two weeks after we arrive there, you all attend, and wish them well, or let them remain in Aginfield, locked away, then word will spread, scandal will ensue, all because of your pride. I'll give you a couple of minutes to think about it instead of you resorting to hysterics, Mrs. Bennet and you resorting to cynicism, Mr. Bennet. Now I wish that I could respect you at the moment, yet you have given me no other choice but to grow very vexed and disappointed. The two simply want to get married. So, let them and be done with it. Come Elizabeth."

I stood up and followed him out, yet before we did so completely, I leaned my head back in and looked at my parents.

"I love you both, truly, and I respect you as well. Yet all that my husband said—very true it all is."

I closed the door behind us and followed Darcy out to the yard.

All was agreed to most readily. My parents saw the wisdom to the scheme, and though they were anything but pleased, nothing could be done for it, and we all moved with alacrity.

In the work of an hour's time, Richard and Kitty had been informed, they moved all the furniture back to the places where they were, unlocked the door, and prepared themselves for immediate departure, which they were content to do.

Upon first seeing Kitty, I wish that I could have slapped her, yet she was smart about approaching me. She was repentant in attitude, apologizing and not looking me in the eye and therefore forcing me to feel pity for her. Then afterwards, she thanked me for carrying her point and ensuring her happiness sooner, making me feel no anger toward her, because I saw how content she had been made. It is hard to deny the truth of the matter, yet when in regards to love, you wish to always comprehend the flights of fancy it can bring.

Colonel Fitzwilliam however was not so fortunate. Darcy decided to strike him down with a punch across his face. Afterwards, Darcy straightened up and continued his stoic manner and slow stance.

Before we left however, Mr. Bingley and Miriam, who were leaving a day after us, accompanied us to the carriages.

"Mr. and Mrs. Bingley," Kitty said, "I am sorry for any trouble I may have caused you. It was most unconsciously done, and I regret ever putting you in the middle of something that you did not deserve."

"I can forgive you, Kitty," Miriam said, "for following love to whatever end." Miriam and Kitty embraced. "Yet, to be earnest, do not ever do that again!"

"And the same goes for you, Colonel," Mr. Bingley said to Richard.

"Very true," the Colonel said. "Though I am still content in that I achieved what I desired."

"You both are hopeless."

I embraced Miriam as well and was happy to know that she did not bear us any ill-will. Nor did she seem shocked in any way.

"One of my sisters eloped with a navy man," she whispered. "That is why I am not so very vexed or surprised at all. To be truthful, I thought they were going to resort to even more drastic measures than these."

"I am happy they did not."

"Yes, you should be."

I then turned to Mr. Bingley.

"Mr. Bingley, thank you for allowing us to remain this one last time in Aginfield. I daresay that we shall never dwell here again now that it is to be sold."

"I am not so certain anymore," he answered. "While I would like to find a home in Kent, giving our children a chance to grow up with one another, I worry that I will grow to miss Aginfield. I have rented it in little time, yet so much has happened since then. I am a sentimental fool, and memories tie me to things. If I cannot find a home in Kent, then perhaps Mr. Bingley will remain in Aginfield."

⚜

My husband gave a warm farewell to his friend and his wife, then Colonel Fitzwilliam, Jane and I remained in one carriage, while Darcy, Georgiana and Kitty were held in the other. The seating had been arranged so in order that there would be gentlemen in both, but Kitty and the Colonel would remain separate.

As we rode through Hampshire, I turned to the Colonel, and he noticed as well, for he turned to me in the next.

"Still irate and annoyed with me?"

"No," I replied. "I should be, yet I am resigned. And you look happy with yourself."

"For I am. I respect your parents, this is true, yet in their situation, there is a valuable lesson to be learned. And I do believe that they learned it."

"And what is that?"

"That, when I put my mind to it, I am a force to be reckoned with. For the better or for the worse."

❧ 14 ❧

A MARRIAGE WORTH THE EARNING

The journey felt longer than normal, yet eventually we arrived at Pemberly and I rejoiced to be home. In the short duration that I have been mistress there, it had grown to be the most peaceful of refuges to have and the most comfortable of domiciles to live in.

Mrs. Reynolds was there to greet us, as well as having wonderful news.

"You will be overjoyed to see that we have been hard at work," she proclaimed. "For we have finished all preparations for the wedding, the altar and everything of minor detail."

"Have you?" Kitty cried. "I wish to see it as soon as we are settled."

"We hope you are satisfied with the lot of it. Now before I speak more on the subject, let us get you all inside and Mrs. Darcy, oh, you should rest after so long a journey."

"I am well," I said, patting my belly. "And though he, or she, sometimes gets unruly, it's mostly sleeping it seems."

"Oh, you look exquisite. Good and large."

"Elizabeth," Darcy whispered in my ear. "I would prefer it if you rested. Please do this, for me?"

"Very well," I replied, then I submitted to Mrs. Reynolds and went off to my room while she had refreshments brought up.

When I retired to my room to rest, Darcy joined me less than half an hour later.

"The altar and decorations look wonderful," he replied when he entered. "That was where we had all been. I have left their company, yet worry not, for Jane and Georgiana are now under my express commands to not let the lovers out of their sight."

"Thank you, my dear. Then all of Mrs. Reynolds's work looks amazing?"

"Elizabeth," he said, sitting down, "it is so lovely but homely that it is even making me excited."

"It is?" I laughed.

"Yes, and a little jealous, for if the weather agrees with them and we won't have to postpone it for any reason, it seems like the perfect way to wed. It was not ostentatious, but still colorful enough. The altar was built out of wood, there will be flowers woven into it, but all around it are apples hung from wooden staffs that are dug into the ground to be stationary. The seats are all wood as well and will be set out for when people attend. A large canopy has been made and placed over everything, to protect it from rain."

He lay down behind me and wrapped his arms around my belly, running his hands over it.

He gave a sigh of contentment. "You are so wonderfully large, and I am not afraid anymore for you. You are a strong woman, Elizabeth, and I know you will survive this."

I smiled. "Thank you for having faith in me. I will survive this, or at least fight to do so, and we shall raise this baby together. He, or she, will be a joy to our lives."

"Yes, they shall."

The days leading up to the wedding seemed to roll on with thunderous speed, for one day we had the arrival of **the** Bingleys, then there was the arrival of my mother, father, Lydia, and Mary another day. Then my Aunt and Uncle Gardiner arrived the day before the wedding, yet there was still no evidence of the Fitzwilliams, and we were all growing apprehensive.

When my parents arrived, I realized that they had never seen Pemberly before and their reactions were as it was for everyone.

"Upon my word!" my mother cried as she exited the carriage. "I cannot believe it. This is a house to put all other houses to shame. Pemberly! I'm sure there is nothing to match it and it suffers no rivals to equal it."

"I am happy that you like it so," Darcy said when she turned to him.

"Like it? Oh, Mr. Darcy such expensive furnishings you must have. And I shall like to see all of it, every room!"

My father nodded to Darcy yet did not know how to receive him since their last encounter, where Darcy gave him a well-deserved lecture, making my father's pride greatly affected.

Lydia and Mary had two different reactions. Mary, though impressed, was doing her best to appear indifferent about all the wealth that she beheld before her and Lydia looked at Pemberly as if she were star-gazing.

"It is more than anyone could ever dream!" Lydia cried. "Mary! Say something."

"It is a lovely house, Mr. Darcy," Mary offered. "Yet you must understand, home is where the heart is. So, while Pemberly is a fine home that is perfectly situated, I look to the occupants of the house as the main reason to rejoice."

Lydia groaned and rolled her eyes. "Oh, do be quiet. They know we are happy to see them, yet we should still offer our compliments."

"You both still love to bicker," Colonel Fitzwilliam noticed.

"Yes," Mary replied flatly. "Apparently it is a requirement of ours to make fools of ourselves. Or at least, Lydia believes so."

"And you still have not told anyone that you are happy to see them," Lydia admonished. "Come Mary..."

"Oh, very well. It is wonderful to see you all. Truly it is."

We tried to stifle our laughter but then, despite it all, we could not contain ourselves and all laughed at Mary and Lydia's entrance.

◌✺◌

The day progressed and still there were no signs of the Fitzwilliams, and I worried that they would let the schism in the family cause them from paying respects to their own son. However, Lady Catherine did arrive, and while she was not much liked, she was the sort of woman who would always have people willing to cater to her and be relieved at her appearance, for at least she appeared.

Yet an hour before suppertime we heard a carriage ride down the front road, and we all filed out of the house in hopes of it being those expected, and they were.

The carriage stopped and Lord and Lady Fitzwilliam stepped out of it, followed by their youngest son, Acton. It angered me to not see Henry Fitzwilliam in the lot, for it showed that he took this disappointment too far. Yet perhaps it was better that he did not attend, for there was the chance of an altercation occurring once more and I did not desire another duel to the death on our beautiful fields.

"Well," The Earl of Matlock said as he stepped down and helped Lady Fitzwilliam follow suit. "You seem happy to see us."

"We are, Father," Colonel Fitzwilliam said, "for we worried that you would not come then."

"And I was quite put out!" Lady Catherine said. "What do you both think you are about, arriving so late in the evening? It is highly improper."

"Catherine," Lord Fitzwilliam warned, "as much as I like your need to lecture—wait, no I do not like your need to lecture, you have not given me time to explain. We are simply delayed because there were a few fallen trees on the road, and we had to find another route."

"Well, I am still filled with unrest."

"And, as the one who is the oldest, you are not to lecture me."

"Age does not breed wisdom."

"It does in our case, Catherine."

When assembled, the Fitzwilliams looked on us.

"Well," Lady Fitzwilliam said, "it is nice to see you all once more. And my son?" Lady Fitzwilliam went up to the Colonel and kissed his cheek. "I am proud of you."

"Thank you, Mother. That means much to me."

Acton then walked up to his brother and clapped him on the shoulder.

"You have gotten yourself into some trouble," Acton said, then turned to Kitty and kissed her hand. "Yet I see that it was worth it. For Miss Kitty, you are truly a face that could launch a thousand ships."

"Thank you, but I must ask, does being charming run in the family?" Kitty laughed.

"Oh, unfortunately," Lady Fitzwilliam said, looking at her husband, "it has been known to skip over a generation."

The Earl of Matlock chuckled and pointed at his wife.

"This is how she woos me."

"Oh, for god sakes you both," Lady Catherine chided. "Let us progress inside instead of continuing with this ridiculous conversation."

"There is one ridiculous person in our family, Catherine," Lord Fitzwilliam replied, "and I can assure you it is not me."

"Then who is it?"

We all entered the house as Lord Fitzwilliam answered Lady Catherine's query.

"The one who always thinks that they are perpetually wise. I shall give you three guesses, Catherine, yet even that will be too little, for to everyone else, it is obvious, yet for you, it will be so hard that you won't even find the answer even if you looked in the mirror and asked the question to your own reflection."

⚜

The next day came, luckily it did not rain, and all had been set properly. Our family had the front rows of seats, while the rest of the tenants or neighbors in the village, who had been invited, all came to fill the field. It truly was a magnificent turnout.

"I cannot believe it," Kitty cried as she had finished adjusting the veil on her beautiful wedding gown. "All of these people are here for the family."

"They are here for you," Jane said merrily. "It is your day."

"It is not just for me, as the day is not just mine. Oh no, they are here because they admire all of us. Because we have done things worthy to be admired."

"Kitty," I began, "before mother comes in, I just wish to say that you look beautiful, and that you have grown into a marvelous woman."

Over Kitty's shoulder, I saw Lydia sit down, looking despondent, but not out of selfishness. It was clear that Lydia knew that Kitty had made the match that she had always dreamed of, and now would never get the chance to achieve.

Mary on the other hand, held Kitty's bouquet and we all turned to her.

"Sorry," Mary said. "I just like flowers."

"Do you?" Kitty asked.

"Yes, I suppose that I do."

"Mary," Jane said, "are you showing signs of emotion?"

"Oh, no! I just... Kitty I... you are very fortunate, and I suppose, as was the case with Elizabeth, I am happy for you. And you deserve the best in life."

"Well," Kitty answered, "I daresay that you have amazed me now, Mary."

"Yes, I suppose that I have."

Mary handed Kitty her bouquet, and Kitty took it.

"You shall be content," Mary said, "in a way that I will never understand, yet I will try to."

We all were silenced by her admission, then our mother burst in.

"My beautiful girls. Kitty, it is time."

When the rest of us were in our seats, Kitty, her arm linked with our father's, walked down the grassy aisle in between the seats while Colonel Fitzwilliam stood next to Mr. Bolingbroke, our vicar.

Sitting next to Darcy, I looked at Kitty, who looked utterly happy, and then I looked down at the Colonel, who breathed in and out evenly.

"He is worried that he may forget his vows," Darcy whispered in my ear. "And the fear of embarrassing Kitty on her wedding day by falling down. He also cannot understand how he got here, at this moment, at an altar, prepared to marry a woman he never thought he would be fortunate enough to find. He sees her as his rapture, his fortune, his destiny, and knows that, even at their most stressful moment, she will give him peace."

"How do you know what he is feeling?" I whispered in reply.

"Because that is what I felt when I saw you."

My heart swelled with love for this man, and I took his hand in my own.

"Darcy?"

"Yes."

"Do I make you feel rapture?"

"Yes."

"Do I bring you fortune?"

"Yes."

"Am I truly your destiny?"

"It is most decided."

"Then I promise, I shall always bring you peace."

He took my hand and planted a kiss upon it.

◈

The wedding scene commenced with no mishaps of any kind. Lord and Lady Fitzwilliam clearly were happy at their son's wedding, and Lady Catherine, overwhelming us all, began to weep during the ceremony. A part of me wondered, at first, if it was something that had simply got into her eye. Yet it was not so. Lady Catherine, despite her hard exterior, and her perpetual habit of making us all disdain her, did actually have a heart—and it had a spot of softness in it.

When the ceremony ended and Richard placed his ring on Kitty's hand, their kiss was said to be the longest in the church's history—even though they technically did not wed within a church, it was still under the head of Vicar Mr. Bolingbroke. Kitty and Richard turned around as rose petals were thrown into the air and everyone clapped. When she had walked down the aisle, she was Kitty Bennet, yet now turning around, she was Kitty Fitzwilliam.

After the wedding, there were tables that the servants brought food onto and all began to eat at their own leisure.

"I cannot understand," Lady Catherine said to me, "how you could be so remiss in your duties, Mrs. Darcy?"

I gave her a pleasant smile. "Lady Catherine, what need have you to insult me now?"

"Out of pure necessity. Are you so unfeeling that you did not care for the credit of my nephew? You have invited not only the high families here in this village, but also the tenants of Pemberly. Over a hundred people are here."

"Which part are you angrier over, Lady Catherine? The fact that some of these people are common, or that your nephew and I do not care?"

Lady Catherine opened her mouth and then closed it once more. Pursing her lips, she walked away, and I knew that was the closest she would ever get to saying anything nice to me.

After we ate, there was dancing. Kitty and the Colonel were the first in the set, and then many of us formed the line while the rest had to wait for the next dance, because there were too many.

Our fiddler, cellist and flute players were most proficient throughout the ceremony and their skills were quite suitable for the style of the wedding. Before Darcy and I took our places amongst the sets of couples, we were surprised to see that Acton Fitzwilliam approached Mary and asked her to dance.

Mary stuttered as she stood up and agreed to dance. It was quite nice, and I was wondering if she was finally breaching her shell of isolation and gravitas that she loved so much. Yet as we passed them, Darcy touched Acton's shoulder.

"Dance with her all you like," he whispered. "Yet please do not fall in love with her. That would be most inconvenient for the family."

"Darcy!" I gasped as we walked away. "What did you mean, sir, by saying such a thing?"

"Believe me, I did Mary a service. The last thing we all need is him fixating on Mary all because Richard has done so with Kitty."

"You think that likely to happen?"

"Matrimony is a contagious concept sometimes, and if Richard did it with a Bennet girl, then I would not be surprised if Acton were to follow suit. And the last thing Mary needs is another Fitzwilliam boy falling in love with a Bennet girl for the wrong reasons. The name Bennet has become an enigma now, and I wish to oversee the rest of you. This is why the last thing I will ever let Henry Fitzwilliam do, if he ever overcomes his pride and re-connects with us, is meet Lydia."

"Are you in earnest?" I laughed as we got into the line of dancers. The music struck up and we began our set, which was the Country Dance.

"Oh, most certainly I am. I would not trust him near her with a ten-foot pole. I could very easily see him transferring his disappointed hopes from Kitty to her younger sister who is married to a man who is never around. Yes, Elizabeth, I may sound paranoid, but believe me, the tendencies of people are astounding."

Along the lines, I saw Mary dancing with Acton, and she laughed at something he said.

"Yet what if Mary was beginning to change? What if she is beginning to want more of herself?"

"Then I shall decide if Acton is good enough for her," he replied. "And if he is, I might consider allowing him to begin to feel for her."

"You now believe you can govern other people's hearts?" I smiled, amused. "Oh, you are a dreamer. Yet we need not fear. They are just dancing, and Acton was just being a polite gentleman in doing so."

"Yes, I suppose you are right. I'll apologize to him after the dance ends."

"Very good, my love."

The next dance I had Colonel Fitzwilliam as a partner while Lord Fitzwilliam danced with Kitty.

"So," I teased, "congratulations Colonel, you got your way."

"Yes, I did. As I do in all things."

"You sound spoiled."

"And you know me well enough to know that I am not."

"No, you are not. This was a wonderful ceremony."

"It was nothing compared to Kitty's beauty."

"I wish you both joy."

"We need no wishes, yet it is nice to have it all the same. It is an amazing thing, is it not? All that has occurred over the last year. It has been so much in so little time, yet I believe on the chessboard of life, the pieces began to move when you and my cousin discovered one another."

"Were we so much like dominos that when we fell, everyone fell around us in a pattern that suited all?"

"Yes, I believe it to be so."

"Then I am glad."

"As am I, for this truly was a marriage worth the earning. And it very narrowly slipped out of my hands."

❧ 15 ❧

NEWS OF A GOOD AND BAD SORT

The wedding ended and all retired. Yet years from now, it would be a wedding that all would remember and talk of.

The wedding couple retired in one of the nicest rooms in Pemberly while the rest of us did so in our own rooms, hoping them to have joy. All that remained before they would fully start their new life together was the Pemberly Ball.

A week from then, it would take place, yet I was getting too tired to oversee it and Georgiana took over the preparations for it along with Lady Fitzwilliam, who seemed to revel in such planning. Personally, I found planning for a ball to be a great nuisance; therefore, it was wonderful to have them take it off my hands entirely.

Three days after the wedding, I was sitting in my study and I began to write a letter to Maria Lucas, to begin our machinations of allowing her brother to send Deborah Darcy his letter. Yet, as I had written it, I heard a shout come from the sitting room.

I stood up but found that the weight of my belly was too much, and I moved slowly. I managed to get to the door, opened it and walked down the hall. I was come upon by Lucy, who had rushed to where she heard the noise, but she saw me.

"Mrs. Darcy, are you unwell? It's the baby, is it not?"

"It is beginning to kick more Lucy, and it is hurting me."

"I cannot believe…" I heard Lydia cry.

"You should be in bed," Lucy said, ignoring the shout. "Here please let me take you."

"I want you to help me to where my sister is crying out from. Lucy do not worry over me, just support me."

I took Lucy's arm, leaned on her and together we walked down the steps in the direction of the sitting room, where I kept hearing sobbing. When Lucy and I entered, Lydia was sitting down, holding herself while there was a letter by her side on the sofa. Our mother was there, and so were Kitty, Georgiana, Mary, Aunt Gardiner, Uncle Gardiner, Jane, Miriam, and Lady Fitzwilliam. I did not know where the rest of the men were, but looking at Lydia's disturbed state, I was happy they were not present, for it was a frightening sight.

"Lydia?" I exclaimed, "Dear lord, what has happened?"

Lydia looked up at me, half-laughing but also crying.

"He is gone! And I am free!"

"What do you speak of?"

Aunt Gardiner took the letter that was beside Lydia and handed it to me.

"She has just received word. George Wickham is dead."

"What?" I gasped.

"The letter was forwarded from Longbourn where it was first mailed to. Read it, she doesn't mind."

I took the letter and began to read.

Dear Mrs. Wickham,
   My name is Colonel James Rolfe, I was the commanding officer

in your husband's regiment. I regret to inform you that on the day of June 1st, 1811, your husband was shot during our counter-attack that was brought forth in defense of the outer borders of Portugal against French forces, and he was taken wounded to the nearest medical station. However, he was pronounced dead on arrival, and we most humbly regret your loss. He died in defense of his country and therefore, he fell an officer of the highest honors.

I pray for him and for you, good lady.

Respectfully,
*   Colonel Rolfe*

I lowered the letter and looked at Lydia's shaking form.

"Oh, my poor Lydia," My mother cried, rushing to her. "I am so sorry for your loss."

"I have lost nothing," Lydia whispered.

"What do you mean, child? I know you wish to hope that he still lives somehow."

"I do not hope that he lives," Lydia whispered, shuddering at the thought of it. "Rather I fear that the report is not true and that he still lives somehow, and he still haunts me. I hope that letter speaks all that is real, because that means Wickham is dead and gone, and I am free."

"Lydia," Aunt Gardiner cried. "You mustn't say such things."

"But I must," Lydia replied. "Or I will never again find the courage to. May all the George Wickhams in this world die in such a way."

"Lydia," our mother gasped.

"He was terrible to me, Mother. He was cruel and capricious. He did not love me. He had others. Other women, and when I got angry over it, he hurt me. And then he grew to realize that he liked hurting me whenever I did something to displease him. He was belligerent. He was violent. He was a demon."

Every woman in the room had their own reaction of horror, yet Georgiana's was the most alert. She sat down after hearing Lydia's confession and covered her mouth out of shock. My uncle, who was by all accounts a warm man, his face drained of all color and a cold resentment washed over him. It was too late to protect Lydia from all that Wickham had done to her, yet he still would wish to have done something.

"I..." Our mother began, and then she closed her mouth. "Oh, my poor girl."

"I made a mistake, Mother," Lydia said. "And now I am free from it. And I do not apologize for saying so. I do not have to fear anything anymore."

Lydia stood up and rushed out of the room. I tried to go after her but ended up stopping after a couple of seconds and holding my belly, short of breath.

"Lizzy," Aunt Gardiner cried. "Stay there and everyone see to her."

My mother and Aunt Gardiner rushed after Lydia while my remaining sisters tended to me as well as Lucy and Mrs. Reynolds.

⚜

Lydia remained in her room with our mother for the rest of the evening, taking her dinner in solitude, as well as I. Shut up in my room, I found the baby was kicking away and seemed to be livelier than ever, and I was not at all at peace.

"If having a baby is this much of a trial, I wonder if I should have any more afterwards."

"I've heard too many women say that and it never comes true," Mrs. Reynolds replied as she poured me some water and handed it to me.

"Thank you."

"It is very little. Wine also may help so I shall call for a glass of it to be brought."

"Thank you, but I do not prefer it at this time."

"Very well."

Lucy also remained in my room, waiting to be needed.

"I should not be here," I said. "My sister needs me now."

"Your sister has three other sisters who can do the duty well enough," Mrs. Reynolds replied. "And a mother as well as an aunt. This is the time for you and your baby, therefore take some time for yourself."

I closed my eyes and lay there for a time before Mrs. Reynolds began to speak once more.

"Mrs. Darcy?"

"Yes, Mrs. Reynolds?"

"I am so sorry."

"For what?"

"For Mr. Wickham. For all that he grew into."

I opened my eyes and Mrs. Reynolds looked repentant, yet there was no reason for her to do so.

"I do not understand, he was not your child."

"No, he was not. He was merely my nephew."

"What?" I gasped.

"I cannot believe..." Lucy gasped, and then she closed her mouth.

"Forgive me for not speaking of it," Mrs. Reynolds said, "yet after his fall, I had no desire to ever speak of him again. Especially after what he did to Miss Georgiana. He was my brother's son. My maiden name was Ariana Wickham, and his own excellent father, my brother Jeffrey Wickham, was Mr. Darcy's steward at the time. Back then I was a simple maid in the household, but the late Mr. Darcy was always so kind to me. When Wickham's mother died from pneumonia, he was only four years old, and I therefore took up the challenge of trying to be a strong maternal figure for him. It was through his father and myself that helped the late Mr. Darcy choose George as a companion to Master Fitzwilliam when they were children. And to Georgiana as well a bit."

She took a handkerchief from her apron pocket and wiped her eyes. "And that was the beginning of the late Mr. Darcy growing attached to George, looking on him as a second son, and developing a bond that was so steady it would still remain even into George's adulthood—even after he did nothing to deserve it.

"When he was a boy, he was a good child, you must understand. And I do not know what had happened. I thought that I did right by him, and I could not be there for him often, yet he had a very strong foundation, many who loved and nurtured him—the man he became was not created through us. The evil was not something that was born with him, but rather it was something that he made all himself. He was charming, it was to be sure, yet he grew wild, reckless, and vain."

She sniffled anew and blew her nose. "He drank, gambled, and was quite hedonistic and extravagant in his desires. He was a villain in the end, and I watched the monster grow in him, not knowing how to destroy it. Yet his charm carried him onward. However by that point, Wickham's habits had grown so dissolute that I did not condone it, so I urged my nephew not to take the post that was granted him in the late Mr. Darcy's will, but rather ask for the sum instead of the living. This way we would be rid of him. He took my advice and I thought that it would be the last I saw of him. Master Darcy thought so as well, and he commemorated my plan and I felt better for having offered it. I rid Pemberly of my disgusting relative and as a woman who did her best to love him as a mother, it was all I allowed myself to feel."

"That is understandable."

"I know it sounded cold."

"It does not in the slightest."

"Thank you. I thought I had done right. We all did."

"But Mr. Wickham returned to Pemberly."

"Yes, he did, and I realized that I was in error. He came to demand more money of Master Darcy, who righteously denied him anything. My nephew was a licentious scourge if there ever was one. The blackguard came to me after Master Darcy denied him, and then ordered me to speak on his behalf and do my best to convince Fitzwilliam to give him some more money. I refused, and then he grew vicious, bitter. To this day, I wonder if he would have attacked me if it had not been for Jefferson coming upon us."

"Jefferson protected you? Of course, he did."

"Yes, of course it was him. He had been following Wickham since he had arrived. It was Jefferson who personally drove Wickham of the grounds. Yet that was not the end of it, for the terror of Wickham continued and he would re-enter the tale under the most unpleasant of circumstances. No doubt you are aware of his trying to elope with Miss Georgiana at Ramsgate."

"Yes," I whispered. "And I suppose it was a miracle that Darcy arrived when he did, or she would have been another victim in his schemes."

"And she would be permanently fixed in a most terrible fate," Mrs. Reynolds said. "Yes, it was a miracle that she was saved indeed. And now he is dead, and I cannot mourn him, for all the damage he has done, I cannot repent him—my own blood and I cannot. And to think, all of this has occurred because of me."

"How so?"

She hung her head, "Because I failed."

"How could you have possibly failed?" I gasped, trying to raise myself up on the bed.

"Because at some point, I have to ask myself, how did I take part in raising such a terrible man? At what point did he become a phantom of Pemberly, and I could not save him, or at least frighten the malignance from out of him? Expel the wildness. Or if there was one action that his father and I had altered, from offering him as a companion to the Darcy children, to not encouraging the late Mr. Darcy to favor him so, or to keep him from paying for his schooling rather than forcing him to learn a trade.

"We spoiled the boy and created the monster. His excellent father, my brother is dead and gone, yet I linger here, and no one else is to blame but I, I am to blame."

"You are not to blame," I said. "No more than Georgiana, Darcy, or anyone who has been deceived by Wickham. Others are culpable, but you are not to blame, Mrs. Reynolds. Your nephew's actions speak for his character, and not your own."

"Thank you." Mrs. Reynolds then turned to Lucy.

"You never spoke of it," Lucy gasped. "You never mentioned one word of it."

"Because I wanted to forget it," Mrs. Reynolds replied. "And the Darcys let me. I never spoke of my nephew once he left Pemberly, and never wished to."

I looked between Lucy and Mrs. Reynolds. Lucy's face looked as if she had just been stricken.

"Is there something else that I am not being told?" I asked. "For I demand to know it."

"Yes," Lucy murmured, still looking at Mrs. Reynolds. "Before he left, he kept pursuing me. It was only through Master Darcy that I remained protected. Wickham originally never left me alone. He was your nephew! Why did you not reprimand him? Why did you not protect me?"

"Who do you think it was who asked Master Darcy to move you to being Miss Georgiana's maid at first, so that you would always be in the presence of other women," Mrs. Reynolds said. "I did my best to protect you, truly."

"I... yes, I suppose that you did." Lucy still looked disgusted, and my heart reached out to her. Here were two women who were hurt terribly by the same man, while my sisters Lydia and

Georgiana were also elsewhere and equally as tormented by such a villain. Even in death, Wickham's shadow still eclipsed the light, and a gloom filled their hearts.

"I am so sorry for you both," I offered. "Though I know my condolences mean nothing in the grand scheme of your disappointments and inner torment."

Lucy gave me a watery smile. "It still helps all the same. I care not how it makes me appear. Thank god he is dead!"

With that, Lucy left the room. I turned to Mrs. Reynolds, who looked twenty years older due to the despair that had weighed heavily upon her. I lifted my arm, and she approached me and took it.

"Be comforted. You did your best with him, and he and he alone is responsible for his own choices. The beast that he was is not your weight to carry, therefore your burden is lifted, and your secret is no longer a cross that will remain on your shoulders. Welcome to brightness. He is gone, and you, Lucy, Georgiana, and my sister are now free of his shadow ever returning."

"Yes, we are now free."

"Mrs. Reynolds, if you like, I shall make the same promise that my husband made, and we need never speak of Wickham again."

"Thank you. My nephew will rest and may my shame rest with him."

❧

When finally left alone, I could not rest for my mind was full with all the revelations that had been revealed to me.

Mrs. Reynolds was Mr. Wickham's aunt.

Lucy had been another one of his few victims.

My sister was also tormented by him.

And Georgiana almost was.

A scourge had been removed from the world, but the scar that was left was permanent. How it must've weighed heavily on Mrs. Reynolds to have a boy left to her guardianship turn out in such a way. It would be something that would weigh heavily on her soul till the end of her days. How many moments that she must've spent thinking on him and how she had failed in some way, even though she had not.

Looking down at my stomach, I thought on my own baby, and I wondered at it. What sort of child would I have and if evil was not born in a person, but made, then how could I keep it from becoming so? How could I teach my child principles and be certain that they committed to them? My child had to learn that every action they made affected others in some way, whether good or bad, and therefore they must always do their best not to hinder the paths of others—and appreciate what they were given. How could I save my child?

I worried that there would be nothing I could do in the end, but surely all would not be lost. It would be hard, but I had to teach them love, happiness, and kindness, but I also had to teach them fear—for only fear of things can teach them to understand that they had limits and their actions had consequences that they could not escape.

Yet that day, where I heard a compilation of news of the good and bad sort, they were all revelations that were worth learning, and well worth learning from.

✢ 16 ✢

A GOOD GRANDFATHER

I felt a hand on my stomach, and I was roused from my sleep. When I opened my eyes, the sun was setting, and I rolled over and looked into my husband's face. He must've climbed into bed when he returned from the fields.

"Hello," I said, kissing his chin.

"Hello, he replied. "You look exquisite, but I cannot get near you for there is someone in between us."

I looked down at my belly and smiled.

"Yes, a large person clearly."

I ran my hands down his face.

"When you returned, were you told the news?"

"Yes. Wickham has passed away."

"Yes, he has."

"There have been many tears over the news, but none were tears of sadness, I can assure you."

"I confess that I feel no remorse."

"No one can. He has given us no choice but not to feel anything but relief."

"Darcy, I will never mention this again to anyone else, but you. Mrs. Reynolds has told me the truth. About him being her family."

"Yes, I am sorry for withholding it from you."

"I understood your reasoning."

"Thank you. I had made a promise, and it hurt her terribly to have to remember him."

"And he also hurt Lucy."

"Yes, poor Lucy. However, I protected her to the best of my ability. She did not suffer as long as others."

"Now you are referring to Lydia."

"Yes, Mrs. Reynolds has spoken to me as well. She overheard your sister's confession to you all in the sitting room. Elizabeth, did you know about this?"

"I have learned little of it, but I have begun to do so. Lydia did not wish to speak of it openly till now."

"She was embarrassed."

"Embarrassed?"

"When a person falls in love with a disgusting person and then links themselves to them, then one does not wish for the person's true form to ever become too apparent to all around them. You see, their villainy doesn't make you look like a martyr for taking it, but rather it makes you look worse. For you chose this person, who by all accounts is a scourge, which makes you appear a fool, or a person who condones such evil. To raise up a villain and have called them a hero makes you appear as the worse villain in the end. They often get away unscathed, yet you, no, you end up inheriting their crimes and you ultimately get blamed in the end."

"Is the world really that foolish?"

"Yes, it can be."

"You are too wise."

"I have only had the misfortune to experience the even-handed dealing of the world: a world that claims to praise good, yet only raises up the superficial and degrades the good folk for being honest and not easily swayed by the populous."

"Goodness can be prized, Darcy. The lives that we lead prove that often. How much happiness and good deeds we have seen go praised and noticed by the multitude. Do not fear the world, even the parts of it that are what you claim, for one reason."

"What reason?"

"Because for every man and woman who is a Wickham in the world, there will always be the Fitzwilliam Darcys who will rise against them and show the world that honesty, loyalty, and compassion are the true sources of what is just, no matter how much such fine qualities get secretly ridiculed."

He took my hand, and we ran our fingers through each other's.

"Then I shall not fear the world."

⊙⊁⊙

All the occupants of the house soon learned of Wickham's demise, and none were saddened over it. It is something extreme to behold when a whole household of gentlemen, gentlewomen, maids, servants, and stablemen do not regret the loss of a man. To have many enemies can still mean that a person is good; they simply have no fear in opposing some. However, to have all enemies and no one to mourn you, then that means you have not one fine point to your character.

When my father heard the news, and the news of Lydia's reaction to it, he was even more ashamed of the first time that he learned of Lydia's plight with Wickham from Brighton so long ago. And the knowledge that she had been so abused was too much for his own tendency toward apathy, and he was not only shocked, but also greatly disturbed.

When I found him, he was sitting alone in the library, but not reading.

I walked up to him and sat down.

"Hello, Father."

"Hello," he said, looking at the table and avoiding my eyes. "I find that I cannot read anything right now. I wish that I could. Yet I cannot. Books will not save me from this one. Nothing can."

"You cannot blame yourself for this, Father."

"Yes, I can, and I will. The blame is mine, and I ought to feel it. And here I sit, once again, heartily ashamed of myself for not protecting you all better, and Lydia especially now. I never was the man I should have been—one of strength, a constant guardian who shielded you from external threats. Mr. Darcy was right...we were negligent parents. It makes our worry of Kitty's simple kissing the Colonel appear as such a terrible overreaction. We were so quick to show our willingness to punish, that we failed to see that we were punishing the wrong child. We always did not punish where the punishment was due. I should have realized this the moment your mother blamed Kitty for coughing so, assuming she did it out of her own amusement."

I placed my hand over my father's.

"The past cannot be changed," I began. "Only the present and the future. You have your goodness now, father, so cling to it. Chase after it. And be a good grandfather."

"Be a good grandfather?" he said, his eyes looking up at me and then his gaze rested on my large belly. "Yes, be a good grandfather."

"Yes."

"I do believe...soon I shall be able to read again."

✿ 17 ✿

LOOK TO THE HORIZON

The night of the Pemberly Ball was upon us and, due to my state, I was unable to attend. Darcy was annoyed at having been obliged to still host it for I was not present, but Georgiana was able to step into the role with great ease and I welcomed it.

While I was at first upset over the fact that I could not host my own sister's ball in honor of her wedding, but to be alone and resting was a great comfort, and I enjoyed the solitude. Unfortunately, the music and the dancing and many voices of the families at the ball were enough to not allow me to fall asleep. However, I was content to read or write by candlelight.

One thing I had done in my time was read letters that I had not been able to do so during the day, and to my happiness, a letter from Maria Lucas was in the pile. It felt weightier than a usual letter, which boded well. I opened the envelope and leaning closer to the light from my candle, I began to read.

Dear Elizabeth,

    How are you? Getting larger in girth, I hope. Oh, it must be so nice to be the mistress of Pemberly. Oh, and I have some wonderful news! Jane Austen has finished the first draft of her novel 'First Impressions', but she acknowledges that she should let it remain by the wayside for a bit so that she can return to it with a more objective eye. She hopes to have improved her writing style from her previous work, and she is wishing to be more dialogue driven than descriptive. Only time will see if she will ever complete it. As for Northanger_Abbey, she is quite decided to give up getting a publisher for it in the near future. Personally, I think that she should finish her short work 'The Watsons'. It began as promising, but then she gave it up altogether, and I still do not know why.

Also, how was Kitty's wedding? I know it must have been a wonderful event. And to marry such a man as Colonel Fitzwilliam. I should wish to be so lucky myself.

Yet I do have a request. I am to go to Hunsford to visit my sister, and there I am to meet Lady Catherine de Bourgh. It will be most wonderful, yet I am terrified, and I should like to have a companion. I was wondering if you could ask Mary if she would like to join me in visiting Charlotte, for I will not be half so frightened of Lady Catherine if she is beside me. And tell her that it will be to her benefit, for she can help play music at the church ceremonies, we can escort Charlotte around the village where we will visit and aid the poor, so it will be most beneficial to her desire to do a duty. We shall be most industrious, I promise. So please ask her, Lizzy, for me.

As for the more pressing matter to my letter, as you can see, I have sent Samuel's letter in my own—and I confess to liking being in everyone's confidence. Samuel will not tell me much, but is it a love letter? I am certain that it is. Oh, what a joke. To find Samuel so lovelorn that he has decided to take such a step is most romantic and unexpected. I wish my life had that sort of intrigue. Either way, I shall maintain the secrecy that has been stressed of being of great import—my lips are sealed on the matter.

I hope you are well, Lizzy, and while your fate is a fortunate one, I do so miss when we were all here together in Hampshire, for we were quite a happy lot. Single we all were, yet we never seemed the lesser for it.

Sincerely,
    Maria Lucas

Soon after I finished the letter, there was a knock on the door. I put Samuel Lucas's letter back with Maria's and stashed it under the covers.

"Who is it?" I asked.

The door opened and it was Lydia.

"Lydia?" I asked, startled. "What do you mean by coming in here? Are you not enjoying yourself at the ball?"

"I am having a well enough time," Lydia said, entering in her ball gown, "but I do not particularly feel like celebrating."

"I can understand that, for you have gone through much."

"Yes, and I do not think that being in a room of people suits me just now."

It was such a tragic sight. Lydia, whether I approved of her behavior or not, was a lively girl once, until she had married Wickham. Now, all of that energy and vitality seemed utterly spent, for before me was a woman who looked and felt defeated. All life seemed drained from her and a soberness arose in its place. For some, that would have been regarded as an improvement, yet I, who knew her previous personality, would have been happy if she maintained a sobriety of manner and rationality of thought, but had also still kept her liveliness in a manner that made Lydia Bennet 'Lydia Bennet'.

"Therefore," she added, closing the door, "I came to check on you, as well as to see if I might talk with you a little. That is only if I am not a hindrance to you."

140

"Not at all," I rushed out. "Come and sit on the other side of the bed."

"Thank you."

Lydia moved to the other side of the bed and laid down on it.

"It reminds me of being back in Longbourn. When I was a child, and very much afraid of the dark, I would crawl into your or Jane's bed and you would let me sleep alongside you. I felt safe back then."

"And you were, for Jane and I made it our talent at fending away night demons."

"It turned out that it was not the night demons that I had to worry over, for it was the demons during the day that would prove to be more fatal."

"Lydia... I am so sorry for what you have gone through. To have lived under such torment and terror for so long. It must have been horrible."

"It was—and I was the one who brought that fate upon me. Lizzy, it was such an embarrassment, to live everyday knowing that you thought such a terrible man was once the hero. It made every action I made seem erroneous. And it was. Then the pain came, the agony, and the fear of him."

"Yet you are safe now, and we shall make certain that you always will be."

"Thank you."

For a moment we were quiet, and then Lydia cleared her throat.

"Looking back on my life, I wonder, and look for that point. That defining point of where it all went wrong. You know? That moment where you ask yourself when did I first begin to slip? Was it when I was thirteen years old, and my body began to physically mature? Was it when I first was told that I was beautiful and then believed it so utterly that I did not see how I made myself appear ugly with pride? Was it when our mother allowed me every luxury and encouraged my behavior? Was it when I did not believe that I could ever be wrong?"

She turned her head and looked at me. "I remember that moment, Lizzy. It was my fourteenth birthday, and I was walking along a pathway, a man tipped his hat to me, then bowed, and said that I was so lovely that I could put any queen to shame. I felt the compliment so keenly, that I believed it. And even let him kiss me, which was his aim and the only reason that he had said it—even though I was just a girl really. Yes, that was the moment that I told myself that I could do no wrong, and I had been telling myself so ever since. Which means that I had been making wrong moves all that time. And I did not know it. I did not know it at the time. And that day, that was the beginning of me losing my way."

Lydia then began to weep, and I held her. Her hair pressed against my cheek, her body shuddered as it did its best to allow her emotions to unwind.

"Cry all you like," I whispered. "Cry, Lydia, for believe that they are the beginning of letting go of everything that had once held you so bound—so lost."

Lydia continued to cry on.

"I shall not go back to Longbourn after this," Lydia said when her crying ceased. "Yet I know that I cannot remain here."

"Lydia, you cannot wish to return to Newcastle."

"No, I am not. Yesterday, Kitty told me that she and the Colonel will travel to America for their honeymoon. I humbly asked her if I might join them."

"You wish to join them on their honeymoon?" I asked, uneasy, for it might hinder Kitty and the Colonel's intimacy.

"It is all well," Lydia explained. "For they have told me that they are to visit the American Darcys. Well, by going I can assure them of privacy, for as they did with you and Darcy, if they ever wish to have time alone, I can be a substitute for their absence amongst our American cousins. I will not be in their way, and as hope would have it, they have both accepted me as my sister's companion. Naturally, we will not be able to inform the Darcys of this, and I will be a surprise, but Kitty tells me that Cousin Emilia will not be put out by it and will do her best to accommodate me if I simply apologize for inviting myself."

"Cousin Emilia will love it. For Kitty is now married, and you are recently widowed. If there is anything Cousin Emilia loves, it is making a good match, and she will love that you have given her something to do."

"Then I will be happy to know that I will not be a hindrance or serve as baggage that is swung about people's heads out of annoyance. I hope she will overlook my self-invite, and I will do all to make that family like me."

"Lydia?"

"Yes?"

"Be good, is all that I ask. Be happy but be good."

"Yes, I know."

"Well then, I hope you find some happiness in America, or a bit of yourself that you feel you have lost. And do not look to the past for your pains, Lydia, but to the lessons that it has taught you, and then look to the horizon and welcome all that it will teach."

✣ 18 ✣

ANOTHER DETAIL

After the ball, Kitty and Colonel Fitzwilliam retired to their bedroom in the early hours of the morning.

Kitty let out a great sigh. "Admit it. Though the ball was a success, you secretly wished for it to end by midnight."

"Too true. Though I am amazed at how much fun it had all been, I thought of being alone with you often."

"Well then." Kitty smiled archly. "Do you still have any energy left within you?"

Colonel Fitzwilliam smiled mischievously.

"When do I not?"

He quickly removed his boots and rushed over to Kitty, lifted her up and carried her to the bed. He laid her down and began to remove her stockings slowly.

"Why the ease of pace?" Kitty asked playfully. "Taking your time has never been your way before."

"Because I want to take my time this night. And I want you to enjoy yourself."

"I always enjoy myself."

"Then may I prolong it, I hope?"

With a saucy salute, she said, "Very well. Proceed then."

Slowly and surely, the Colonel removed every bit of clothing from her body and looked down at Kitty's nude form as she lay there.

"How long will you leave me unsatisfied?"

"Not long." He leaned down and kissed her passionately. He quickly removed his clothing but when he began to unbutton his breeches, Kitty rolled on top of him and pressed him down on the bed sheets.

"Feeling like the monarch, my dear." Richard smiled, cupping her breasts in his hands, and caressing them.

"Thank you, Richard, for marrying me."

"Thank you for having the courage to propose."

"Well, you are welcome, and I also congratulate you. It takes a strange sort of man to find the beauty in a woman who will propose to him."

His smile was so warm it melted her heart. "You merely anticipated me. How could I feel intimidation in that?"

Richard raised himself up, pressed his lips against her breasts and began to gently nip at her nipples with his teeth. Kitty's back arched out as she ran her fingers through Richard's hair, falling into the pleasure that Richard's lips brought her.

"I love you, Kitty Fitzwilliam."

"And I love you my dear, and I love being with you always in this manner."

Kitty ran her hands down Richard's chest and within his breeches while she kissed his neck. Richard laid down enjoying the attentions, then kissed her breasts again, then rolled Kitty on her back, running his lips down from the softness along her neck, around her breasts, down to her stomach, and then he wrapped her legs around his neck.

"Oh, Richard!" Kitty cried out while he lowered his head and began to caress her with his lips in the most intimate of places between her thighs. Deeper and deeper he kissed her, her back arching out of pure ecstasy. Rocking from crest upon crest of romantic sensation, Richard felt her body stiffen, but was so desiring of licking her till her body ached from the pleasure. Her cries of joy fueled him, and the intoxication he got from her body stimulated him to no end, as did the taste of her beauty overwhelm any doubts he ever could have had in the security of their union.

When he had finished, he raised himself up, then he asked, "Do you remember the first time we made love?"

"How could I forget?" Kitty whispered, out of breath. "Yet it still feels new. It still feels perfect."

"I know, and here we go—having our first time again and again... and again."

Richard entered Kitty, and now two united as one, they pressed against and into one another, reveling in their union.

As Richard looked down on his new bride while she writhed underneath him, he wondered and marveled at her. From her beauty to her fine figure, her voice, eyes, smile, laugh and disposition, he enjoyed the peace that he found in her arms, which was unlike any other earthly pleasure he had experienced. For so long, he thought he had experienced everything that life had to offer and was aware of every surprise fortune could bring him; he believed he knew the world and that there would be no more shocks that would make him falter or not know himself.

Yet looking on Kitty, she was not only a perfect wonder to him, but something he never could have foreseen entering his life. How had he got the courage, he asked himself, to have walked up to such perfection and grabbed it, then made it all his own. Kitty was devoted to him in ways no other woman had been, and it did not frighten him in ways that it frightened more senseless or foolish dandies he had known in the army—he had walked up to truth, sincerity, passion and true love rather than suffer a love that the world would have praised, but a love that was not real or worthy of the name it claimed to be.

Richard had found his reality—not an image of it, but the actual thing—and destiny had proven him to be the most fortunate of all his brothers, it had seemed.

Together, they continued moving within each other, moving back and forth between waves of emotional contentment, then with one final thrust, Richard reached his pinnacle and Kitty had embraced him all the more.

"Do I make you happy?" She sighed as Richard lay on top of her, having his fill.

"Yes, very much so," Richard replied, closing his eyes. Kitty wrapped her arms around his shoulders and ran her fingers gently down his back. As he lay on top of her, Kitty looked down his body and noticed the scars he received from his battle injuries. Her heart went out to him as she remembered how close he was to death, and how she had almost lost him before anything would ever begin with them.

Further down his back, right near the scars, she saw a marking, a brand and while she had noticed it after their first night together at Aginfield, she neglected to ask him about it. Yet now that she was comfortable enough to do so, she wanted to take the initiative and ask him before his eyes closed from exhaustion.

She traced it with her fingers. "Richard, what is that branding on your back?"

"Oh, you noticed my mark."

"Yes, where did you get it?"

"I had it drawn on me when I was posted in India."

"You were posted in India once?"

"Yes. There was no action involved there, but when I went, I had this branding placed on me."

"It is permanent then?"

"Yes, very much so."

"Why did you want it?"

"Because it's a symbol."

"A symbol? For what."

"For our family."

"Your family? You mean to say that all you Fitzwilliam men have this?"

"No, we do not. Just the soldiers."

"Richard, could you possibly be more elliptic?"

"Very well, my dear, and sorry, for I am just so exhausted after our activities. It is rare that any of us actually gets the brand, and we only do so if we are officers or soldiers in any way."

"Officers?"

"Yes, it's been a story passed down from generation to generation that every Fitzwilliam got this brand, be they male or female. This had to have been from ancient medieval times, naturally, and not any recent time period, for back then such traditions were not regarded as being barbaric.

However, over time, it was said, that tradition was only passed down through the male side, so that no matter how far a Fitzwilliam man traveled, we could always find each other and know who the other one was. Then it was a custom that got even more reduced. Fitzwilliam men could get the brand if they wanted to mostly, but the only ones who getting it was mandatory, was the ones of us who became soldiers of any kind."

"Really, why so?"

"Somehow the brand, as well as symbolizing our family, it symbolizes strength and the nature of a warrior. We all know what the symbol looked like because it was passed down from person to person, then from person to book, and then to family crest or emblem, and now it's something we all know of, but is never more than a memory. Until me. I have been the first Fitzwilliam son in a few generations to go into the army. And therefore, I believe I am the first one to get drunk one night in India, and then think it a marvelous idea to get the brand. It hurt like hell, yet I am the only Fitzwilliam in the last fifty years to uphold a tradition that seems to have been in existence since a time we do not know, and that has been long forgotten."

"So, you come from a long line of heroes then?"

"I want to believe so, but there is the grim truth that I probably am not. All I am is Richard Fitzwilliam."

"And what is Richard Fitzwilliam but a hero in his own right?" Kitty smiled. "A man who has faced death, looked it in the eyes and said, 'do your worst, for I will certainly do mine'. You have courage, and even if the world did not see it, I do. Look kindly on yourself, Richard. A man such as you had to have been spawned from greatness in one quarter. Let that quarter be your history."

"You are determined to think me a romantic classic." He ran his hands in between her thighs and stroking her while she sighed out in ecstasy.

"You are a modern man," she breathed, trying to speak through his pleasing attentions. "That much is clear. But I will believe that you come from a romantic classic. For there is too much about you that seems like a grand adventure."

Enjoying her compliment, Richard stroked her more and more, taking pleasure in the look of her body as he caressed it.

"I'm a grand adventure, am I?"

"Yes, and we did not even have to leave the bedroom. Therefore, let me enjoy that I now know another detail about Colonel Fitzwilliam."

"Oh, my love, you will have much more to enjoy besides that."

Gathering up some more energy, Richard raised himself up and began to kiss her thighs. Then he rolled her over, ran his lips from the nape of her neck down the curves of her spine, and over her bottom, caressing every soft place of it with his mouth and hands.

Kitty moaned out and welcomed his attentions once more.

"Richard?" she gasped.

"Yes, my love," he said in between his actions.

"I am very greedy. Please do not cease to do so at the present time, and please do not choose to fall asleep for another half an hour."

"I can do so."

"Then I shall reward you."

When he was done kissing her, he raised himself up and entered her while she remained with her stomach lying on the bed.

"Kitty!" he cried as he began to spend himself within her. When reaching the pinnacle, Richard felt the eclipse that occurs whenever he arrived within her, and he collapsed, rolled her over and began to caress her in between her thighs again, enjoying the look of her body arched underneath him while she was completely at his mercy.

When they finished, both out of breath and appeased, he said, "You must always be open to me," Colonel Fitzwilliam insisted. "Let it always be like this."

"I shall, and you must always forgive me when I make a fool of myself."

"Of course I shall."

"You must also see the good in me."

"I can do that. And you must always want me as you do now. I am a hungry man, and I am in love with you. Therefore, I shall always desire this."

"Another detail of yourself that you had left out before we exchanged our nuptials?" Kitty laughed, and then she moaned out in pleasure. "Yes, my love, I am hungry for you as well. I shall want you like this always."

"Then you complete me. Yes, my love, another detail about me that eclipses them all is that I love you terribly. And I will never stop."

"Nor shall I," Kitty replied. "Never will I stop."

Kitty and Richard kissed once more.

19

THE BETTER PARTS OF MYSELF

The day after the ball brought the gift of solitude and intimacy but took away the gift of company. All had ended, from the wedding to the ball, and therefore one by one, our guests were leaving.

The first to leave was my Aunt and Uncle Gardiner, who we promised could come back to Pemberly and celebrate Christmas with us. Jane accompanied them temporarily, for she wished to spend some time with them in town. She promised her students that she would return in two months' time where she expected them to have still remembered their studies and enjoy their holiday for their lessons would return in full vigor.

The second to leave was our parents with Mary, who was happy to know that Maria had use for her and that she could travel to Hunsford to assist Charlotte and Mr. Collins—I still cannot believe Mary actually liked him once in sincerity.

Then the Fitzwilliams left, and Acton was no longer angry at Darcy for ordering him to not fall in love with Mary when he was just trying to be cordial.

The last were the Bingleys to leave with Kitty, Lydia, and the Colonel—yet therein was the next surprise.

"I have spoken to Kitty and the Colonel," Georgiana said, "and they have agreed that if Lydia is allowed to go to America without being invited first, then surely one more will not be too cumbersome. After all, in for a penny, in for a pound."

"Georgiana," I gasped, "are you implying that you invited yourself along their honeymoon as well?"

"Yes," Georgiana said, looking down bashfully. "I know that it sounds foolish, but if you hear me out, then you will see how my traveling with them is for the good of all."

"All right," I said, sitting down on the sofa in the sitting room. "Begin to try and convince me."

"Elizabeth, you are with child, and I am respectful of that, as well as overjoyed on it, so do not think that my leaving you is me not wishing to care for you. However, I know very well that you would much rather prefer being tended to by Mrs. Reynolds and Lucy, while also having an empty house for once where you and my brother can finally have each other all to yourselves."

I looked down at my hands, for she was correct. I did want my husband, and my husband alone.

"And since you have married, neither of you has gotten that chance to just enjoy each other," Georgiana said. "Now, I shall give you your chance. For if I remain here, yes, I can assist you, but I will also be in the way, when you really just will want to be with Fitzwilliam and your baby."

"Thank you, Georgiana. I had not wished to speak of it, for fear of sounding vicious, yet since you have anticipated me, that shows great intuition on your part."

"And this way I can make certain also to keep an eye on Lydia for you," Georgiana said triumphantly. "I do not understand why I am the only one to have noticed this, but Lydia will need a chaperone, and Kitty and the Colonel should not have to be so on their honeymoon. If I go, then they can have plenty of time to themselves and never have to see to her if they do not want company. I can go with her everywhere. Even if she gets annoyed with me, I will never shy away from my duties."

I did not even need a moment to see the logic of everything that Georgiana had said.

"Georgiana, that was brilliant."

She gave me a triumphant smile. "I know. In unguarded moments, I can be quite a schemer, if I put my mind to it."

⚜

And it all came to fruition.

Georgiana was able to pack everything she needed with alacrity. She joined the party to London, I gave Samuel Lucas's letter to Kitty, who would give it to Deborah Darcy, and with the Bingleys and Georgiana in one carriage, and Colonel Fitzwilliam, Kitty and Lydia in the second, they were all off to London.

At London, Kitty, Lydia, Georgiana, and the Colonel would catch the ship called The June Flower, and the Bingleys would remain in their townhouse.

We waved goodbye to them and while I should have felt very forlorn at their going, I knew I would miss them, but felt oddly comfortable and at peace.

"My dear?" my husband asked while we watched their departure.

"Yes, Darcy?"

"While I know it is customary for a woman to want her family to be near her during her final weeks of being pregnant, I am happy that you did not care for it."

"Yes, I did not. For we actually have all of Pemberly to ourselves for the first time."

"Yes, and I am greatly looking forward to it."

"It is too bad that I am the size of a walrus."

He gave me a wicked smile. "Yes, too awful, for if not so, think of all the uncivilized things that we could have gotten up to."

"I already have thought about it, for we still have that lake on the edge of the estate to take a swim in."

"Oh, do not fear, beloved. I have not forgotten about that one."

※

The days at Pemberly rolled on by, ever blissful and with no mishaps or misadventures to them. Darcy and I were left to enjoy each other's company in peace aplenty. While doing so, I was worried that he would grow bored with me, yet it proved to be otherwise. He treasured tranquility and ease in his household. He enjoyed conversation, yet he also found comfort in the quiet that comes with not having to speak with someone when you have found peace with them.

He spent his days tending to Pemberly or to other business while I either remained resting or was looking at the nursery that Mrs. Reynolds and I were preparing.

"A part of me regrets not painting the room to a more childlike color," I said as Mrs. Reynolds had some men bring in the rocking baby basket. "Oh, that is the basket?"

"Yes, Mistress," Mrs. Reynolds said. "First it saw Master Darcy in it, and then it was also used for Georgiana when she came. Now it shall be for the heir of Pemberly, the next generation."

Lucy had entered with some tea and cakes for me.

My stomach growled. "Oh, thank you, Lucy. I haven't eaten in thirty minutes and that felt like too long ago."

"You're welcome, miss, and that is good to hear you say."

Lucy served me the food and then stood back against the wall, seeming as if to make herself as invisible as possible. There was also clearly some tension between her and Mrs. Reynolds.

"Is there something else bothering you both?" I asked them. They looked at each other and then eyed me nervously. I knew that I was being impertinent, yet my current state led me to sometimes having mood changes that made me direct and pushy. "No, truly, do you both harbor unease between each other?"

They both continued to not respond.

"I promised you both that I would never speak his name," I added, "and I will not. Yet he the man, nor the memory of him, is worth discord growing between you. He is gone, and I care for you both. Therefore, do not carry the weight of him around with you when he should be set down and never thought on again."

They both nodded, and then Lucy looked up at me.

"I'm sorry, ma'am. You are right and yet—it is all so strange."

"What do you mean by that?"

"I mean that, when you hate someone so, it takes a hold on you, and you can't leave them behind as you ought. For some reason, they remain with you, like a demon and I... I cannot release him from my mind so easily. I want to be free of him, but I have hated him for so long that now it has become an obsession of mine."

"Oh. I had not thought of that."

"I do not mean to make any excuses."

"I know that you are not. You just reminded me of the thing that cannot be escaped. Clinging to a hate is as contagious as clinging to a love. And if it has become a part of you so, moving on shall not be simple, yet I implore you both now to not let it come between you and move on from this. Can you both attempt to do so?"

"Yes, we can, and we shall," Mrs. Reynolds replied confidently.

"Very good," I said, standing up. "Now we may—oh!"

I faltered and stumbled back into my seat. Mrs. Reynolds and Lucy rushed to me as well as the other servants who assisted them.

"Mistress, are you quite well?" Lucy asked, but then she looked at the ground and Mrs. Reynolds followed her gaze.

"Oh, Mrs. Darcy's water has broken!" Mrs. Reynolds then looked at me, "Mistress, we must get you to your room."

I was carried to my room by the servants while Mrs. Reynolds ordered Lucy and another maid in the household to see to me, others to boil water and bring clean rags while Nicholson was sent to fetch the doctor. Another stableman was also sent to retrieve Darcy from the part of Pemberly he was overseeing, and I was left to the pains and aches that labor was beginning to present.

"I cannot do this," I cried. "This is too terrible!"

Fear gripped me, for as I was laid down on my bed and Lucy and Mrs. Reynolds tended to me, I began to have horrendous doubts. Doubts that I couldn't survive such pain, fear of what lay ahead and pure physical agony at all the torture it felt that I was experiencing.

"Breathe out and in, mistress," Lucy said, wiping a wet rag down my face to wipe away the sweat but give me moisture.

The two of them then began to remove my clothing. Some of it was too cumbersome to remove, therefore they cut them off and I was left in my chemise.

After a few minutes, Doctor Hamilton arrived, and he began to prepare me immediately for going into labor. He touched my stomach to make sure that the baby had turned properly to make certain that I would be safe for delivery. When he was satisfied that the baby had done so, he gave me some ointment, had Lucy prepare some yards of white muslin to wrap the baby in, for he said that my contractions were reaching their peak and that it was soon time. Yet those contractions felt like I was being stabbed over and over in my stomach, for which it was unbearable. And my back. Spasm after spasm weakened me, and I wanted it all to end. I wanted it to all be over and that I should be released from such torment.

Through all the sounds and my own cries, I heard footfalls and then Darcy's voice rang loud and clear.

"Elizabeth!"

"Darcy!" I cried out. "Darcy!"

The next second, the door burst open, my husband entered, and then froze upon seeing me.

"Mr. Darcy," Doctor Hamilton said. "You must leave this place, sir."

"No!" I cried. "He will stay. Darcy, please stay with me!"

"Of course, I'd be damned if I didn't." My husband rushed to my side and he took my hand. I looked deep into his dark eyes, which were filled with alarm and concern.

"Husband..."

"My Elizabeth," he moaned, kissing my cheek. "My strong wife, I'm sorry for this pain you feel."

"My love...in a moment, you shall see me cry out, but please do not leave, do not look away. You give me comfort."

"I shall remain, I promise you."

To have him beside me! All then had changed, for though I might not survive this, I knew that I was not alone. I knew that I could at least give it one last fight, and if my eyes were to close and never open again, at least I had seen him for one last time.

"I am ready," I said to the Doctor. Hamilton nodded, got himself into position and then he readied me.

"Mrs. Darcy, right now, I need you to push. Now push!"

❧

Holding Darcy's hand to the point of breaking it possibly, I cried out as I pushed with all of my might. I felt rather than saw that I was expelling something, and the doctor had been sounding optimistic all the while.

"You are doing wonderfully, Mrs. Darcy," he encouraged. "Its head, shoulders and stomach are visible. All we need is another push and all will be well. Come on! One more go."

I looked into Darcy's eyes, almost lost in them.

"I do not know if I am strong enough."

"Elizabeth," he whispered desperately. "You are the strongest woman I have ever known. You found me, you freed me, and then you saved me over and over. You have strength enough for anything. My love, you can do this."

Finding energy from his encouragement, I nodded and proceeded to push one last time and then—

"Well done, Mrs. Darcy," Doctor Hamilton said. "And... my god."

"What is it?" Darcy said desperately, worried over the doctor's exclamation. "Is she going to be—"

"There is another head!"

"What?"

"Mrs. Darcy, I know you have little strength left, yet you must continue to push. Another infant is coming."

"Another one?" Darcy croaked.

"Yes, sir. She is giving birth to twins."

⚜

The shock in hearing this was overwhelming to say the least. My body felt as if it could go no further yet hearing that I would bring two into the world held me in wonder and fascination. Within me was a desire to bring the second one to the world safely, whether it kill me or not. I therefore took Darcy's hand once more and pushed till all energy was drained from me.

"It is out as well!" the Doctor cried, handing the second child to Lucy while Mrs. Reynolds had wrapped up the first one. Doctor Hamilton then cleaned up the afterbirth and ordered water to be brought. Lucy, while holding my second child, gave me a glass of water. Darcy took it from her and raised it to my lips while I drank it. Doctor Hamilton then smiled down on both of us.

"Congratulations, Mr. and Mrs. Darcy, you have two beautiful baby boys."

"Boys," I said, beginning to weep. "I do?"

"Yes, you do."

I turned to Darcy and was amazed to see a tear roll down his cheek.

"My darling, you are a father now."

"I cannot..." he whispered, at a loss of what to say in return. "I am a—how could it have been..."

I turned to the doctor, Lucy, and Mrs. Reynolds.

"Please let me hold them."

"You are weak now," the doctor said.

"Then I will hold them for the both of us," Darcy snapped. "Let me hold our sons."

Lucy and Mrs. Reynolds, knowing my husband would brook no opposition, walked over to him, and put a baby in each of his arms. He looked down on them and a smile spread across his usually serious face. The sight was breathtaking.

He then bent down and placed them next to me. I did my best to roll over and I looked at both of them.

They took my breath away. "They are beautiful."

"Yes, they are. Look, Elizabeth, you have given them to me. My love, I am so grateful."

"Yes, you are their father now," I whispered, my eyes closing. "May they become as you..."

"Elizabeth!"

"Oh," I said, my eyes snapping open. "Forgive me, I did not mean to frighten you. I am simply exhausted, but I feel well."

"Mrs. Darcy," Doctor Hamilton said, "you can rest, but try to stay awake. Mrs. Reynolds, get her some food, it'll help her mind stay alert. If a woman lets her energy be drained from her, then she is more susceptible to not... well, just get her some food and Lucy, continue to give her some water."

Mrs. Reynolds rushed out and soon returned with bread, cheese, and cold meat which I ate with alacrity. The consuming of food did help to energize me, and I felt my strength rising. However, my thoughts strayed never close to myself, for all my attention was turned toward Darcy and our two babies that he held beside me.

"Oh, my husband. How could we be so fortunate?"

"I do not know, my love, but we are. And it makes me so glad."

When Doctor Hamilton was certain that I was out of danger, he allowed me to rest and fall asleep, yet he stayed overnight to guarantee my safety.

The next morning, I was woken by Mrs. Reynolds who helped me into the washbasin so that I could clean myself up, then she instructed me to return back to my bed, for rest, which I did not deny I needed much of. Soup and bread were made for my breakfast and it was delightful. However, soon after I was reclined in my bed once more, I had her bring my sons to me.

"Oh, dear," I realized, "that means we have to get another baby basket."

"That is already being seen to, Mistress. We shall have one by the end of the day. Till then, Lucy loves to hold one and Master Darcy loves to hold the other."

"Does he?" I smiled.

"Yes, and you shall see for yourself."

Very soon Lucy entered, carrying one of my sons in the basket, and Darcy entered carrying the other. Oh! To see him there, such a tall, strong, and proud man, now holding his tiny infant with such affection. It moved me deeply and I could not be more at peace than when I had glimpsed him in such a way.

"Please," I said, "let me hold them both."

"Of course, my dear."

Darcy sat down beside me and placed one child on my left arm while Lucy placed the second son on my right.

"They are so little. And yet they are also so strong it seems."

"They must get that from you." He nodded to Lucy and Mrs. Reynolds and they both left, closing the door behind them.

I was still incredulous. "Twins. Who would have believed it?"

"I could not, even in my wildest of dreams."

"And to think all that my parents attempted seven times to have a male heir, and we were lucky to have done it on the first try."

"Fortune has been very good to us. Mrs. Reynolds also says that we need not worry for confusing them both, for they do not look alike."

"Oh, she could tell that?"

"Yes. She has seen many children, and she claims that they luckily look very different in features, which will be good for them."

"Yes, it will be."

"Have you considered what we should name them?" I asked.

"I have and though we have thought on it before, it was mostly the girls' names that I liked, and not the boys. So, what shall we consider? I enjoyed the name of Henry once, but now it has been quite ruined for me.

"Yet, I do like the name of Hector. However, I prefer it as a middle name."

"Very well, one will have the middle name of Hector."

"And you are still wishing to not use the name Fitzwilliam?"

"Of course, I am still against it. That name is a scourge."

I laughed at that.

"How about Alexander?" he said.

"Unfortunately, no. I once knew a man named Alexander, and I hated him, so that name is altogether ruined for me. How about Peter?"

"Unfortunately, the first man to get into a fight with me when I was at Oxford was named Peter. He gave me a black eye and I gave him a bloody nose."

"I never knew you got into a fight when you were at school."

"It is university; every man gets into a fight at least once. Too much intelligence was flying around, and when it does so, people are so busy thinking themselves smart that they do not see they are being stupid."

"So, Peter is not allowed then." I laughed. "Yet there must be a good strong name that can fit these two. Wait, can we not take the better parts of your name? Can we not name one William?"

"Ah, William."

"Yes, he can have your spirit, and the name stands for greatness so often. Just think of William the Conqueror."

"Very well. And for the second one, how about Dorian, or Arthur, Percival, or Abraham."

"Abraham is a good one, but overused. And do you think the name Merlin is too fantastical?"

"Merlin!"

"I know, I know. What can I say? I always liked the name. And did you not once say that you liked the name Victor?"

"I did, yet now I am undecided, for the name Victor sometimes strikes me as a mad doctor-like name. Though I might be strange for thinking so."

"Well," I said, "I chose the name William for one, and I shall not let you go by without having your say in this important matter."

"Thank you, you are correct. So, I have the names Victor, Dorian, Arthur, Percival—and not Merlin."

"Very well, not Merlin."

"And yet... Caiden."

"What?"

"Well, it is not a very common name, and it sometimes is described as the name that has no origins or meaning, which might suit him well."

"How so?"

"In naming one William, we give one the right to be a leader, and with the other, we give him the right to make his own path and become whatever he likes."

"Caiden," I considered, liking the explanation as well as liking the name. "My dearest, I like your choice and think it a thoughtful one."

"Very well, this one is William Hector Darcy, and this is Caiden Arthur Darcy."

"William and Caiden. Caiden and William. Yes, they will do perfectly for our strong and fortunate boys."

❦

When we were done naming them, Darcy cuddled next to me and we placed our babies in between us. I had grown exhausted, yet before I had lost all my energy and fell into a deep sleep, I noticed Darcy looking at our babies.

"What are you feeling?" I asked him.

"I am feeling particularly terrified. Elizabeth, what if I am not up for the task that is laid before my feet? What if I disappoint them? Or am not the shining example every father ought to be. What if I fail them in some way?"

"You are worried of being a bad parent," I concluded softly.

"That is precisely so."

"Dearest," I began, trying to offer solace, "I have a little news for you: there is no such thing as being a perfect parent. Just as there is no way that there is such a thing as being a perfect child. Now, I may not have any firsthand experience at being a mother, for I did not become so until of late, but I know at some point, our children are not going to like us, we shall have to come down on them, we might unexpectedly favor one over the other, yet we must endeavor to never stop trying. And you must prepare yourself, as shall I, for sometimes children reach that point in their lives when they will grow to despise their parents, and it is only a phase. I onetime knew a man who did something and his father reprimanded him. The son replied bitterly, claiming that he hated his father. And the father then said, 'I'm your father, I don't have to be liked, but I will be respected, and you'll learn to see everything I did for you in the end.' You will fail sometimes, and so shall I, but we must never stop trying."

He sighed out and looked ahead of me.

"I still am frightened."

"Of course. We are meant to be. I am quite terrified myself."

"Would I be strange for wanting to maybe have a daughter as well?" he asked sheepishly.

"Darcy! That was hell to go through once; I don't think I can do it again."

"My dear, at the rate of our lovemaking, you must admit that there is a likelihood that it will happen again."

"Oh, very well. I suppose it must be if you put it like that."

"There is really no other way to put it."

"Yes, there is no other way. Though if it were possible, I would very much like to be able to have my way with you often and not have to worry about offspring as a byproduct."

"If it one day does come to pass, it will not be within our own time period. Therefore, we must make do."

"And endure the suffering," I moaned. "You men have no idea how lucky you are."

"Oh, we know."

I sighed as I beheld Caiden in Darcy's arms, and I began to guffaw at an apparent irony.

"I suspect that you will favor Caiden in the end, and William will be the apple of my eye."

"It is very possible. He rests so well in your arms already."

Silence reigned on us some more, then Fitzwilliam looked at Caiden as he began to fall asleep in his embrace.

"Elizabeth?" he asked.

"Yes?"

"They...they are so beautiful."

"Oh." I breathed, almost beginning to weep.

"And I want to be there for them," he said. "I want to always be there to protect them from anything and everything that could harm them. I want to know that they will grow to love us, that they will be small at first, but have my height—though if they be short I would not object either. Yet for them to have your heart, your mind and disposition. May they have your goodness. And with me, my need for loyalty, my desire for family. May they learn from my mistakes, and not commit them themselves. Or if they do, may they fix them. I will love them, even though I will feel lost sometimes. And you will be beside me, and we shall make it. We shall live, they will grow, and I hope, that they will be all the better parts of myself. This is what I feel."

I leaned over to Darcy and kissed him.

"What a beauty you are," I whispered. "And such an incredible thing. Do not fear, my love. They will see it as well. All who are around you will see it."

✣ 20 ✣

FRIENDLY SHORES

Kitty looked out as their ship, the June Flower, rolled into the harbor of the Delaware River, on the edge of Penn's Landing. As she watched, she beheld Philadelphia once more before her very eyes. The last time that her eyes rested on the place, she assumed that she would never return there again, for they would not be wanted. However, fortune had turned away from conflict, it seemed, and looked towards peace. For here they were, in the land she once looked on with fondness.

"I hope they shall be happy to see me," Georgiana said, "and will forgive our oversight of the self-invite."

"May they," Kitty replied. "But if not, hopefully we can distract them with news. Cousin Emilia and Cousin Thomas always enjoyed a good story. Well now we have many of them. And it does follow, I wonder how my sister and your brother fare right now. I wonder if Elizabeth has had the baby yet."

"If she has, I do fear for her health," Georgiana said soberly. "Childbirth is such a dangerous thing."

"I do not actually. Whether it is out of stubbornness of wanting to not believe her to be in any danger, or because of intuition, but

Lizzy is strong. She was always active, ate well, healthy and hearty. I cannot see a delivery being something to take her from this world. In fact, very little I believe has the ability to take her in such a permanent way."

"May you be right."

"Yes. I suppose for the sake of my peace of mind, I firmly believe she is."

Further down the deck of the boat, the Captain roared out for his sailors to drop anchor, and Richard came rushing up to his companions.

"It is time. Be prepared, for we shall go ashore."

Further down the deck, Lydia was standing with a group of people, gazing out at the city before her in wonder.

"Philadelphia," she whispered. "Please be kind to me, for here is where I wish to lose and find myself."

৩৯৫

When the June Flower made berth and the walkway was lowered, Colonel Fitzwilliam, Kitty, Lydia, and Georgiana left the sea vessel, carrying their luggage and began to look around.

"How will we find them?" Lydia asked, looking to and fro.

"If I am correct," Georgiana said, "and I hope so, they will find us before we ever even see them—"

"Kitty and Georgiana!"

For those who knew the voice, the call and the tone behind them was a welcome one. They turned and beheld Cousin Thomas and Cousin Emilia Darcy approaching them.

"Cousin Thomas and Emilia!" Kitty cried. "You found us."

"Oh, it was easy as ever," Cousin Thomas replied, approaching with his wife on his arm. When both sets of individuals drew near enough, Cousin Emilia opened her wide arms.

"Let me embrace you both."

Kitty and Georgiana rushed to her eagerly and they all hugged one another with sincere affection.

"Your eagerness to see us can only show that you missed us," Cousin Emilia said.

"All too true," Kitty said. "And as you can see, we come with more to our company than we claimed."

"Indeed," Cousin Thomas said. "And I am waiting to hear how this story came to be. And there is one that I do not recognize here," he said, gesturing to Lydia.

"Oh," Kitty said, standing straight. "It's time for introductions. This is my younger sister, Lydia Wickham, who has come to visit."

"Wickham? Then you must be married then?" Cousin Emilia hinted, "And pray, where is Mr. Wickham and how dare he not think it right to come as well and pay his respects?"

"He might have done so," Lydia explained. "But for a prior engagement. He was serving in his majesty's army when his militia was called to the continent. He fell in battle a couple months prior to now, and I am recently widowed."

"Oh, my dear heavens!"

"We are sorry for your loss," Cousin Thomas said. "And if there is anything we can do to offer you sincere solace, then we shall be happy to oblige."

"Actually, there is one thing you can do very well," Lydia said. "If you would be so kind as to forgive Georgiana and me for inviting ourselves and then pardoning us coming without giving you any notice of our doing so, that would be most wonderful at easing my grief.

"You must understand, I heard so many wonderful things about the American Darcys and about Philadelphia,that I hoped to fall into the many diversions here as well as finding the comforts of family."

Kitty and Georgiana eyed Lydia with surprise at her response, which was so humble, honest, and simply put, that one would not believe that it came from Lydia herself.

Kitty raised an eyebrow. *Could it be that terror can actually be a teacher in the end? Was Wickham's evil so frightening that it humbled Lydia, that it forced her to awaken to the worst parts of herself and overcome them? His tyranny did not kill her, yet it did make her stronger. I do so hope that this transformation is for permanence and not temporary.*

"Well, that is all very well and can be done most easily," Cousin Thomas said, smiling. "You seem to be much like your sisters, and that can be nothing more or less than the best of blessings."

Georgiana said, "And this is not false flattery. They actually mean what they say."

"And Georgiana," Cousin Emilia cried, "even without giving us notice, we are overjoyed to have you, for it is nice to see that you have not lost your liveliness." Cousin Emilia turned to Lydia. "In our household, we prefer liveliness, for it makes conversations by the fire more enjoyable."

"Then you shall love me," Lydia cried. "I have a hard time not talking."

"Oh, thank goodness! I do not enjoy women who come to our home thinking they must stand on ceremony and act demure. We are family, for Christ sakes, not beaus to put you on display like brood mares. And now, to this handsome gentleman who is standing next to you, Kitty. Could this be my cousin, Richard Fitzwilliam?"

"It is indeed," Colonel Fitzwilliam replied. "And I bring with me a bride that you clearly already know and love."

"And I am not surprised," Cousin Thomas said. "These Bennet girls seem to be made for our family, do they not? Now, I have not seen you, Richard, since you were this tall," he said raising his arm three feet off the ground. "And you are grown to a strong man it seems."

"That is one quality amongst many," Kitty replied for him. "He has grown into what could be described as intelligent, confident, well-deserved, well-rounded, filled with conversation, heroic, and a particular favorite of mine, handsome."

Richard gave her a warm look. "Oh, Kitty, you know very well that I am not handsome."

"You are to me. Or would you prefer I not call you that?"

"I never implied that. Call me handsome again."

"You are handsome, Richard."

"Yes. Now say it again."

"No!" Kitty laughed.

"Oh dear," Cousin Emilia said. "You are truly perfect for one another. I shall be quite distracted with how you suit each other so well. And to think, the first time that you had come here, if someone said that you would marry one of my family, I would not have known what to reply with—and to see you here now, so perfectly suited...it's just that I do so love a happy ending."

"And who could possibly be so cold to disagree with you?" Colonel Fitzwilliam replied. "I think there is none."

"Well," she said, kissing his cheek, "if Kitty says that you are a good man, you had darn well better live up to your good name. Yet you are doing a good job already."

"I hope so. Though giving a good first impression is not so hard, but it's the second and third impression I give that I am frightened for."

"Oh, quiet yourself." Kitty gave him a gentle punch on the shoulder.

"And as for you," Cousin Emilia said, hugging Lydia, "that is to make you feel more at home."

"I believe I do now," Lydia said. "And it feels nice to be on friendly shores as opposed to being dashed against rocks of coldness and solemnity."

21

CANTERBURY

The party walked along Penn's Landing and approached the carriage that Cousin Thomas and Emilia traveled in. It was large enough to fit them all, the luggage was stored in a second carriage where their carriage men stowed it all safely.

When all was secure, the party was off and traveling down Market Street. Lydia, who was enjoying the layout of the city, leaned forward over and over, looking out the carriage window.

"I can see this is Lydia's first time in our city as well?" Cousin Thomas asked.

"Yes, it is," Lydia said, her eyes wide with wonder. "And it looks lovely so far."

"We do not live in the heart of the city, but further out in the more rural parts of it, yet we are still close enough to it that we do not have to worry about ever being far from the pleasures it has to offer."

"We come from Hampshire," Lydia cried. "And that is in the heart of the country."

"I have heard this. Did you love living in Hampshire?"

"At first I longed for a more cosmopolitan living."

"We all did at one point," Kitty added.

"Indeed," Georgiana added. "It is the way with people to believe the grass is always greener on the other side. Mr. Bingley once said that when he was in the country, he wanted to be in the city, and when in the city, he wanted to be in the country."

"Ah, how are Mr. Bingley and his new bride?" Cousin Emilia asked.

"They are both very well," Colonel Fitzwilliam replied. "We left them in London, and they were enjoying the delights of the city while also the delights that comes with being newlyweds."

"A delight you now have."

"A delight I hope to have long after we cease to be newlyweds."

"Oh, you little devil," Kitty joked.

"I am a devil."

"And a most adorable one." Kitty then turned to her cousins and continued trading news. "Elizabeth, as you know is with child."

"Has she delivered before you all came to your honeymoon?"

"No, she still has over a month of time before the baby was expected. When we left, she was still not close to the date."

"But around the time of your arrival, she should have given birth."

"Yes, now would be around that time."

"Then that is wonderful news. When you are all settled, I shall write to them to inquire what gender and manner of baby it is. For now, I desire to know very much. They must be overjoyed to be on the brink of becoming parents."

"Yes," Cousin Thomas added. "One thing that could be said for Elizabeth is that she is a natural born mother. Fitzwilliam is a different matter."

"Oh, dear what could that mean?"

"It means that while I am sure that he is happy to have an heir, it does not always follow that he will want to share Elizabeth with anyone. You remember them when they were here, my dear. He was bound to her in full, and he might suffer as I did at first. Elizabeth will have to share her attention between him and their baby. He might miss being the only object of affection in her eyes. I did with our first child."

"Oh Thomas, you never told me!"

"I did not because I was ashamed of my feelings. What father wants to admit being jealous of his own baby? Yet Fitzwilliam might be more vocal on the matter than I. You know how truthful he is." Cousin Thomas then recalled that he was in the company of Fitzwilliam's sister and cousin. "Oh, forgive me, I meant no offense to your brother, Georgiana, and if it appeared so, then I am mortified. I was merely making a comparison towards him and myself."

"There was no offense taken," Georgiana rushed out. "For it is no offense for a man to want his wife's attention. And that does sound like something Fitzwilliam would do."

"Yes, he is a devoted husband to say the least of him," Cousin Emilia confirmed. "Yet onto yourself, how are you my dear, and are you still not engaged?"

"No, I am not actually."

"Well then that is wonderful. You know my ways and habits and you will give me something to do."

"I have no inclination to marry at present," Georgiana answered with a chuckle.

"I know my dear, yet you know that shall never stop me and my incessant scheming. And as for Mrs. Wickham here," she turned to Lydia, "I must apologize in advance."

"What have you to apologize for?"

"It is my way to always see young ladies on their way to falling in love and tying themselves to it. I shall do my best to recall that you are recently widowed, yet if I do not and begin to encourage gentlemen to meet you, then you must understand that sometimes I cannot help myself."

"You remind me of our mother!"

Kitty pursed her lips, for she had had the exact same thought when she first met Cousin Emilia as well all those months ago. And it made sense, for Cousin Emilia possessed the same amount of volume, flightiness, volubility, and beliefs of Mrs. Bennet. Cousin Emilia simply had a better outlook on life and wider views to maintain her energetic ways from ever becoming vulgar.

"Do I?" Cousin Emilia asked. "Good, for that is what I am, through occupation. Therefore, now that most of my children have left me, I am in need of more work. Ladies, you can fulfill that void quite easily."

"We shall do with great alacrity," Georgiana encouraged.

"And how are your children?" Kitty asked.

"Oh, they are all what they are: perfectly fine without knowing it. It is the habit of humanity to always think they are falling behind when they are in the perfect place or actually quite ahead of many."

"Too many have a trajectory of only going up rather than staying in the same place," Colonel Fitzwilliam added. "It makes the angle on which they are looking become askew."

"You speak like a soldier perfectly, cousin," Cousin Thomas said.

"It's easier than sounding like a gentleman."

"Anything is easier than sounding like a gentleman."

"Oh, one thing is harder," Kitty added. "Believe me, sounding like a gentleman's daughter is even more of a trial."

"Oh, now that is very true," Georgiana agreed.

"If you do not mind me asking," Lydia added, "I have heard of your children, yet they are so much in number that I cannot recall their names. How many are they again and what names do they contain?"

"Oh, there are my sons Henry and Joseph. They both live here in Philadelphia. Joseph is married, but Henry is still living the dedicated life of a bachelor."

Georgiana and Kitty looked down at this detail spoken, for they recalled how Henry had proposed to Jane, her rejection of him, and the disastrous aftermath of it all.

"And yet," Cousin Thomas said, "being single suits him well, for the present, for I firmly believe that he lacks the ability of how to be a husband."

Kitty and Georgiana smiled at Cousin Thomas, for the father clearly spoke openly of his son's faults for their benefit. He also did it to acknowledge that he did not blame Jane for the incident, nor hold ill will against any of them. Or maybe at least he found Henry to blame in the end.

"And those are our two boys. Then there is our oldest, Samantha, who lives with her husband in New York. Then there is Molly who is also married and lives in Boston, Massachusetts. Then there is Victoria who is wed and lives in New Jersey. Felicity and Helena live here in Philadelphia. Felicity is married, yet Helena has brain damage and remains with us at home. There is also Esther, who lives in Ohio with her husband, and the last is Deborah, who has taken orders and—"

"And is a nun," Lydia finished, looking at Kitty. "I have heard of her. She knew our neighbor, Samuel Lucas."

"Yes, she did."

"And Cousin Emilia?" Kitty asked. "As soon as it is proper, might we visit Deborah at her convent?"

"Of course, you may, and she would be delighted." Emilia looked around, trying to act coy and then failing at it, she decided to remain in the direct approach. "She told us that she went to the landing to see you all off during your last visit."

"Yes, she did."

"Good and sweet Deborah. Always doing her duty so well. Yes, she would have made someone a proper wife."

Kitty gave her a warm smile. "Still saddened over her choosing love for faith over a marital one, I see."

"Still. Always."

The carriage pulled down a lane and Cousin Thomas perked up.

"Oh, prepare yourself, Cousin Richard and Mrs. Wickham. Here is our home and estate, Canterbury."

The carriage rolled around a set of trees and Canterbury appeared.

"Oh!" Lydia cried.

"Stop the coach, Smith!" Cousin Thomas called out to his driver. The carriage slowed down, and Lydia and Richard were able to take in the estate to its advantage. "Well, cousin and Miss Lydia, what do you think?"

Canterbury was as Kitty and Georgiana had remembered it, large but very well designed, looking elegant while also simple.

"I..." Richard was impressed. "It is lovely. You have a wonderful home, Cousin Thomas."

"Thank you. And how do you like the house, Miss Lydia?"

"I... I like it very much. Indeed, after Pemberly, I do not believe that I have seen a house more perfectly situated. How long has it remained in your family?"

"It has been in our family for six generations, and mark my words, we shall always make certain that it remains in the family. I was able to get it removed from its entail."

"Entail?" Richard asked.

"Yes, for so long it could only be passed down from father to son, therefore a male heir had to be produced. I went to court when I was a middle-aged man, argued my case and won, having my attorney open the option, making the estate passed down to the eldest in the family, whether they be male or female."

"Our home was entailed away to the male line," Lydia said. "When our father passes away, Longbourn shall be inherited to our cousin, Mr. William Collins."

"Oh, that must have been dreadful for you," Cousin Thomas

replied, "to spend your lives knowing you could lose your home at any moment if something happened to your father."

"Yes, we had to be forearmed against the worst, and the only way to do so was to marry."

"Therefore, that pressure was put on your shoulders at a young age to do so, was it not?" Cousin Emilia guessed.

"Yes, it was."

"Each life carries its own heavens and its own hells. I'm sorry that was the Inferno you had to bear."

"Life has shown us that there are worse fates to have," Kitty replied. "And love won out—some of us fought our way to the better path."

"Yes, you have. Drive on, Smith!"

The carriages rolled down the lane to the front of Canterbury. They entered and Cousin Thomas ordered the servants to prepare two more rooms for Georgiana and Lydia while the other manservants brought their trunks to the proper rooms.

They all entered the sitting room and Cousin Emilia had tea brought in with cakes. Lydia, famished, took the cake with eagerness, and ate to her heart's content.

"You were all famished, I see," Thomas said.

"Oh, forgive me," Lydia said. "I am always hungry."

"Are you? You are not a large woman, so where does it go?"

"Probably due to my chatty nature. I spend so much energy in talking, that maybe that is where it all goes."

"Deborah loves to eat, and so does Joseph."

"Henry is different," Emilia added. "When he was growing up, I sometimes had to remind him to eat."

"What young boy forgets to eat?" Lydia asked. "It is all the children I have met think of doing."

"Yes, Henry is the strangest of oddities."

"What is odd can be welcome."

"Yes, it can. An oddity can keep people interesting. And for a long time, Esther was the one who felt guilty about eating meat."

"She likes animals?"

"Yes, and when she was young, she had the most alarming habit of always bringing stray animals home. You have no idea how many times I found a kitten or squirrel under her bed."

"A squirrel?"

"Yes, oh bless me. Well, squirrels were quite the idea for an ideal pet once so..."

"Squirrels?" Kitty, Georgiana, and Lydia said simultaneously.

"Oh, so that was never a trend in Britain? Well, there was a time when people would domesticate squirrels, raising them from their birth, and therefore taking them in as pets."

"That is marvelous," Georgiana said. "And I would like to have seen that once."

"I did see it once at its fullest," Thomas said. "An actual government official had one and I was over at his house once when I was young. He paraded his squirrel around for us all to see. Its name was Pondi."

"Pondi?" Richard laughed.

"He couldn't think of any other better name for him."

"Well, it would be complicated for a squirrel."

"Yes, I would have just named him Nuts, or something more foolishly obvious. Yet Esther did try to domesticate the squirrels and our maids always had to search her room and drive the squirrels back out to nature where they belonged."

"And to think our parents were upset with me trying to keep a cat," Kitty said. "And I liked that cat!"

"What happened to it?"

"Oh, our mother would not let me keep it, but it remained on our land and I would sneak food to him, and I also made a small house for him that would shield him from the cold and weather."

"Wait, that was what you were making?" Lydia asked.

"Yes."

"Why did you not tell me?"

"Because I was worried that you would go ratting out to mother. You never knew how to keep a secret, Lydia."

"Oh, shut it!"

Cousin Emilia and Thomas laughed at the sisters bickering.

"Oh, sorry for our argument," Lydia said.

"Not at all. This is most amusing."

"And here we are talking of the past," Kitty added, "when we should be complimenting you on your constantly good hospitality."

Lydia lifted her shoulders and sighed. "Very well. I acknowledge that I have been improper, and I have been remiss in my complimenting your home. It is a wonderful seat, placed advantageously, and such comfortable furnishings."

"Comfortable furnishings!" Came a voice from behind them. They all turned, and Henry Darcy stood in the archway. "Yes, that is the thing that is needed of every fine home. And nothing less could be worthy of Canterbury."

❦ 22 ❦

WHERE THE STORY UNWINDS

enry Darcy took a few steps closer to the company, stiff and apprehensive. All the guests rose when he entered while Richard bowed, the rest of them curtsied.

"Oh, timely met," Cousin Thomas said, standing up and looking at his son with a warning look, indicating for him to behave. "You remember your cousin Georgiana and Kitty."

"Yes, I do," Henry said, bowing curtly. "Ladies it is... a delight to see you once more."

And more untrue words could not be spoken, Kitty thought to herself. Her findings actually were quite true, for Henry Darcy's cold gaze seemed even more stone-like than she remembered. Henry Darcy's mind was a complex one but also one that was easy to read. The arrival of Kitty and Georgiana brought a reminder of his disastrous proposal to Jane Bennet, for both women saw his shame for themselves, and now with their eyes upon him, he felt naked—exposed to a memory that he would rather have forgotten. And now, as long as they remained at Canterbury, he would remember it every day. Therefore, while he would be as polite as his will would allow, he looked forward to the day that they would leave back for England.

On that day, he thought, *when I finally never have to see these women again, goodbye, and good riddance!*

And Kitty, being well acquainted with his mind and manners, sensed every thought that he had. Lydia however, who had never known him till that moment, did not know what to make of the *Goliath* that stood before her. Not knowing why he was glaring so hard at her sister and sister-in-law, Lydia accidentally shifted in her place and everyone's attention fell on her.

"Forgive me," she whispered, and then she saw the look in Henry's eye as it fell upon her. While his glare was light at first, now it turned more severe and even colder, and it made Lydia freeze and feel an immediate disdain for him.

Why does he look so meanly upon me? Lydia asked herself. *What have I done to deserve such scorn? He looks like a miserable sot!*

"And Henry," Cousin Thomas continued, "here are both old friends and new ones come to visit. To join Georgiana and Kitty is your cousin Colonel Richard Fitzwilliam, whom Kitty has just married, and her younger sister, Mrs. Lydia Wickham."

Henry tore his eyes away from Lydia and bowed to the Colonel.

"Good day, Colonel Fitzwilliam."

"Oh, we are cousins, sir." Colonel Fitzwilliam bowed. "You need not be so formal with me. Richard shall suffice."

"Then you may call me Henry," he stated, still not smiling, "if that is your pleasure."

Richard did not falter yet could tell that Henry was being severe —and without a reason for having that severity.

Henry then turned to Kitty. "And Mrs. Fitzwilliam now?"

"Yes, Mr. Darcy. Or Henry."

"I offer you my congratulations."

"Thank you, and my sister Elizabeth is with child as well."

"Then that side of the Darcy family appears to be given many gifts."

"I am certain this side has its shares as well."

"It can be."

"And if the Darcy line is so lucky, then our side of the Bennets must own to being no less fortunate."

"Yes. For Elizabeth caught one Mr. Darcy, and now you seize his cousin."

"And I embrace her proudly," Richard interjected, with a firmness in his tone that made Henry cease. "Yet you are correct, Henry, the men on our side of the family are lucky."

Henry nodded his head curtly, and then he turned to Lydia.

"You are the youngest of your sisters, I presume."

"Yes, Mr. Darcy."

"Remember," he said with a hint of edge to his voice, "I am to be called Henry it seems."

"Right," Lydia replied, trying to restrain her temper. "Henry. I am the youngest, as you are the oldest."

"Ah, we are both extremities."

"And how does being the extremity of age make us so different than those in the middle?"

"You can tell yourself there is sameness, yet I can assure you, for us oldest, there definitely is not. And for you youngest, there is a definite distinction, whether you admit it to yourself or not."

"And what difference would that be?"

"The youngest is usually the favorite, and some would even go so far as to say that the youngest could be spoiled."

"Any of the children can be spoiled, so that statement is half-true, I confess. Besides, there are side effects to being spoiled."

"And how so?"

"One does not learn humility or self-doubt."

"And do you know those things?"

"How has Philadelphia been since we left it, Henry?" Georgiana asked, changing the subject immediately. "I take it that it has been nice."

"It has been Philadelphia."

"And what does that mean, Henry?" Cousin Emilia asked with emphasis. Henry took her meaning, and he bit his lip, then he smiled gently.

"It means, Georgiana, that all has been well, and that I am happy that you are all come at this time."

"Thank you, Henry," Kitty replied, smiling, but still on her guard. "We are happy to have come as well."

⚜

"I cannot believe that impertinent imbecile!" Richard exclaimed when he was in their guestroom with Kitty. "The way he spoke to you, Kitty, made me wish to drive a stake through his heart. Dear lord, I wonder at the pride of that man!"

"Yes, and I do confess to him hating me as much as I do him."

"Oh, you hate him? Why did you not tell me that there was discord between yourself and one of the household? I would not have consented in our coming."

"I am not afraid of him."

"Yet I am not the sort of man who can sit by and watch him think he can disrespect you. And you have seen me, Kitty, I can fight a duel in a moment."

"Yes, you can, yet you need not be alarmed. Thomas and Emilia will speak with him and force him to recall his honorable side. Besides, his disgust towards me is not a personal one, but one owned through wounded pride."

"Wounded pride?"

"I saw him fail at something, and so he cannot forgive me."

"What did you see him fail at?"

"I saw him be rejected. When we were in America before, our holiday here was filled with bliss, until Henry began to fancy himself in love with Jane."

"Your older sister?"

"Yes. He believed himself so much in love with her that he proposed to her after a short acquaintance. And she rejected him."

"Really?"

"Oh yes."

Richard sat down on the bed next to Kitty and stared ahead.

"You look disturbed." Kitty chuckled, taking in his expression.

"I suppose I am. It is just so strange. Jane is such a kind and serene creature, that I cannot ever imagine seeing her saying no to anyone."

"Yes, it was quite the bold action on her part. However, he did not take this rejection as a gentleman ought to. Not only did he not walk away from it with grace, yet he informed his parents and even cornered Jane, asking for an explanation of why she refused his hand."

"He did that?"

"Yes, he did. Mr. Bingley, Georgiana and I were present when he did this, so she was not alone, but it was still a terrible form of harassment—and bullying."

"It was lacking any refinement or manners. Should I say something to him?"

"For the present, please do not, but if Henry ever were to lose his way to his own temper again, then we will need you to save us, Richard. Though I hope you will not need to. Yet still, the truth remains that Henry will look on Georgiana and me with disdain every now and again, and I know that look. He is embarrassed that we saw him fail in so disgraceful a manner. And knowing Henry, he will feel his shame fresh every time he beholds us. This means that he will not easily forgive us—all because we remind him of his bad moment."

"Right. Are you going to tell Lydia all of this?"

"I will have no choice, but I will do my best to stress keeping this all a secret. And hopefully she will keep it, for she has changed enough to warrant me license to believe in her more."

"Yes, she ought to be warned. Do you know, when I had first seen Henry, he reminded me of Darcy?"

"Did he? Oh! Now that I think on it, there is a similarity in stance, posture, attitude and awe-inspiring. Yet now that I know Darcy better, his coldness has abated completely and there is so much warmth to him than he allows the world to see."

"Yes, he unfolds when he is around people he loves."

"With Henry, I never saw him unfold around Jane in the way that Darcy unfolds around Lizzy. Henry was a fool. He did not love Jane in the way that love is meant to be felt, I believe. It never appeared in his eyes. And that is where Darcy and he are so different. Elizabeth may have been the makings of your cousin, but he was willing to open up eventually. With Henry, I see no opening up. I see nothing."

"Which means that whatever woman Henry chooses next...will have her work cut out for her."

"Or he would consume her with his coldness and eat her alive."

"Yes, making me happy that Jane refused him, for he would have attempted to reign over her, and she would never stand up to him. Whoever does choose him in the end would have to be a truly bold woman."

⁂

The next morning, before attending breakfast, Kitty dressed and went to see Lydia in her bedroom. When doing so, she unfolded

Henry Darcy's history with Jane, thus revealing the source behind his discomfort with her and Georgiana.

"He proposed to her?" Lydia said. "I can scarce believe it. Not at anyone who would propose to her of course, but he seems so cold, so severe, and he was in love with her all the time."

"It was not love, believe me. I have seen the real thing, and it was not so with him. He was in love with the idea of her, but he never actually became acquainted with her true spirit and nature."

"Yes, he would have been tyrannical over her. It seems to be his way, at least."

"That was what we all suspected would happen. But you do not blame her for refusing him, do you?"

"Blame her, oh no! A woman should not be forced into a union where the man loves a concept of her, but not the real thing. You and I know that it will never do."

"And now you are speaking from your own experiences?"

Lydia looked down at her hands, and Kitty sat down next to her. "Lydia, how are you feeling?"

"I am well. And now being so removed from it all, I hope—I believe that I can put it all behind me."

"I am sorry for how Wickham hurt you. It must have been awful."

"Awful was a euphemism for it, Kitty. And yet, when I looked back on it all, I thought of what moment, what action had pushed me to that fate that I had received. What was most humiliating was there was not one action, but several that were taken, and they all were done by me. It was I who chose to fall in love with a man who clearly did not care about me at all, even a little. It was I who took the invitation to go to Brighton, then abandoned all her friends to elope with a man who was covered in lies. How could I have believed that he planned for it to be so? There was never truth, honor, or compassion to him. There only was charm."

"Charm is dangerous," Kitty offered. "And lethal, for it is hard to see past, and easy to fall in love with. Wickham was handsome and captivating, and as Georgiana has shown, you are clearly not the only one who had fallen prey to him."

"And then I chose to marry him," Lydia continued. "And many times, through all the horrors, I wondered what it would have been like if I had chosen not to. Would it have been better to have lived in exile somewhere rather than suffer the fate I chose for myself? And it would have been, Kitty. It would have been a much better destiny to have lived in infamy, rather than live above reproach from society but below happiness from within the home."

"Lydia, Elizabeth and I do not pretend to be perfect. We had broken our share of rules for the men that we loved, yet we did so because they deserved it. They showed the ability to understand sacrifice, or at least identify the error in their ways."

"I was a fool."

Kitty patted her sister's hands. "We are all fools in love, and you are not alone. We all were blind at times; therefore, all that I can say is remember your faults and do your best to correct them. Then, when you have discovered that in earnest, the next step is to find the one who is worthy, the one who can own to his mistakes. Wickham's evil was actually a very simple one. It was not illness of temper or intentional malignancy. It was the stubborn belief he had that he was never wrong to do anything, and therefore, he thought himself correct to commit any evil and be right to do so."

Kitty took Lydia's hands in hers. "Lydia, just promise me one thing; do not listen to what we were taught. We are not doomed to marry above all, even if the man is not well-suited for us. Marry properly or do not do it at all. Marry someone who will listen to you, who will inspire you to want to improve yourself, who has conviction, but also humility... and who knows kindness. He will not always be charming."

"Richard is charming."

"I was fortunate to find a man who allowed charm and sincerity to go hand in hand. Yet do your best to look at what the man is underneath and see that what he says is consistent with what he does. Improve yourself as you go along and command nothing less."

"Yes. I am heartily ashamed of myself. Yet I have been saved somehow. Therefore, this feeling shall pass, and no doubt more quickly than it should."

❦

Kitty left to join Colonel Fitzwilliam before they all went down to breakfast. While she did so, Lydia, who had finished dressing and being tended to by a servant, left her room and began to make her way to the dining hall. However, before she arrived at the top of the staircase, she heard voices coming from a doorway. At first, she thought to ignore it, but then she heard a voice mention Kitty's name. Allowing curiosity to get the best of her, she walked up to the door, which was mostly closed but not fully. She pressed her eye against the crack of it and was only able to see barely a little. But the owner of the voice became clear. It was Henry Darcy, and he was in the library, accompanied by another man who she did not recognize.

"Henry," the man said, "calm yourself."

"Calm myself? Why do you always tell me to do so, Joseph, when I hardly ever shout?"

"It is not your volume that I ask you to keep in check, but it is your tone and temper. You are too easily moved, Henry, and you do your best to hide it behind a veneer of stone. However, brother, with you, still waters run deep. And sometimes easily troubled."

Oh! Lydia thought to herself. *That's who the man is. It is Joseph, Henry's younger brother.*

"I am simply... Joseph, I confess that I am still bitter toward the lot of them."

"And why so? You cannot blame Kitty and Georgiana for Jane's refusing you. Nor should you."

"It is the shame of it."

"Oh, yes, the shame that comes with them knowing your secret, for you made your humiliation public."

"Joseph, are you content to ridicule me over things beyond my control? And how would you have felt for a woman to have rejected you in such a manner? It is easy to claim that you will act like that of a gentleman, but when you are in the circumstance, the emotions take over, and one's pride is affected."

"Do you still love Jane?"

"No, not at all. I am just resentful. I feel as if I have been dealt a great wrong, offering my hand to a woman who ought to have been grateful for it, and instead I was rebuked as if I was not good enough—for her!"

"Yes, you did deserve better."

"Yes, I did. And to see them now, Kitty happily wed to my cousin, when it is in that family to be so impertinent. Mark my words, Joseph, they are all the same. We both warned Elizabeth to not engage in getting acquainted with Miriam Goldman, and she did the reverse. And now Mr. Bingley and she are married, and very soon, the poor girl will be subject to society looking down on her for her background. Yet no one understands that sometimes one must be cruel to be kind."

"Hopefully, we were wrong though, and maybe we deceived ourselves there."

"Hardly. The world is not ready for such a change. Yet Elizabeth was stubborn, willful to the point of blindness, then Jane proved to have the same failing, Kitty has it as well, and now we have another one: this Mrs. Lydia Wickham."

"Have you made her acquaintance yet?"

"Yes, and from the little that I have seen, she is just like her sisters, and perhaps even worse. Believe me, Joseph, she will be like a flame that burns much. And I do not like such dangers."

Lydia balled her fists, gathering an immediate dislike of Henry Darcy that was well justified. Every word uttered from him was not only derived from wounded and misplaced pride, yet it was inspired by a cold and cruel prejudice that he placed upon her and her sisters. Lydia ground her teeth, for he was wrong to speak so! Every crime he claimed the Bennet girls committed was a gross injustice against her family, for they were all innocent of the flaws he claimed. She and her sisters were not ignorant to the point of blindness—well she, Lydia, had been, but that was her sin alone. Each of them had courage, and a will to believe in something, and the right to speak, and be heard as opposed to not be listened to. And who was this Henry Darcy to make such claims? He was nothing more than a bitter and repulsive man who blamed others for his mistakes.

'I may not have owned to my mistakes before,' Lydia thought, *'yet I do now. And therefore, I am greater than him.'*

And Lydia's pride not only was affected, as well as her feelings, yet there was also a wish to defend. He had insulted Jane, Elizabeth, and Kitty, who were all above reproach—who had all accepted her after she had done nothing to deserve it. Whatever flaw they had, it should not be laid at Henry Darcy's feet, for at their very worst of moments, never would they be as low as he was being.

Feeling her anger rise up from within her, Lydia desperately wished to walk up to Henry Darcy and kick him. However, she refrained from giving way to her sensibilities at the moment. But her body still had an impulsive physical reaction and she let out a gasp.

She covered her mouth immediately, trying to stifle the noise, however, it was enough to be heard, and she saw Henry Darcy turn and his eyes fell on her. They looked at one another, his steely gaze penetrated her confidence and struck fear within her nerves and she was rooted to the spot. For both, beholding each other felt like an eternity, yet in actuality, it was no more than a couple of seconds till Lydia regained her courage and rushed from out of the doorway. She heard quick footsteps make their way through the library, knowing them to be Henry's. Gathering her weight so much that her footsteps made no sound, she rushed down the steps and to the first floor before Henry could even open the library door.

When feeling herself to be safe, she stopped and took a breath.

Everything that Henry had said ran fresh through her mind and the words still stung as if she had just heard them recently. If anything else, they had stung more than at first because now she had more time to allow her feelings to be affected by them.

Lydia did not need a second impression to feel as if she hated the man. For he lent himself toward that sensation so much that she knew herself to be justified in every feeling of disdain she could hold for him. And yet, she was within the home of Cousin Thomas and Emilia. Therefore, she had to remember to keep her words select and subdued—at least in their presence—for she did not want to become an unwanted guest who was sent home in a solitary state because she upset her hosts. No, she reasoned, she must allow the change that had begun within her to take hold and reshape her fully. For only part of her former self was reformed, and the rest was still quite fragile.

She entered the breakfast hall where all were assembled except for Henry and Joseph. When she entered, they all looked up at her and Cousin Thomas smiled.

"There you are! Sit down and eat your fill. And tell us how you slept."

"Thank you," Lydia said, sitting down with grace. "I slept very well, and my bedroom is quite lovely, comfortable, and all that I would wish."

"I can see that you are wishing to inject every possible

compliment you can into that sentence, but it is not false flattery, and I enjoy a good compliment."

"As you should," Colonel Fitzwilliam said. "Being around so many women, compliments become something I always enjoy."

"Oh good," Cousin Emilia said. "I like a man who can stomach women's attentions. Indeed, there are too many men out there who for some reason, when a woman compliments them, they become closed off, as if the pleasing attentions we give you are too overwhelming."

"Oh," Cousin Thomas said, "as much as I hate generalizations placed on my species, for they are usually monstrously inaccurate, that is one that can be often very true. And I do not understand it! I love when women cater to me, and I actually demand Emilia here to do it often."

"You do not demand me to do anything, you liar!" Emilia laughed. "I do it of my own choosing!"

"Ha! See, this is why I married her, and simultaneously tricked her into saying precisely what I wanted her to without ordering it."

"Oh, you bugger!"

"You see, Richard," Thomas said, turning to Colonel Fitzwilliam. "This is how you find peace in a relationship. You do not have to order the woman, yet through quickness of mind, you can passively hint at what you want her to say, and then use trickery to your advantage."

"Richard, you had better never use that trick on me," Kitty demanded, chuckling all the while.

"I apologize in advance my dear, for I have already done it to you multiple times."

Everyone laughed.

"That is a lie," Kitty objected.

"Not at all, after all was I not the one who was able to passively get you to propose to me?"

"What?!" Was everyone's reply.

They were all surprised however when they heard footsteps and Henry and Joseph Darcy entered.

⚜

"Oh, there you both are!" Cousin Emilia cried. "You both truly take delight in vexing me, being so late to breakfast. My dear cousins, we have a wonderful addition to our breakfast. This is my other son, Mr. Joseph Darcy. He came down early so to join our meal."

"Hello Joseph," Georgiana said. "It is nice to see you once more."

Kitty offered her hellos as well.

"The pleasure is all mine," he said bowing. "Forgive my early arrival, but I felt there to not be a moment too soon for me to come and make the acquaintance of this new addition to your party."

Lydia smiled, but felt all the falseness to his words most keenly. She recalled how he allowed his brother to speak earlier, and while not speaking the most severe of insults himself, by allowing Henry to voice them made Joseph look equally as guilty.

"Cousin Richard," Joseph began, "we haven't seen each other since we were children, yet it is no surprise to me that you have gone into the army, for you always had a soldier-like way about you."

"That had better be a compliment." Colonel Fitzwilliam answered with a laugh.

"Do not worry, it was!" Joseph then turned to Lydia and bowed.

"And this must be Mrs. Wickham."

"Yes, this is my sister, Lydia," Kitty said.

"And the family resemblance is not lost on me. You have the same beauty that the rest of your sisters possess, for Kitty is proof how potent it is by catching my cousin for a husband."

"Yes, but while my wife's Bennet beauty must be given credit," Colonel Fitzwilliam said, "I also must take some accolades, for to win such a woman takes incredible skill. And to win a *Bennet girl* takes much greatness of mind, and those lesser cannot hope to achieve such a prize."

Most of the table laughed at this, thinking it was spoken in jest, however Lydia and Kitty both were able to see through the Colonel's lightness of tone. Colonel Fitzwilliam had meant to wound Henry, probably as a result of Henry's sarcastic tongue the day before—and he was successful, for Henry's jaw held a tension that he did not hide well. He was offended, and the Colonel meant it to be so.

"Tis true," Joseph Darcy said. "A man does deserve credit for catching a wife."

"And speaking of such," Kitty added, "where is your love, Mrs. Darcy?"

"Oh, my wife remains home for the present. She is very ill."

"Oh, I am so sorry."

"Thank you, I will tell her you offered your condolences, however her state is hopeful, and I know she will recover with much rest. Believe me, she will be well enough to receive you in our home very soon."

"All that matters is that she recovers," Georgiana said. "She need have no worry for us."

"Aye," Cousin Emilia said, "for we have many abilities to entertain them, and you can help us this morning by sitting down and making them comfortable."

"Very well, Mother," Joseph said with mocking gravity, "I shall endeavor to do so."

Joseph and Henry sat down, and they all began to eat. Despite her desire to not look on him, Lydia could not deny looking at Henry Darcy every now and again. She could then tell, by the look in his eyes, that he was wondering who had been the one to overhear him. For he saw little of her, only one of her eyes, and therefore the mystery was upon him. Lydia promised that she would do her part to never make him aware of the answer.

However, it was clear that Henry felt that he was under even more rocky terrain, for he would spend all their days there wondering which woman was the one for him to put on his guard for, and if she had told what she overheard to everyone else in the company.

Lydia was aware of his fears, for the apprehension showed in his eyes. It was of a man worried that he was found out, and that he made an even worse impression than before.

As for Henry, there was that apprehension that was mingled with anxiety. He was of a taciturn disposition, this was true, but he did not enjoy being fundamentally loathsome to his entire company no more than anyone else would. His words were meant to be spoken in confidence with his brother and his brother alone. Yet all that was needed to push his character back into the role of the antagonist was one more bad report upon his person.

His eyes looked on Kitty at first, for she was the most like Elizabeth, and would be the most unafraid to listen to his coarse words.

Then he turned to Georgiana, who if she overheard, she would have the least fear of him because they were directly cousins, and therefore she would have suffered no consequences.

He next looked on Lydia, who smiled and laughed at everything that Cousin Emilia said, yet her eyes would every now and again fall upon him, and then look elsewhere. However, that expression could signify anything.

Yet in an unguarded moment, while Henry appeared to be looking to her left, Lydia did look on him and her eyes filled with resentment before she leaned down and took another piece of bread. And that was when Henry favored the notion that it was Lydia who had overheard him. For his actions, though terrible the night before, did not deserve such a glare, but that day, his words could have warranted such a response.

Thinking on her history, he recalled that she was recently widowed, and accompanied her sister, not seeing the coldness it showed of her to be on holiday so soon after her husband's death.

This is where the story unwinds, Henry told himself. *Lydia Bennet... I was correct. She contains the same blindness and tendency to follow her own will as her sisters have. I have no patience for them. None at all.*

❦ 23 ❦

HARSH WORDS

The first day was spent in rest and within the home. Thomas and Emilia allowed their cousins to rest if they were still tired from their journey, which all were happy to do. Then after the mid-day meal, she gave them a tour of the house. Kitty and Georgiana, though having seen it before, were now enjoying it once more, for it was with two others who were new to it all. Henry did not join them for it, but instead, he and Joseph did some hunting throughout the day, bagging many birds in the process. Cousin Thomas left to see to the farm and see to the tenants on the estate. Their company was left alone with Cousin Emilia, for she was always so open.

"And," Cousin Emilia said as they walked through the house, "here was the room where the children would receive their lessons. They were the unruliest children and I felt bad for our governesses. Yet one thing I can say for myself, is that I never sided with my children if they were clearly in the wrong. Some mothers are so dense and believe their children were angels. Well, my children had angel-like qualities to them, but overall, they could also be devils."

"We could be as well," Kitty said. "I did my best to get away with many pranks when I was younger."

"Oh, and what was your crime as children?"

"I would break my sisters' thread when they tried to sew."

"I would pour ink on their clothes," Lydia added.

"And I poured ink in my brother's tea," Georgiana added.

"Ink?" Everyone all laughed.

"And me as well!" Richard cried. "You poured it in mine as well!" Everyone laughed harder.

"Oh, I do so miss my children being that age," Cousin Emilia said. "We mothers complain, but we secretly enjoy it."

"I can see why. It keeps you on your toes."

"And it gives you a story to tell. Oh, and if you do not mind, I will have Helena sit with us at dinner tonight. We believe that she has gotten over her inability to sit at the table."

"Oh, that is wonderful," Georgiana said. "The poor girl."

"Yes, it is so unfortunate, but she has such a strong will to her."

Once the tour ended and there was still more time, Emilia offered the option of visiting Deborah's convent to see her, or to remain and rest at Canterbury. While all secretly wished to sit in the drawing-room and enjoy each other's company, a duty that must be done could not be done too soon, and they all agreed to go and see Deborah Darcy, who also went by Sister Mary Ignatius.

❦

"Georgiana and Kitty!" Deborah Darcy cried out as the whole company entered the convent and she met them soon upon their arrival. "And is that my cousin, the Colonel?"

"It is indeed," Georgiana and Kitty exclaimed, hugging her when they met. Once affection was displayed fully, Deborah turned to the rest of the company.

"And this one looks like you, Kitty," she began.

"Yes, this is my sister, Mrs. Lydia Wickham."

"Well good day,, Mrs. Wickham."

"And good day, Sister Ignatius. I have heard so much about you that I feel as if I know you."

She pulled a comical frown. "Yes, I hear that a lot. That must mean that I speak too much."

"I speak a lot as well," Lydia added.

"Oh, how refreshing." She turned a bit and looked at Richard. "And this is my cousin, Colonel Fitzwilliam?"

"Yes, and you most certainly can call me Richard."

"Well, Richard, when I first look upon you, I want to like you. Please promise me that you are a good man."

"I want to believe so. Yet being a 'good man' is a title that can vary from person to person, and I do not wish to disappoint you if my measure of goodness is not as wholesome as yours."

"You think because I am a nun that I do not laugh? Clearly I have shown the opposite already."

"Yes, you have, but I still do not wish to do myself too much credit."

"Oh, for god sake's, man!" She gasped, which would have startled the company had they not been so used to her frank and open nature. "There is nothing wrong with thinking oneself good, as long as it is true."

"And it's true," Kitty confirmed. "I would not have married him if he was anything less."

"You are married?"

"Oh yes," Richard and Kitty said at once.

"How perfect this is," Deborah said. "And you must promise me now that you will always deserve each other."

"We promise," Richard said. "I believe I quite like you, Sister Mary."

"Oh, call me Deborah. Even god could not deny you are justified in doing so, for we are cousins."

"Very well, Deborah."

She gave them a warm smile. "Now, I know that one of you bears a letter for me."

They all looked startled at her saying it so publicly.

"A letter?" Cousin Emilia asked.

"Yes, Mother. Elizabeth wrote to me that she would send a letter from a mutual acquaintance of ours, and I believe that one of them has it."

"That would be me!" Kitty confirmed, removing the letter from her purse, and handing it to Deborah Darcy.

"Thank you very much for being the letter bringer," Deborah said, taking it. "And forgive my impatience, for I know that one should wait to read a letter when a company has gone, but I was in hopes that you would let me read it, and if it would require a reply, then I could write it while you are here. I would need you to mail it for me as well, for we do not mail letters from out of the convent unfortunately. You must forgive me for my haste."

"We understand," Georgiana said. "And I have no qualms with walking around the field here and looking around your convent gardens."

"Thank you. The gardens are quite bland in my eyes, but do your best to enjoy them, if it is in your power to look past the mediocrity."

They moved away from Deborah Darcy as she sat down and began to read while they walked around the gardens.

Eventually they came upon her again and were startled to find that Deborah Darcy was weeping.

"Deborah!" Cousin Emilia gasped, rushing to her daughter. "Is something amiss? Is there bad news?"

"Oh, no!" Deborah cried, not afraid of showing her feelings. "There is nothing unfortunate of the kind."

"Then the letter is sanguine? Why do you weep, my child?"

The rest of the company had the impulse to walk away and leave mother to offer solace to her daughter, but the look in Deborah's eyes rooted them to the spot, as well as Deborah's lack of fear in displaying her emotion made her naturally hard to look away from.

"I am not weeping out of sadness. I just learned some wonderful news."

"What news?"

"He loved me!" she cried. "Samuel Lucas truly did love me all the while!"

"What?" Cousin Emilia gasped.

"It was the past love of mine, Samuel Lucas. Nothing ever came of it, you know, but I had Jane Bennet give him a letter of mine, telling him that I forgave him long ago for his not offering me a proposal. And he has written back...he loved me all the while. And he had never forgotten me! And he has never forgiven himself for it."

"What?" Cousin Emilia repeated and took the letter from her daughter's hands and began to read it with alacrity. When done, she wielded on us with a fury.

"You still know this Lucas boy?"

"Oh," Lydia said, startled. "He is our neighbor in Hampshire. His sisters Charlotte and Maria Lucas—well, she's now Charlotte Collins, are our close friends."

"Cousin Emilia," Kitty whispered. "Please do not be upset with Jane and us for exchanging their letters."

"No, Mother please do not!" Deborah cried. "It is not proper for ladies and gentlemen to write letters to one another, but I am a nun, and am above any form of impropriety, do you not think?"

"I am not angry with them for doing you such a service!" Emilia cried. "I am simply angry, now that I know his feelings were sincere, that this Samuel Lucas did nothing to further his position!

Why did he not propose? What a fool! Deborah, do you mean to say that you would have married him?"

"Mother, he was the only man that I would have married. I am happy for my fate, but he was the only one."

"Oh, now I really hate him!"

Unfortunately, Cousin Emilia spoke her last sentence so loud that other nuns passing by noticed. Luckily, they had the goodwill to keep walking and pretend to be deaf.

"Then," Lydia asked, feeling very empathetic toward Deborah, "you will write back to him?"

"Of course, I shall. I'm no spineless ninny! Being a nun requires great courage, you have no idea!"

Lydia laughed at first, and then she stifled it.

"But what will you say?" Emilia asked.

"That I was happy to know that he loved me. Then I will encourage him to fall in love elsewhere and find happiness. He has asked for forgiveness of me, and therefore I owe him my blessing to be content for the rest of his life. Yes, that is what I shall do. Though I would have liked to have seen him one last time."

The company waited for Deborah Darcy to finish her letter, and then she saw them off as they rode from the convent. As they did so, Lydia looked back at her as she watched them depart, for she could not help but wonder at the spirit that moved such a woman, and marvel at her.

As they drove down Arch Street, Emilia looked out the window, lost in thought.

"Cousin Emilia," Kitty said hesitantly, "forgive me if you wanted to keep to your own counsel just now, but I simply wanted to make certain if you wished to talk of what you are feeling or if not."

"She would have been a wonderful mother," Emilia whispered. "And though I am proud of her calling, I do not deny that I would have preferred a different life for her. No," she began to weep. "I do not fear admitting it."

Sitting next to her, Georgiana wrapped her arms around Cousin Emilia and held her as she wept quietly. She did her best to end her tears soon, however, and then she turned to Colonel Fitzwilliam.

"Well, Cousin Richard," she said, smiling through her tears, "are you an officer, as you so claim to be?"

"I am."

"Well then, you are the only gentleman present, and a gentleman can always write to another gentleman." She handed Richard the letter that Deborah had written.

"Please write a letter to this Samuel Lucas explaining the content of my daughter's missive and store her letter in yours. Have Kitty write the address and send it as soon as all this is done."

"I shall do so, with all the immediacy as if the Queen of England had ordered me herself," Colonel Fitzwilliam said, taking the letter and storing it in his vest. "Cousin Emilia, if I might be so bold, you have a remarkable daughter in Deborah Darcy."

"Yes, yes I do. And I feel the luck of it most keenly."

They rode along and Lydia watched Emilia grow quiet, feeling such compassion for her state, and she wished to offer solace to the best of her ability. Understanding that nothing would fully suffice, she felt it best to deliver a lighthearted quip.

"Well, Cousin Emilia. Nothing could take the place of having such a daughter as Sister Mary, however if you need temporary release, then Georgiana and I would very much allow you to throw us in the paths of many men that you would see fit. As long as you do not blame us for when we return without a fiancé, which will happen often. If anything, it should make you most happy, for after one plan fails, it gives the ability to try once more."

To Lydia's happiness, this had the desired effect and Emilia began to laugh.

"Thank you, Miss Lydia, for that is a great comfort. And I think I might know some very eligible gentlemen."

"Of course, you do."

After they returned from the convent, Lydia, to even her internal surprise, found that she desired a solitary walk on the grounds surrounding Canterbury. When she announced this, Emilia and Thomas permitted it, yet Kitty and Georgiana looked to her dubiously.

"Do not fear," she said. "What trouble could I possibly get into when we are surrounded by trees on all sides?"

"It is not about how long you walk," Kitty said, "but how far you can get."

Lydia shook her head. "I would not do something so foolish now. Lighten yourself already!"

"Very well," Georgiana said, "but limit your walk to an hour."

"Thanks, Mum!"

"Oh, get along with you," Georgiana answered with a grin.

The day had grown a little warmer, and Lydia was able to leave without a cloak or cape but did have a small spencer jacket that fell below her bust, buttoned, and then she was off, walking around the yard at first. As she paced around, she wondered at Deborah Darcy, or Sister Mary Ignatius, and she took comfort in the fact that love was not simple for many people. After seeing Elizabeth obtain true romance so easily—very well then, not so easily—and Kitty obtaining it even more simply—though Lydia casually forgot the fact that Kitty fled to the continent just to see him before he possibly died in battle—made Lydia apt to wonder if love was easy to find for everyone but herself.

True love appeared to be something she was without, or not allowed to obtain at least, and every day that she was married to Wickham made it more apparent that she was in error when she thought her happiness lay with him. All too soon into their marriage, she quickly began to realize that her destiny clearly was to be miserable, in torment, and one that would be devoid of anything good. And her inadequacy woke her from her ignorance very quickly.

Yet now, seeing Jane apparently single indefinitely, seeing Mary spend too much of her time wallowing for a man who went after her sister, and then meeting Deborah Darcy who became a nun after the man who she loved offered her nothing even when he gave her encouragement—no, it was not her fate to suffer disappointment alone. Many women had it. And she, Lydia, had the good fortune to at least escape hers before she was tied down to agony for too long. Maybe, if one looked at it from a positive circumstance, Lydia Bennet had been lucky. Wickham was a name she shed away from herself long ago. Now, she could return to the woman who she once was and start again from there.

Wandering around in her musings, Lydia aimlessly began to move through the trees that bordered the estate, and she was so wound up in her own thoughts, that she did not notice anyone entering her path till he was right in front of her.

"Mr. Darcy!"

"Mrs. Wickham," Henry Darcy said in reply. "Oh, I did not think to find you walking here."

"Well yes, my appearance can come across as sudden, I suppose," she replied evenly, not wishing to give him encouragement with a smile, nor discouragement with a frown.

"I simply never took you for a very good walker."

"How could you take me for anything when we have barely met?"

Lydia flexed her hands instinctively, and not trusting herself to talk to him for too long without losing her temper, she curtsied to him and then began to walk in the other direction, through the trees.

At first there was no sound, but then soon she heard footsteps behind her.

"Well then..." Henry Darcy began. "I see that you do walk."

"Yes! And I am alone!"

"Well, not so much. For I am here."

"Oh, are you?" Lydia wanted to kick herself, for the thing she most dreaded had occurred. She was beginning to show her animosity for Mr. Henry Darcy.

"Yes, I am," he replied heatedly. "Can you not tell?"

"No, all that I can tell is that you assumed that I was not a great walker, after meeting me in so short of a time, and thought yourself correct to do so. Indeed, you seem to think yourself right to judge many even before you have allowed a proper enough allowance of time to define a person's character accurately, from all that I can tell."

Henry Darcy stopped pursuing Lydia while she kept walking on, coming to a revelation.

"It was you then! You were the one who was listening in while I spoke with my brother."

Lydia stopped in her tracks, closing her eyes in frustration. She did not want to reveal that she had been the person, but as always, her words came tumbling out as if she had no filter. In that short amount of time between Henry Darcy's appearance on the walk and that second, she realized that she had not changed as much as she would have liked. Lydia still found that she could not refrain from saying what she felt, and therefore now she appeared to be an eavesdropping fool.

"I do not know what you are talking about," she began, trying to lie to cover herself before it was too late. "And I should think—"

"Do not lie to me!" Henry Darcy interrupted, his brow furrowed and making him appear more frightening. "It was you, wasn't it?"

She decided to come clean. "It was an accident. And if you were both smart about it, then why did you not close the door fully? Any person with any common sense would have understood that concept."

"We are not in the habit of always having to close doors when we wish to speak between each other," he said spitefully. "For we are not used to having impertinent snips about."

Lydia felt her blood begin to boil. "How dare you call me so?"

"I call you what you have appeared to be. How dare you eavesdrop? And in someone else's home?"

"And I might ask, in reply, how dare you find yourself so far above your company that you cast judgment and disdain upon us all? You said terrible things about my sisters, and they did not deserve to be slandered so. And nor did I."

"Slander requires defaming someone publicly."

"I widen the definition to mean any ill words spoken against another and lack truth. And I can see from your response that you think me stupid. I am not so!"

He arched an eyebrow. "Are you not?"

"Do not mock me."

"Very well."

"It was a vile and malicious act, speaking such things about all of them. Elizabeth should not be ridiculed for being kind and giving. Jane should not be sneered at for being guided by her own infallible instincts in matters of the heart. Kitty should not be defamed because she stood up to you! And is this the even-handed dealings of men always? To think they have the right to judge others most excessively, yet when time comes for them to be judged, you call us impertinent and unsound."

"You are prejudiced against men it is all too clear."

"Am I?"

"Yes, for if you saw clearly, you would notice that women do the same thing."

"You talk as if you are a man who sees clearly yourself, when it is evident that the case is otherwise. If you were so wise, how did you not see that with my sister Elizabeth, you were in error to tell her not to reach out to Miriam because of their differences? With Kitty, how could you offend her, your cousin's wife, and then not admire her for standing up for herself? And with Jane. How can you call yourself perceptive when it was probably clear to all but you that you were proposing to a woman who never desired you?"

Henry Darcy faltered at her speech, feeling as if he was stricken across the face.

"No, Mr. Darcy, I am not candid. Because you are not. Why are you so relentlessly unpleasant? And why must you now make me into the villain for provoking me so? Let me guess, you believe yourself to be smart?"

"I believe you to be a great nuisance and I will waste no more words upon you, Mrs. Wickham. Talking with you is to be talking to a woman who will not listen to sense."

Lydia stood her ground. "What you and I define as sense must differ greatly."

"You do not see that you make the foundation of your argument on me not out of anger against what I said about your sisters, but out of scorn for what I said about you. If I had hurt your sisters' good name truly, then my faults by your calculation must be great indeed. But perhaps these offenses might have been overlooked had not your pride been affected by my admitting that I found you to possibly be base and vulgar. Can you deny that you are not?"

She looked at him, wide-eyed. "And these are the words of a gentleman?"

"No these are the words of a taciturn fool, which is what you call me."

"What have you to be so angry for?" Lydia cried.

"Your sister hurt me."

"She hurt your vanity, not your heart. You said it yourself in not so many words that you no longer desire her, which means that your love for her was not that deep."

"What do you know of the heart? You cold woman, you do not even speak of your husband and it is obvious that you do not miss him. How can you claim to know me when you do not even know yourself?"

Lydia turned away, and then felt a sudden desire to tell the truth. Turning around, she wielded on him with a turn of her countenance that startled even him.

"I know what it is to love the wrong person. And I know the heart of a woman whose husband, the man who swore to protect and honor her, was abusive. I have the heart of a woman who married a man who never loved her—and then who committed acts of violence upon her."

Lydia's admission startled Henry Darcy and his expression altered from one of resentment to shock and bewilderment.

"Yet I tell you this, Mr. Henry Darcy, all the cuts and bruises on my body are minimal to the lacerations he left on my heart. And this is the man that you ask me to cry over? Well, I will not cry! I will not weep for him! Call me what you will, raise you voice, be quick to label me, and I still will not weep."

She fought angry tears. "And you say that I am prejudiced against men. Well perhaps you are correct, but it's not out of bitterness. It is out of fear that you will always do what you call to be 'right', and get away with it, no matter how wrong it is. So, I say, Mr. Darcy, that until you learn humility, I can firmly say that Jane was correct to deny you—and that you are the last man in the world any woman could ever be prevailed upon to marry."

"What...what did you say?" Henry asked, flinching.

"You heard my words. I will not repeat myself."

Lydia curtsied to him and then left, not regretting the harsh words that she had spoken. Yet nor did she feel content in saying it all either.

❦ 24 ❦

MUST WE FORGIVE ONE ANOTHER?

L eaving Mr. Henry Darcy under the trees, Lydia all but ran to Canterbury home, went inside, rushed to her room, and closed the door behind her.

Her stomach immediately felt empty, and she paced back and forth.

It was all so strange! She had said harsh words before, yet never had she felt such a way afterward. Never had she felt so sick. At first, she was bewildered by the sensation, pacing over and over, trying to subdue the feeling that she was about to force up her lunch at any given moment, yet it was undeniable.

She had felt guilt!

Guilt over saying such painful things to Mr. Darcy, even though he deserved it. Not understanding why she would possibly feel any remorse for speaking words that he needed to hear, she began to consider her own situation. Her words had not changed, but she had.

There was a time where she did not care what she spoke or how it affected people. She could be flirtatious and engaging, or mean and crude, but never considered the effect she had upon others. Yet now she had altered so in the very depths of her nature—now she was beginning to care about her actions, her words, and how they affected others. She had developed a sense of empathy. As a result, she could not say anything she wished any longer and not suffer any remorse for it afterward.

Finally, after her breathing evened, she sat down and looked at her hands. What was done could not be undone. She would be equally proud of herself for what she had said, and equally resentful to herself.

Lydia Bennet had finally grown up.

๑๛๑

"We have the most delightful news!" Cousin Thomas said over the dinner table that evening. Lydia was looking down at her food for the majority of the evening, afraid to look Henry Darcy in the eye, for he was sitting opposite her. "One of my good friends here in Philadelphia, named Sir William Hillary, will be hosting a dinner party on his estate, Waterfell, in honor of his cousin's wedding."

"What is the woman's name, and is she of any family?"

"Yes, her name is Harriet Price, and she's from England actually."

"Is she?" Georgiana asked.

"Yes, she was raised on the estate of Kellynch Hall, for her father ran the parsonage there and was the younger son of the master of Kellynch. They moved to America when their father died, and they no longer had any domicile of their own. Sir William let them rent the cottage on his estate, Waterfell Cottage. Sir William Hillary was also English born as well. I think you will like them exceedingly, and he has extended his invitation to you all. Might I be able to tell him that you will attend?"

"Yes, we would love to make a new acquaintance," Colonel Fitzwilliam said.

"And in regards to company, you shall like him immensely and his cousins," Cousin Emilia encouraged.

"Indeed, you will," Henry Darcy said so suddenly that all turned to him, and in spite of Lydia's will, she did as well. "For he is a great talker, and you are a lot who has much to speak on." He looked at Lydia briefly before he looked back down at his food and continued eating.

⚜

The next evening came swiftly and they all were traveling to Waterfell where they drove down the lane, following after some other carriages. Waterfell rested at the end of it.

"It is a very elegant home!" Lydia exclaimed. "I like it very much."

"Be prepared to repeat that comment to Sir William when you see him," Cousin Thomas said, "for he loves to be complimented by young ladies."

When they arrived, their entire company consisted of Cousin Thomas, Emilia, Henry, Joseph, his wife, then Colonel Fitzwilliam, Kitty, Georgiana, and Lydia. As they entered the home, they were met by Sir William Hillary, who was warm and as jovial as Cousin Thomas.

"Thomas!" Sir William said, coming forward and clapping Thomas on the shoulder. "It is good to see you, and I see you bring a merry party with you."

"Yes, we did, Sir William! They are my family from England. These are my cousins and nephew Miss Georgiana Darcy, Colonel Richard Fitzwilliam and his lovely wife, Mrs. Kitty Fitzwilliam, and with her is her sister Mrs. Lydia Wickham."

All bowed and curtsied as Sir William bowed in return.

"It is wonderful to meet you all." His voice boomed and echoed in the room. "And to have my fellow countrymen and ladies here.

You must tell me all about England, for I have not been back there for years now."

"We shall tell you much," Kitty replied. "Yet it might be safe to say that it is the same as when you left it."

"True, England will always be England."

"And may we compliment you on your lovely home," Lydia added.

"Oh, I love a good compliment."

"We were told so."

"And I was the one who told them," Cousin Thomas added with a laugh.

"Very good and keep telling them so. Well, let us give you introductions to all else in the room, but first let me introduce you to my cousin Harriet and her new husband. Do not fear or be nervous, for you will love them both."

The Canterbury party followed Sir William through the throng of attendees, and they accosted the center of the party: the married couple.

"Ah," Sir William exclaimed. "Our new friends from England are here to meet you lovebirds. Party from Canterbury, this is Mr. Parson Persons with his wife and my cousin, Mrs. Harriet Persons. And Mr. and Mrs. Persons, this is Mr. Thomas Darcy's relations, Colonel Richard Fitzwilliam and his wife, Mrs. Kitty Fitzwilliam. Also, Miss Georgiana Darcy and Mrs. Lydia Wickham."

All bowed and curtsied to one another, but when Georgiana took a close look at Mr. Parson Persons, she gasped.

"You!"

Parson Persons turned to her and the familiarity came back to him.

"Oh, we do know each other slightly, do we not?"

"Yes, you were the actor that we met when we saw *Timon of Athens* at the Briar Theater."

"Oh, my stars," Kitty said, recognizing him. "Yes, it was you that we saw."

"Yes, it is coming back to me now as well," Mr. Persons added. "You were a merry party. And amazing, is it not? For the world to be so small that we run into each other again."

"It is."

"Yet I wish to know what you speak of," his wife Mrs. Harriet Persons said, "How do you know each other?"

"Oh," Georgiana said. "Well..." she stopped her narration however and gazed upon Harriet. "Is this the woman that I reminded you of, Mr. Persons?"

All looked on the triad in curiosity of what was being spoken of.

"Yes," Mr. Persons replied, turning to his wife. "My dear, one night after a performance, Mr. Darcy here asked me to meet his party who had seen the show. Their party included Mrs. Fitzwilliam here and Miss Darcy. When I rested my eyes on Miss Darcy, I was reminded of you, for as you can see, you both look similar in feature."

Harriet and Georgiana looked on one another and laughed, amused at the coincidence.

"Yes," Mrs. Persons interjected, "there is a bit of a resemblance."

"No wonder you stared at me with such astonishment," Georgiana said to Mr. Persons. "For I reminded you of the person who stole your heart."

"Yes, you did. And it amazed me. Especially since I feared that I might never obtain her."

"Well, you did," Harriet Persons said, taking his hand and kissing it. "Well done, sir."

"We offer our congratulations then," Kitty said. "And your husband is quite the actor."

"Yes, he is. I started out as one of the thespians in his company."

"You were an actress?" Lydia asked.

"Yes, I was. Yet I must ask, you belong to the name of Darcys from England. Would you by any chance know a Mr. Fitzwilliam Darcy and Mrs. Elizabeth Darcy?"

"Yes!" Colonel Fitzwilliam said. "Mr. Fitzwilliam Darcy is my cousin, Miss Darcy's brother, and Mrs. Elizabeth Darcy is Mrs. Kitty and Mrs. Lydia's older sister."

"Then it is a small world indeed!" Harriet Persons cried. "For I have met them."

"Have you?" Kitty gasped.

"Yes, it was on the road for when I left with my family to England. I came upon them when they were defending a Freed Woman and her family from being dragged away by a Slave Catcher."

Kitty was amazed. "That was you who my sister spoke of? I can scarce believe it."

"Believe it, for it was frightening. Such an amazing coincidence. And I can truly say now that life is a curious thing."

"Yes, it is."

"Then let me introduce you to the rest of my family."

A few individuals stepped forward and Harriet turned towards them.

"Members of Canterbury, this is my mother, Mrs. Elinor Price, her sister Mrs. Fanny Price who is married to my uncle, Mr. Henry Price, who is the master of Kellynch hall, and—oh, where is Emily?"

"Coming, Harriet!" They all turned and a young woman who was handsome and resembled Harriet to a fold approached them.

"Harriet and Parson, I am sorry but there is a group of the younger adults who were wondering if they could start up a dance."

"Well, I am fine with it, if Sir William is. Oh, before you go on your errand, you must meet this family. Everyone this is my sister, Miss Emily Price."

"How do you do?" She curtsied.

"It is nice to meet you, Miss Price," Lydia said, and all the names were exchanged before Emily was able to continue after what she sought.

"Yes, Emily, of course they can dance," Sir William said, clapping his hands together. "I enjoy such entertainment, you know this."

She gave him an engaging smile. "But I still must always ask permission, this you also know. But Harriet and Parson, you must be the ones to start off the dance, for this is clearly your party."

"We can oblige." Harriet laughed, then she turned to Kitty. "Yet you are newlyweds as well, are you not?"

"Newlyweds enough, yes indeed."

"Then will you begin our set as well? It would be a great honor."

"We would be delighted." Then she turned to Colonel Fitzwilliam. "Yes, I spoke for us both."

"You little imp."

Very soon, part of the room was made clear so that a dance floor could be made, and it was soon made known that Georgiana was an expert pianist, so she was asked to play for everyone as the dance began. She took her place at the pianoforte, which was a Broad wood Grande, and the dancing commenced.

<hr />

Having no partner to dance with, Lydia at first sat down, but she tapped her foot to the beat as the music commenced.

Watching the couples move around each other, she was reminded of her carefree ways before she had gotten married and become Lydia Wickham. Many a time they were in the drawing-room at Lucas Lodge, she would hound their sister, Mary, to play something jolly so that they could dance. At first, Mary would resist, but Lydia would taunt her so until she gave in. Being so far away, she wondered if she and her sister bickered because they were comfortable enough to do so, or did they do it because they bullied each other? Perhaps, when Lydia returned to England, she and Mary could find some way to be at ease around each other.

While she sat there, she saw Sir William Hillary approach Henry Darcy, who was standing in a corner near her, still as a statue.

"Ah, Mr. Darcy," Sir William Hillary began. "What a charming amusement for young people this is. There is nothing like dancing, after all! I consider it as one of the first refinements of polished societies."

"Certainly sir; and it has the advantage also of being in vogue amongst the less polished societies of the world," Henry replied, not looking at him.

"Sir?"

"Every savage can dance."

"Yes, they can, quite so. However, Mr. Darcy, do me the honor of not being yourself just now. I fear that of all times for you to be you, do not do it at a dinner party."

Lydia had to stifle her laughter but fearing she would not be able to do so, she stood up and began to move away.

"Ah, Miss Lydia!" Sir William said when he saw that she was near. He walked up to her and took her hand. "Why are you not dancing? Forgive me, but I am comfortable enough around you to think you worthy of a partner." He then led her to Mr. Henry Darcy and Lydia, blushing, looked to the floor.

"Mr. Darcy," Sir William Hillary encouraged, "you must allow me to present this young lady to you as a very desirable partner— you cannot refuse to dance, I am sure, when so much beauty is before you."

"Indeed sir," Lydia said, flushed from embarrassment. "I have not the least intention of dancing. I entreat you not to suppose that I moved this way in order to beg for a partner."

"Actually," Mr. Henry Darcy interrupted, "I would be most honored of your hand, and dancing with me, Mrs. Wickham."

"Thank you," Lydia said, looking up at him with severity. "Yet I am not inclined toward dancing at present."

"You look as if you excel so much in the dance, Mrs. Wickham," Sir William said, "that it would be cruel to deny me the happiness of seeing you; and though Mr. Darcy dislikes the amusement in general, he can have no objection, I am sure, to oblige us for one half hour."

"Mr. Darcy is all politeness," Lydia replied, smiling archly.

"He is indeed—but considering the inducement, my dear Mrs. Wickham, we cannot wonder at his complaisance, for who would object to such a partner, eh Mr. Darcy?"

"Forgive me for rejecting his hand then." Lydia smiled to Sir William. "Yet I would hate to be what he regards as one of the 'unpolished societies'." With that, Lydia turned away and walked to the other side of the room, finding an empty seat, and sitting down. However, before she did so, over her shoulder, she had overheard Sir William speak to Mr. Darcy.

"See, Henry? I told you not to be yourself just now."

Lydia sat there in careful contemplation, yet when Mr. Henry Darcy appeared at her side, she was neither startled nor able to leave. For if she did so, it would have been apparent that she had slighted him. Therefore, when he sat in the seat next to her, all she could do was cross her hands and prepare herself.

"You rejected my offer to dance," Henry said.

"You sound surprised."

"I am. You seem like the sort who would love dancing."

"Oh, I love dancing a great deal, however, it was the partner that I objected to."

"You are just saying that to hurt my feelings."

"Was I successful?" She grinned wickedly.

"Yes," Henry said, grave. "Yes, you were."

Immediately feeling remorse, her smile faded.

"Then I am sorry. I did not know my words would be felt so keenly."

"I am not surprised. For it is clear to me that you believe me to be devoid of any proper feeling."

"Are you?"

"I know not what I am." He sounded so miserable.

"Mr. Darcy..."

"Yes?"

"The reason I rejected your hand in dancing is because I knew that you did not want to dance with me."

"Then you were wrong."

"Was I?"

"Yes, I would not have asked if I did not wish to, in the end. I did wish to dance with you."

"Why so? I would have thought that you would not wish to be near me."

"At first I did not. Yet your frankness in nature has led to me not being surprised by you."

"How so?"

"We have already argued with one another, therefore what do I have to fear from you, for we have already seen the worse sides of each other."

"Are you saying that you feel more comfortable around me because we had such a tumultuous beginning? You are a strange sort, Mr. Darcy."

He actually smiled. "So are you."

"I! I... oh, I see your point. Yet make no mistake, I want you to respect me, and until you do so and find some warmth to your speech, we shall always be at odds."

"Yes, we just might be."

"You are truly such an enemy to peace?"

"When peace is boring, yes. Yet when provocation leads to more stimulating conversation, then I do turn toward that instead."

"I worry that if I remain close to you, I shall lose whatever goodness I have left within me."

"It is not evil I speak, but honesty."

"Evil is a form of honesty."

"Mrs. Wickham?"

"Yes?"

"Would you mind if I called you Lydia from now on?"

"Oh..." Lydia was at a loss of what to say to that, for what could he mean?

"It has occurred to me," he continued, "that you might not like your last name at all."

"Oh. I did once, yet now you are correct. Now I do not. Not in the slightest. You may call me Lydia, if that is comfortable for you."

"It is well. Would you find comfort in calling me Henry?"

"While I like the name Henry, I also like the name of Darcy. Therefore, I shall call you Henry in some moments, and then if you approve, I might slip back into calling you Mr. Darcy in other moments. Would that be to your liking, or have I committed an error?"

"No that is all very well. Henry or Mr. Darcy, as long as it is not 'relentlessly unpleasant'."

⚜

The dinner party went by with much success. They made the acquaintance of everyone there and were offered invitations for tea and luncheons amongst some of the families in the neighborhood.

Therefore, when the Canterbury party retired back to their home, much good was spoken of that evening, and nothing negative.

The next day, Lydia went to find a copy of Shakespeare's plays in the library so that she could read *Taming of the Shrew,* in hopes of rendering herself open to learning about what other people discuss. Struggling through the beginnings of it, she looked up at the sound of footsteps.

"Do not fear, Georgiana," Lydia said. "No books have attacked me and—"

She stopped her speaking when to her utter surprise it was not Georgiana, but Mr. Henry Darcy.

"Expecting someone else, I see."

"Yes, I was," Lydia said. "You come for a book."

"Oh... yes."

"Well then, I see."

"Yes." Henry did not move.

"You did not come for a book, did you?" Lydia sighed.

"Um, no I did not."

"Did you come for me? Because if you wish to argue, I am still not afraid of you."

"I know you are not. And that makes it easier."

Lydia couldn't stop a chuckle. "I must say you truly are taking this whole 'not threatened by me because we have already fought' concept to a whole other level."

"You feel comfortable around me as well. You are just in denial of it."

"Am I?"

"Yes."

"Henry, why do you come here?"

"Because..." Henry paced back and forth a bit, then sat down, and then got up again.

"Henry?"

"I'm trying to apologize. Give me some time to harden myself to the idea and form my words correctly."

"You are trying to apologize?"

"Yes."

She cocked her head at him. "And doing so takes this much of a struggle?"

"Well...yes."

Unable to help it, Lydia burst out laughing.

"I fail to see what is so funny—truly! I fail to... fail to..." Despite himself, Henry Darcy began to laugh as well. At first it was a silent guffaw, then his gurgle became louder, and he was laughing in earnest. Eventually their chuckles ceased, and they were left looking at each other.

"Henry I am still waiting for your apology."

"Oh, right. Miss Lydia, I humbly apologize for any and every offense I may have made against you and your blameless sisters. It was wrong of me, and whatever my history with the eldest Bennet, none of you deserve my wrath, resentment or my wounded pride."

"And in return," Lydia began, "I apologize for any offenses I had given as well."

"Thank you."

Lydia sighed. "You were correct; apologizing is quite painful."

"Yes, sometimes being at odds with someone does feel simpler."

"Yes, for now I feel quite exposed to the world."

"Me as well," he answered.

"Right."

"Right."

"Henry?"

"Yes?"

"Why did you feel inclined to apologize? It does not seem like you."

"You are correct. It was not like me. I do not know exactly what caused my desire to do so. All I can say is that... I suppose it is never too late to dramatically change the course of your own nature."

"Then you have beaten yourself?"

"I cannot claim to have done that yet."

"It is possible, so do not fear. I have found victory over myself on a couple of occasions. They are all recent victories, mind you, but still. You find me trying to defeat myself as we speak."

"Why? What are you attempting?"

"I was never a great reader, and I most certainly am not great when it comes to Shakespeare. I was reading *Taming of the Shrew*, in hopes of being able to discuss it with Mrs. and Mr. Persons if I ever saw them again—in hopes of improving my mind by extensive reading—and yet I see that I am out of my element and very much not up to the task."

"You are looking at it from the wrong perspective."

"How so?"

"Shakespeare's plays are like plays in general. They are most enjoyed and understood when they are seen, or heard, but not read. Here, if you won't mind."

Henry pulled up a chair and sat down next to her.

"I'll take one character if you take the other," he said.

"Should you not have asked me first if I was interested in this scheme of yours?" Lydia asked, raising an eyebrow.

Henry Darcy ground his teeth and then relaxed his jaw.

"Lydia, would you mind if I offered my services and read with you?"

She gave him a warm smile. "Better, and I do accept."

"Oh," Henry said, clearing his throat. He leaned over her and Lydia flipped to the front page so that they could begin.

"We can alternate characters as we go," Henry said.

"Very well." Lydia turned back to the scene that she was reading. It was when Petruchio had first met Catherine, who he intended to woo.

"Good morrow, Kate," Henry Darcy began, 'for that's your name, I hear."

"Well, have you heard," Lydia read, "but something hard of hearing: they call me Katharine that do talk of me."

"You lie, in faith; for you are call'd plain Kate, and bonny Kate, and sometimes Kate the curst; But, Kate, the prettiest Kate in Christendom; Kate of Kate-Hall, my super-dainty Kate, for dainties are all cates: and therefore, Kate, take this of me, Kate of my consolation; hearing thy mildness prais'd in every town, thy virtues spoke of, and thy beauty sounded—yet not so deeply as to thee belongs—myself am mov'd to woo thee for my wife.

"Mov'd! in good time: let him that mov'd you hither remove you hence. I knew you at the first, you were a moveable.

"Why, what's a moveable?"

"A joint-stool."

"Thou hast hit it: come, sit on me."

"Asses are made to bear, and so are you."

"Women are made to bear, and so are you."

"No such jade as bear you," Lydia continued, "if me you mean."

"Alas! good Kate, I will not burden thee; for, knowing thee to be but young and light—"

"Too light for such a swain as you to catch, and yet as heavy as my weight should be."

"Should be! Should buz!"

"Well ta'en, and like a buzzard."

"O slow-winged turtle!" Darcy continued to read. "Shall a buzzard take thee?"

"Ay, for a turtle, as he takes a buzzard."

"Come, come, you wasp; i' faith you are too angry."

"If I be waspish, best beware my sting."

"My remedy is, then, to pluck it out."

"Ay, if the fool could find it where it lies."

"Who knows not where a wasp does wear his sting? In his tail."

"In his tongue."

"Whose tongue?"

"Yours, if you talk of tails; and so fare-well."

"What! With my tongue in your tail? Nay, come again. Good Kate, I am a gentleman."

Lydia lowered the book and turned to Henry.

"What is it?" Henry asked. "The scene is not done yet."

"No, it is just...thank you. I do believe that I am understanding it better."

"Oh—well then, you are welcome."

Lydia and Henry both looked away and then resumed reading the play.

After they finished reading the first Act of *Taming of the Shrew*, it was time for afternoon tea, therefore, placing the book back on the shelf, Lydia followed Henry out of the library and down the steps to the sitting room.

"You read very well," Lydia said.

"Thank you," Henry Darcy replied. "In truth when I was younger, I had a stammering problem and my mother had me read aloud to help my impediment."

"It appears to have worked."

"Yes, it did."

"You have a remarkable mother," Lydia acknowledged. "Why do you not appreciate that so?"

"Who says I do not appreciate it?"

"When she offers you company and introduces you to people, you are not happy."

"I am—apprehensive around new people."

"I can understand that, yet every time you offend someone, do you imagine how she feels?"

Henry's brow creased as he was torn between being considerate or being offended.

"And Henry, this is speaking from someone who embarrassed her father often. Every time we, in our older age, do not act as we ought, we do not appear to care for them, because we have no shame in embarrassing them."

"You wish to wound me."

"No, I am wishing for you to learn from my mistakes."

Henry stopped walking and turned to her, giving Lydia no choice but to stop as well and turn to him.

"Learn from you?" Henry repeated.

"Well yes, to be honest. Mr. Darcy, Henry, believe me, the last thing you want to do is embarrass your parents and find yourself within something you will forever regret."

Lydia continued onward and Henry followed after her as they went into the sitting room and joined the rest for tea.

❦

The next day, Lydia walked through the halls of Canterbury and she noticed Kitty, Georgiana, and Colonel Fitzwilliam riding on horses along the fields through the window, and she paused to look upon them.

It occurred to her that there was never much stress on riding lessons back at Longbourn. Jane and Mary learned how to ride a little, though not becoming experts at it ever. She, Kitty and Elizabeth never learned however, but apparently much had changed in Kitty's case, for as she rode along, it became plain that she had become an expert equestrian.

While she stood there, she felt eyes upon her, and she turned to see a woman looking at her.

"Oh..." Lydia said. "You must be Cousin Emilia's daughter, Helena."

"Uh," the young woman said, her neck twitching back and forth, indicating a tick to her mental defect. "I... I am Helena."

"Well," Lydia said, curtsying. "I am Lydia Bennet. Lydia

Wickham actually, but if you would be so kind, just call me Lydia Bennet."

"Bennet?"

"Yes. We were told that we were going to meet you sooner, but then your mother never brought it up again after that."

"I—I was too scared."

Helena then raised her gown and began to curtsy, but she fell down, in the process.

"Oh, no!" she cried, her neck twitching.

"Oh, but it's all right," Lydia said, going up to her and offering her a hand.

"No, it is not!" Helena cried, growing agitated and fidgety. "I fell and I fail. I fail!"

"No, you don't," Lydia said, taking Helena's hands in her own. "I have fallen before when curtsying."

"But I always fall."

"I can show you how not to."

Helena began to stop twitching and looked at her.

"You can? Can you? No, you can't! Or can you?"

"Yes, I can. You see, I fell down plenty of times when I first learned how to curtsy. It all has to do with the footing. Now come on, up you go."

Lydia helped Helena up and continued to hold Helena's hands in her own.

"Now, watch what I do with my feet," Lydia instructed. She moved her feet in the correct manner, and Helena watched her feet as she curtsied. She did it a couple more times and then smiled at Helena. "Very well, now be brave. And let's do it together. Ready?"

"I—want—I—want to be—be."

"Very well, here we go."

Together Lydia and Helena curtsied together.

"See, Helena?" Lydia smiled. "You did it."

"I—did I?"

"Yes, you did!"

Helena laughed, her head moving back and forth wildly as she did so.

"I am..."

Helena moved away from Lydia, prepared herself and curtsied.

"Again—I did it again."

"Yes, you did!"

"Ha!"

Helena curtsied again.

"Well—how do you do, did, do, Miss Bennet Lydia. I mean Lydia Bennet. I am pleased to meet you—you."

"And I am pleased to meet you as well."

"I..." Helena began, her eyes glazing over. "Did not want to meet you all until my curtsy was perfect. I wanted to this time—this time, I wanted to be perfect this time."

"And you were," said a voice behind Helena. Both women turned and Henry Darcy came forward down the hallway. While walking forward, he began to clap.

"You were perfect, Helena," he said. "See, we knew you could do it."

"Yes, you did know!" Helena cried. "You always said that I could."

Helena rushed up to Henry, jumped into his arms and he embraced her tightly. Spinning her around over and over, Helena laughed, and Henry did so as well. Lydia stood there, watching them and did not know what to do, yet it then occurred to her that she had never seen Henry look so happy before. And Helena, she did not know what compassion had awoken in her, but she felt remorse for the unfortunate woman.

After a moment, Henry set his sister down and Helena socked his chin, playfully.

"Should I go and mother show? I mean show Mother?"

"I think that would be a most excellent idea, Helena."

She skipped past him, going down the hall and disappeared behind a corner. When he turned to Lydia, he was surprised to see her looking most confused.

"What is it?" Henry asked.

"Nothing, it is only... I believe that is the first time that I had seen you look so happy."

"Was it?"

"Yes. Why do you not do it more often?"

"Because I find very little funny."

"I find many things funny."

"How so?"

"There is much worth laughing at and laughing with. Or at least that is what I see."

"I confess missing most of the humor that you find so easily."

"Yes well, she loves you a lot, I see."

"She has a good heart. She just was not given a good mind."

"Many of us do not have one. At least she has a proper excuse."

Lydia curtsied and began to walk away.

"Lydia?"

"Yes?" She stopped and turned to him.

"I was thinking of going for a long walk to the river. And at present, I am inclined more toward company than solitude. Would you be willing to join me?"

"I am not the best walker, but I believe I am good enough."

"Then that is a yes?"

"Yes—it is a yes."

Before they left, they informed the butler and a few maids where they were going in case anyone sought them, and then they began their walk.

As they moved along at a leisurely pace, Lydia looked up at the man that she was next to and wondered at how differently he and George Wickham looked. Indeed, there was no similarity. She did not understand just then as to why her mind connected the two gentlemen, yet it was a natural impulse, it appeared.

"What you just did was very kind," Henry began, "and most unexpected."

"Thank you, but I must confess that it is not through any extreme goodness on my end," Lydia confessed, "but rather it is customary. In Hampshire, we have a family we are close to and they have a son who is mentally impaired. Our vicar to our church, Mr. Austen, has a large family and one of his sons can barely speak or comprehend much. I was raised with him, and his sister Jane Austen showed us how to treat him. Helena is more fortunate than he, and you seem to be a good older brother to her."

"It is the way of like-minded individuals. She did not come and see you all sooner because she was afraid, and I know the feeling."

"You are bashful."

"At times, yes very, and have nothing like her excuse. Therefore, when growing up, I suppose I was selfish and used her as my crutch."

"You used her?"

"Yes. If I made myself her companion and was always looking after her, I did not have to mingle with company because someone had to be there for her always. We were a sibling relationship built on co-dependency. She had an older brother who doted on her, and I had a little sister who I could look after and save me from having to always be in company."

He paused a moment. "Especially around women. Being the oldest to such a family, heir to this grand estate, I was a prize for most women, and the whole concept of all eyes being on me was most unnerving."

"We are very opposite then. You wished to once fade into the background, and I once did too much to be in the forefront. Is there a middle path that can be walked? And if so, how can we gain?"

"The idea of being in the forefront enough and then also being in the background at other times?"

"Yes, or maybe it is the pains of living. If you are in the forefront of everyone's attention, you enjoy the concept that you are visible to all and of renown, yet you are also subject to scrutiny and will be exposed to the world for when you do something foolish. Yet if you are in the background, then you lose importance, to the world or to oneself, and you never get the chance to be seen for what you are—but you have peace, you can have contentment in not having to suffer under the gaze of so many critics. You are free of negativity."

"And you have found it, Miss Bennet. The double-edged sword of life. One is content if one has and content if one has not, just as one is sad if one has, and sad if one does not."

"Yes and—wait, did you just call me Miss Bennet?"

"Yes. I heard you tell Helena that."

"Yes, I did... Henry, were you listening in on our conversation?"

"Well, listening in and walking in on a conversation are two different things."

"You hypocrite. You were upset with me and now you do not expect me to be upset with you?"

"Lydia, you were in the middle of a hallway!"

"Oh, fair point. I am still a little vexed, yet I admit, fair point."

"Thank you. But as to that, you really do miss your maiden name as you told me before, do you not?"

At first, Lydia did not reply.

"Lydia...we walk together so you cannot escape me. Please, help me to understand."

"Very well. Yes, I do miss my maiden name a great deal. I do not miss the person I was under that name, but I miss all that it gave me."

"And what did it give you?"

"A clear past. And not a cloudy one."

"Ah, not a cloudy one," Henry repeated. "Your name reminds you of your late husband, doesn't it? Or do you mind me talking of it just now."

"No, it is quite all right, for I have never been very good at concealing my emotions. If anything, my inability to conceal has more often set propriety at naught."

"Has it now?"

"It was my lacking in propriety that led to me falling in love with such a false man to begin with. No, I am not candid toward my late husband's memory. He was a villain, and I was one of the many who called him a saint while he was so."

"He was much loved?"

"What villains ever are not?"

"Fair point."

"I thought George Wickham was beautiful and everything perfect. Yes, love, Mr. Darcy! Love is the most powerful of emotions. So powerful that it makes fools of us. All of his flaws, his inconsistency, his lies, his deceptions and his wanton behavior were there for me to see, hidden behind his charming words, but still visible to the keen observer, were non-existent to me." Lydia clasped her hands behind her back as they strolled.

"I believed him to be perfect. And I was grossly in error. All that can be said is that all the pain that I endured under him forced me into a wiser way, but that was luck—pure luck. I could have gone the other way, you know? I could have let his disregard for me lead me into being more ridiculous, more beyond the reach of amendment. I could have become the silliest girl in England forever!"

"I am sorry that he hurt you, Lydia. Men such as him offend me exceedingly, and such a worthless, vile and cruel libertine—well, you deserved better."

"Everyone deserves better. I was simply one of the more fortunate people who was given it eventually. I have my freedom now, and that is more than I could have hoped for at one point. Now I have found peace, and you have no idea how soothing it is. Therefore, if I may presume to give you some advice, never fall in love with what appears as perfection, for it will never suit you. Marry someone who showed you from the very beginning that they were not perfect, yet they know they are not, and they will always aspire to be better."

"That is a hard individual to find. And you forget, Lydia, I was in love before."

"Oh dear!" Lydia cried, recalling his past heartaches. "Yes, forgive me. How did that slip from my mind?"

"Yes, but it was not just your sister, Jane. I have been in love a few times."

"Have you? Well, what has kept you from pursuing the bond?"

"Well, your sister's rejection was the simplest answer. Yet with the others—I knew that they were not right for me."

"How so?"

"Our personalities did not align so well. And it would not have led to domestic felicity and joy."

"You decided not to marry because the women were too different?"

"Yes."

"That is a foolish reason."

"How so and how can you claim it to be?"

"Like qualities does not always determine happiness. It can, but two people with similar traits are no more or less likely to have a happy marriage with two people of different traits. At the end of the day, it all comes down to a person's ability to yield, I suppose, and not make decisions solely on their pride and belief that they are always right. I thought I was right to run away and elope with George Wickham. Yes, I tried to elope, Henry! And look where that got me. My life, and all the decisions made from within it, could have been reshaped if I had learned to see that sometimes I could be right, and sometimes I could be wrong. And therein lays the truth of it all. All it takes to fall in love is a mutual love and loyalty for one another—and a desire to yield to one another. Or at least, I want to believe that *that* is the way in which two can become one. My sister Elizabeth and your cousin Mr. Fitzwilliam Darcy do it often and look how happy they are."

"Yes, they are happy."

"Very much so."

They walked on a little further before Lydia decided to press another matter.

"Do you feel much sadness of my sister's rejection of you?"

"I did at first, yet I grew to understand that others were correct. My vanity was affected, and not so much my heart."

"Very good, for she did you a service. There was no chance that you and she would have been happy. Mark my words; you would have both been miserable."

"What makes you say that?"

"Your personalities make no sense together. You are too awe-inspiring, too heavy in stance and mood. She is sedate as well sometimes, but her lightness is not of the sort that could shine on you and make you brighter. I do not know what is right for you, but marry someone who brings life to you, Henry, and activates a spark from within. Jane has spark in her, but for her magic to take effect, the man has to have an even greater spark than her own."

"You say I have no spark."

"It is of no offense, Henry, so don't you dare become offended. Your cousin Mr. Darcy has a small spark as well, and my sister Elizabeth has a large one, then she kindles the fire within him. Watch them together and you shall see. Believe me, you were in the wrong, and this is coming from a stance of respect. You had more need for an Elizabeth than a Jane Bennet."

"Your sister, Elizabeth...she and I did not get along."

"And whose fault was that? I could ask for three guesses, yet I believe that I shall only need one."

"Very well, I was in error. And, while I am not saying you have convinced me fully of anything, I will agree that your sister does bring a light to my cousin."

"Then rejoice. In refusing you, Jane saved your life."

They arrived at the top of a hill and the river lay before them.

"It is beautiful."

"Yes it is."

"Mr. Darcy? Henry?"

"Yes?"

"We are no longer enemies at all, are we?"

"No. No we are not."

"It is all so strange. It's quite confusing now."

"How so?"

Lydia laughed, a soft, light sound. "To be at odds is simpler, as you know. Therefore must we forgive one another? Can we not go back to being angry all the time and sharing in the joy of putting another down?"

"No, we cannot and you know it." Henry smiled. "We can tease one another every now and again, but we can never again learn to be at odds."

"Oh, very well, then. We shall have to make do and like one another in a boring fashion."

"Yes. Hopefully, it will not be as boring as we fear."

Standing together, they continued looking at the river that kept flowing along.

25

THE CHOICES OF LYDIA BENNET

"Oh, it is all too delightful!" Cousin Emilia said as they sat down to breakfast the next day. "Girls and gentlemen, I have just received an invitation from an acquaintance of ours, Mr. and Mrs. Kneely who reside near Spring Garden. They are giving a ball in honor of their son returning from the Indies where he has successfully set up a trading business between there and here. And they have extended the invitation to include you all."

"Oh, I do love a ball," Lydia cried. "And it has been so long since I have had the fortune to attend one."

"Well then luck has found you, my dear. Now, am I correct in assuming that you all have never had a ball outdoors before?"

Kitty, Georgiana, Lydia, and Colonel Fitzwilliam looked in between each other in surprise at being asked the question.

"Well, no, of course," Georgiana replied.

"Well, then you shall have a new experience to talk of when you return to England. This ball is going to take place out of doors."

"What?" Colonel Fitzwilliam asked.

"Oh yes. They will have candles on tables, many lanterns hanging from the trees and servants shall carry them as well."

"A ball at night, in a field?" Kitty exclaimed, giddy. "Under the stars? Truly?"

"Do not worry. It shall be stupendous," Cousin Thomas encouraged. "The food will be on tables and you shall go to them when you are hungry rather than being served. There will be seats, tables— yet the weather is now fine enough for summer is on its eve and it is nice and warm."

"It sounds fascinating," Georgiana cried.

"Yes," Lydia agreed. "And how long do we have to wait to experience this beautiful sight?"

"It shall be in a week's time. Let us hope there is no rain that day, for it will have to be postponed."

"Oh, hopefully luck is with us."

"And the elements as well," Henry added quietly before he looked down at his food.

After breakfast, Cousin Thomas asked Georgiana to play on his pianoforte, for he loved to hear her do so. Georgiana agreed and they all sat down in the music room to listen to her.

While she played and sang, Henry, who had placed himself next to Lydia, leaned into her and began to whisper.

"Excited for the ball, I see?"

"Yes," Lydia whispered. "An outdoor ball, how could I resist being happy?"

"I am not censuring your happiness, no, but only wishing to confirm it."

"Do you actually like to dance?"

"I have no choice but to."

"Oh."

"Well... Miss Bennet?"

"Yes?"

"If I might be so bold, may I request your hand for the first two dances?"

Lydia blushed and looked down at her hands.

"I did not take you for the sort to have asked."

"Well... I am."

"Then yes. You may, and I would welcome it, Mr. Darcy. Henry."

"Thank you. That makes the night less daunting for me a great deal."

"Just promise me one thing, Henry."

"What?"

"Do not dare step on my toes."

"Lydia, of course I'm going to step on your toes. Just for the sake of provoking you."

"Then I'll kick you in your knee cap."

"Very well. Very well."

❦

To pass the time, Cousin Emilia took the women of Canterbury to the dress shops to have new gowns made for them. Though they already had gowns, she was demanding for new ones all because of one excuse: why ever should they not want another gown?

Therefore, hiring six dressmakers and seamstresses, they went to work, and the week passed quickly with their gowns being prepared for them. On the night of the ball, Joseph and his wife joined them at Canterbury and all the women came down the steps when they were prepared. Kitty, Georgiana, and Lydia walked down in their new gowns and Cousin Emilia and Thomas were numerous in their compliments, yet Colonel Fitzwilliam was the most open. Upon seeing Kitty on the landing, he walked up to her and kissed her without shame. The last impression to be described therefore was Henry Darcy.

He observed that all women looked equally beautiful, yet his heart was more selective. Whatever beauty that Lydia Bennet naturally possessed was only enhanced by her appearance that night and by the elegant gown that she wore. Exquisite beyond description, she was not a perfect beauty—but she was a complete one. Unable to deny it within himself, he approached her and Georgiana.

"Miss Bennet and Cousin Georgiana," he began, "you both look remarkably well this evening, and I am quite enchanted."

"Oh," Georgiana said turning to Lydia, amused, "I believe Cousin Henry has just complimented us."

"Yes, but to say thank you is not enough," Lydia said. "I believe the best thing for us to reply with is to acknowledge that complimenting us looks quite lovely on you, Mr. Darcy."

"Thank you, Miss Bennet."

After compliments were exchanged in full, they all got into the carriages and made their journey to Mr. James Kneely's estate, Berwyn Briar.

ॐ

The party arrived and the field behind the great estate was already filled with many attendees who looked lovely under the ambiance of the decorations.

"Look at it!" Lydia cried. "The lanterns and candles look like stars that have fallen down to earth and are suspended in the night."

"Yes," Kitty added. "And the people remind you of fairy tales, of stories of elves dancing in woodland glades under the light of the moon."

Colonel Fitzwilliam gave his wife a warm smile. "You wish for magic, Kitty. My love, I see it in your eyes."

"You see well, then. I want to believe that, one time, magic did exist in this world. And your existence is proof of that."

"Me? How so?"

"You have a magical aura about you, Richard. In a way, you

glow, and to possess that ability renders me to believe that maybe there can be something magical in this world."

"My love, you make me blush."

"Hopefully, you will not turn as red as your regimental uniform," Kitty answered with a chuckle as she took his arm.

⚜

The hosts of the estate, Mr. and Mrs. Kneely, welcomed them and not too long after they began to start up conversation with the other ball-goers, the first dance was to begin. Lydia looked around for Henry Darcy, yet her searching was not needed.

"I am right next to you." He took her arm.

Her smile was apologetic. "Forgive me. I was just being paranoid."

"Ah."

They went to the floor, followed by Kitty and the Colonel, Georgiana with a stranger who had asked her to dance, and Cousin Emilia along with Cousin Thomas, joined the many other couples.

The music struck up, the couples stood opposite each other and then the dance began.

"Could you imagine," Lydia began immediately, "if one was to have a dance partner where there was no speaking on either side, or they did not like one another?"

"A whole half an hour in torment it would be," Henry Darcy acknowledged.

"I agree. And the performance would not reflect well on either person in that case."

"No, it would not."

They danced on in silence for a while, and every now and again, their eyes met, and they locked gazes.

"Lydia?"

"Yes?"

"I believe...you look beautiful."

"Thank... thank you," she stuttered, growing suddenly nervous. "And you look handsome as well."

"You flatter me."

"No, I offer you a compliment. A compliment is a convenient truth, and flattery is a good quality that offers more praise than is normal. I offer you a simple truth that is convenient to say."

He blushed. "Right; thank you."

"You are blushing, Henry. That is something I never thought that I would see."

"Well, you now see it."

"And I am glad."

"Are you? Why so?"

"Sometimes you stand as still as stone. And now, so vulnerable in appearance, it makes you appear very human."

"You enjoy this?"

"You cannot find warmth from a statue, Henry. Yet now it can be drawn from you."

"Lydia, forgive me."

"For what?" Lydia said, confused.

"For many things. For my harsh words from before, from my bitterness overwhelming my sense, and for offending your sisters, who deserved better from me and who were, now that I see, quite blameless."

"Take heart, Henry Darcy. You were already forgiven."

"I was?"

"Yes, the very minute you began to change, you were forgiven. As I was, I suppose."

"Then there is a chance for people such as us, Miss Bennet, to find our notions of peace."

Lydia looked down the rows of dancers and saw Mr. and Mrs. Parson Persons dancing together, and it made her dazzled at the idea that life could be so detailed, complex, and intricately woven.

"Yes, Henry, I believe we can find it."

She looked back up at him and felt a sudden change in her soul that she could not deny. Henry Darcy smiled down at her and she smiled in return, feeling her nerves flutter within her. She liked him! The revelation was sudden, so sudden that she wanted to believe that it was a trick of the moment, a foolish whim of her sensibilities, but as they continued to dance, the feeling lingered, and she grew to realize that she had been growing a tenderness for him quite some time.

Through the dancing and merriment, they continued enjoying each other's company.

After the ball ended, they all returned to Canterbury around one in the morning and it was too late for conversation, therefore they all retired to bed as soon as they entered the house. This suited Lydia very well, who along the way home, began to give careful contemplation to her feelings.

Could it really be that I like him? She asked herself as she lay in bed. *And to think I who pride myself on my gathering sense, were to allow myself this slip of sentiment. Dear lord, I do like him, and I might have been for some time, for my feelings now feel as if they had been coming on so gradually that I hardly even know their origin. Yes, I do like him. And it is a most inconvenient thing, for nothing good could come of it. Yes, it is most inconvenient! To begin to gather feelings for a man who was once in love with my older sister, who could therefore have no feelings for me, it is all too senseless! Therefore, I must never tell him, and not allow my feelings to expose me to some very idiotic behavior. No, I must never tell him that I have grown fond of him—and the truth will die inside of me.*

Rolling over in her bed, Lydia allowed her mind to let go of her fears and thoughts, before she was finally able to fall asleep.

The next day, they all dressed and went down to breakfast, but the night of merrymaking and dancing made them all quite sluggish. Therefore, it was with a shock that Colonel Fitzwilliam spoke of their oncoming departure.

"Amazing is it not?" he began. "That we have already been here for almost a month complete and yet it feels as if only days had passed by, for it has been most exciting? And so, it is so strange to know that we shall leave for England in two days' time."

"Two days?" Henry Darcy blurted out. "What?"

"Yes," Cousin Thomas said, alarmed at his son's tone. "They were only meant to stay here for a month complete, Henry."

"So soon?"

"I suppose that it could be described as soon in some ways," Colonel Fitzwilliam said, "and it is nice to see that our company has grown on you so, Henry. It is a great compliment to us."

"Yes—yes." Henry, unable to help himself, turned to Lydia, who smiled at him gently and then looked down at her plate, continuing to eat. After she began to admit her hidden affection for him, his company now made her bashful, unable to know how to receive him without giving herself away in some kind.

"We were happy to have come once more," Georgiana said.

"And for those of us who are new to Philadelphia," Lydia said, "we will always look on our coming here with fond memories."

Cousin Emilia and Cousin Thomas both expressed their satisfaction in hearing it, but Henry Darcy remained silent all the while.

⚜

Lydia was beginning to pack her things to prepare for their leaving in two days—for she had a perpetual bad habit of waiting till the last minute that she did not want to do in this case—when there was a knock on the door.

"Come in," Lydia said. The door opened and a maid named Sarah entered.

"Oh, what is it, Sarah?"

"I was sent from Master Henry Darcy. He says that you are late in meeting him for your daily walk."

"Dailywalk? But we never—" Lydia did not continue, beginning to comprehend that it must have meant that Henry needed to speak to her once more, so she stopped packing. "Thank you, Sarah, and tell him that I shall be down directly to meet him by the gazebo."

"Very good, ma'am."

Sarah curtsied and then left. Lydia looked at herself in the mirror, hoping to look as well as she could, then she left her room and went out onto the grounds.

She found Mr. Darcy waiting for her where she had told Sarah to inform him and when she approached, he placed his hands behind him nervously and folded them.

"So?" Lydia gave him a perky smile. "One final walk then."

"Yes, one final walk."

They began walking down the lane and in the direction of the river.

"Our departure day surprised you," Lydia began. "It was must amusing, for your face turned so white with shock."

"Did it?"

"Yes, you gave two very human expressions in less than 24 hours. It is most unprecedented."

Henry Darcy chuckled nervously and then began to breathe unevenly.

"Mrs. Wickham—Miss Bennet... Lydia?"

"Yes."

"I never wish to say anything to cause you grief, but I cannot—I cannot allow you to leave for England without telling you this. And though I know you may not reciprocate my sentiments, and I have argued with myself to not voice what will be uneasy for you to hear —in vain I have struggled, and it will not due. My feelings will not be repressed. You must allow me to tell you how I ardently adore...and respect you.

"Lydia, I have grown to feel a connection to you, a decided attraction and my mind turns to you often with fondness. And all that I can ask of you is to please remain in America for a little while longer. Allow me the chance to court you and show you that I could be a suitable companion. I know you may not love me now, but have I no chance of succeeding with you?"

"No chance?" Lydia cried. "Mr. Darcy, are you telling me that you could find yourself in love with me?"

"If you would open your affections to try and include me in them, you will see that I could make you happy."

"Henry," Lydia exclaimed. "Why are you so quick to think that I might say no?"

"You...you are not against me then?"

"No, I am not! I... I welcome your attentions. Though I do not know if what I feel for you is love, I do feel a passionate attachment to you that I have just discovered within me."

"Lydia, are you speaking in earnest? Please, you are too generous to trifle with me."

"I am not toying with you! I admire you now Henry, and though it is a strange predicament to begin to fall for the man who once was attached to my sister, I do not wish to care for that, if you will not."

"Indeed, I do not." Henry stopped and took Lydia's hands in his own. "Lydia, you agree to this courtship?!"

"With all my heart, Henry. Let us see where we end, and if it does not end well, please do not become my enemy."

"I will not, but you must allow yourself to try and feel some tenderness to me."

"Are you deaf, Henry? I do feel tenderness to you, but I just have to accept that you might not wish to marry me in the end, and I must prepare for that."

"Prepare for that?" Henry said, a smile forming across his lips. "Then you feel for me truly?"

"Yes, I do not pretend that it is not a recent attraction, but the quickness of the time does not impede nor lessen its sincerity. Henry, could you really like me?"

"Yes, I do. So please, Lydia Bennet, allow me this courtship."

"I do and I will," Lydia cried. "Oh, Henry!" She rushed into him, wrapping her hands around his waist. Though surprised at the sudden contact, Henry realized that he liked it quite a great deal and therefore he wrapped his arms around her, feeling the satisfaction of being granted a chance at a woman he had grown to like, in spite of his efforts to do the opposite.

As for Lydia Bennet, this sudden change of events was quite a surprise to her that would affect her for the better. The night before, she had lost all hope. Yet, she did not shun her feelings, despite how foolish and ill-founded she had thought them to be. But she welcomed the truth of them. Thus, she learned a timeless truth of life which was to admit to oneself their true desires and though wishing for the best of outcomes, never doing anything to hurt or wound another in the process; a dream was worth having, and pursuing, as long as it was the right sort of dream to have.

Therefore, in allowing herself to be courted by Mr. Henry Darcy, not because she forced her affections but simply allowed them to exist within her, she had begun to feel that she had done right, in the middle of her life.

And thus, were the choices of Lydia Bennet that would change the path of all around her. Yet this time, she hoped, for the better.

❦ 26 ❦

REACTIONS

U pon returning to Canterbury, Henry and Lydia sought a private audience with Henry's parents. Upon telling them the news, exclamations of joy were expressed from both father and mother. Cousin Emilia was all in excitement. Cousin Thomas was finally feeling satisfaction at knowing that his son and heir might finally have a chance at a woman that would become mistress of Canterbury and give him even more grandchildren that he was hoping to have.

Colonel Fitzwilliam and Kitty were surprised to say the least, but equally joyous of the news. And Cousin Thomas and Emilia then ordered their party to remain at Canterbury as long as the courtship commenced, for this was a time where family should stay linked to family!

Georgiana was amazed, but also apprehensive, for if the courtship was successful, then it would all be well, but if not, this would be another Bennet girl rejecting her cousin, and tension might rise once more.

Joseph and his wife were both happy for Henry and wished him luck in the courtship.

Helena's response was the most colorful.

"You have to marry my brother, Lydia! For you—you—you are the one who taught me how to curtsy without falling down."

And to add to all this, Canterbury soon received a letter from Pemberly.

"Elizabeth gave birth to twin boys!" Georgiana read the letter aloud to the family. "I have two nephews, we are to be aunts, and the rest of you have two cousins!"

When it was made evident that Elizabeth had survived the labor and was also doing well, cries of joy over Elizabeth and Darcy's new children added to the happiness of the blossoming romance.

Colonel Fitzwilliam, Kitty and Georgiana remained at Canterbury, knowing Lydia could not remain alone, and they watched the courtship of Lydia and Mr. Henry Darcy bloom with every coming day.

Meanwhile letters were sent to England, to Gracechurch Street, Longbourn and Kent.

At Gracechurch Street, Jane Bennet read the letter announcing her Lydia's courtship with surprise and closure. For now, she could overcome her guilt in hurting Henry Darcy and causing a rift between the family.

"Amazing!" she said when she showed the letter to her Aunt and Uncle Gardiner. "Of all the sisters to yield the breach I worried that I had made, I never thought it was to be Lydia who saved me."

At Longbourn however, when the letter was read, the news was met with much more volume.

"Lydia is being courted by Henry Darcy!" Mrs. Bennet cried. "My god, however could this gift have come! My Lydia, she always was one of my favorites. And who would have known that there were two such Mr. Darcys in the world, my dear?"

"Yes," Mr. Bennet replied. "Never would I have foreseen that one. Never would I have foreseen any of this."

With all the reactions that went around the circle of recipients, there was one reaction left to see, and that was in Kent, at Pemberly.

❦ 27 ❦

HOW FAR WE HAVE COME

After Darcy finished reading the letter sent from Lydia to me, he looked up in surprise and alarm. I, with baby William in my arm while Caiden rested in his crib at my feet, sat there, meeting his expression with equal astonishment.

"Elizabeth..."

"Yes..."

"This is all too much."

"I still am amazed that it is even true, my dear."

"For Henry Darcy to court Lydia?"

My husband paced back and forth.

"My dear, should we be worried or content?"

"I think we are allowed to be both," I replied. "My heart finds joy in the fact that maybe, with Lydia's astonishing transformation into a creature of sound mind, sense and compassion, she does love him, and if they unite, then our families will be forever linked in another way. Our bonds will be all the stronger."

"And yet, if they do not marry and the courtship turns sour, it shall cause a rift," Fitzwilliam finished for me. "And we might not be able to recover this time."

"Then all we have is hope," I said.

"Yes...and I suppose, I shall be happy for them."

Our baby William fell asleep, I placed him in his other cradle, stood up, walked over to my husband and sat down on his lap.

"Yes, we must be."

"And yet, it is all so strange."

I snuggled against him. "At this point we should grow accustomed to what is strange."

"Yes, we must, for we have seen our share."

I thought on his words and then my brow furrowed as I came to an interesting conclusion.

"I do believe that we have seen our share of strangeness, because we created it!"

"What do you mean?"

"Darcy, think on it. What has happened that we did not indirectly cause? Our bond forced you out of your marriage to Anne de Bourgh, then it forced us to find allies in America where we met the American Darcys, there Mr. Bingley found his fortune in the most unexpected way, we allowed Kitty to remain here, which was how she met the Colonel and found her destiny in him, you allowed Jane to teach the children in the village to read and write and now she has found her path in helping others, and then our family has gone to America to celebrate my sister's marriage and there Lydia meets Henry Darcy, and they have begun to fall in love."

"All of this has happened, because of us. Because we chose to fall in love. Indeed, who would have known that one decision could have led to so much falling into place for so many more? How can this be, Elizabeth?"

"It can and it is. Amazing, to see it all unwind." And it was. How could our good fortune have fallen upon so many others, affecting them in so many ways that it made me shudder? From our family across the ocean, to our babies that slept at our feet, our decisions had ruled the fate of more than we had anticipated.

"Are you astonished, my love," I said, kissing him, "how far we have come?"

"I am." He returned my kiss. "Yet for all that we have endured, I find comfort in knowing that it is not the end, but better beginnings on the horizon."

"No, it is not the end. For nothing ever fully ends, now does it?"

"No, nothing ever does. And especially not us."

"Mr. Darcy?"

"Yes?"

"May you live forever."

"And may you always have a place for me in your heart, Elizabeth."

"Then we shall live."

"Yes, we shall live. And I will love you always."

"Mr. Darcy... I am very much counting on that," I said, kissing him once more, "And so is my heart. Forever—no, our love is more infinite than that."

"Yes, it is."

"Yes, it is."

The End

Don't miss out on your next favorite book!

Join the Satin Romance mailing list
www.satinromance.com/mail.html

THANK YOU FOR READING

Did you enjoy this book?

We invite you to leave a review at your favorite book site, such as Goodreads, Amazon, Barnes & Noble, etc.

DID YOU KNOW THAT LEAVING A REVIEW...

- Helps other readers find books they may enjoy.
- Gives you a chance to let your voice be heard.
- Gives authors recognition for their hard work.
- Doesn't have to be long. A sentence or two about why you liked the book will do.

ABOUT THE AUTHOR

Ney Mitch has been a long-standing Jane Austen enthusiast, having written forty novels that were inspired by her various works. Since stumbling on Miss Austen's books after graduating from college, she has always dabbled in Austen inspired literature, ranging from writing works for teens to adults. Originally, her desire was to adapt Jane Austen's writing in a way to help young adults connect with her, however over time, she has spread her aims to other genres and styles.

Having received her BA Degree at Desales University, she is a writer, both literary and dramatic, as well as being a Historic Reenactor.

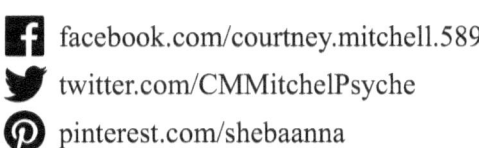

facebook.com/courtney.mitchell.589

twitter.com/CMMitchelPsyche

pinterest.com/shebaanna

The Memory Series

Moments of Moments Past

Moments of Moments Present

Moments of Moments Future

Moments of Moments Infinite

Pride & Prejudice Reimaginings

Rapture & Rebellion

Fortune & Misfortune

Desire & Destiny

Pride & Peace

Chances Series

Chances Are

Chances Come